Lies
Beneath

Lies Beneath

ANNE GREENWOOD BROWN

EMBER

Text copyright © 2012 by Anne Greenwood Brown
Cover photograph copyright © 2012 by Dmitry Laudin

All rights reserved. Published in the United States by Ember, an imprint of Random House Children's Books, a division of Random House, Inc., New York. Originally published in hardcover in the United States by Delacorte Press, an imprint of Random House Children's Books, New York, in 2012.

Ember and the E colophon are registered trademarks of Random House, Inc.

Visit us on the Web! randomhouse.com/teens

Educators and librarians, for a variety of teaching tools, visit us at
RHTeachersLibrarians.com

The Library of Congress has cataloged the hardcover edition of this work as follows:
Brown, Anne Greenwood.
Lies beneath / Anne Greenwood Brown. – 1st ed.
p. cm.
Summary: As the only brother in a family of mermaids living in Lake Superior, Calder White is expected to seduce Lily, the daughter of the man believed to have killed the mermaids' mother, but he begins to fall in love with her just as Lily starts to suspect the legends about the lake are true.
ISBN 978-0-385-74201-6 (hardback) – ISBN 978-0-375-98908-7 (ebook)
ISBN 978-0-375-99036-6 (glb)
[1. Mermen–Fiction. 2. Mermaids–Fiction. 3. Brothers and sisters–Fiction. 4. Love–Fiction. 5. Revenge–Fiction. 6. Superior, Lake–Fiction.] I. Title.
PZ7.B812742Lie 2012
[Fic]–dc23
2011044337

ISBN 978-0-385-74202-3 (tr. pbk.)

RL: 5.0

Printed in the United States of America

10 9 8 7 6 5 4 3 2

First Ember Edition 2013

In memory of my grandfather,

Norman Edward Biorn,

who loved the lake

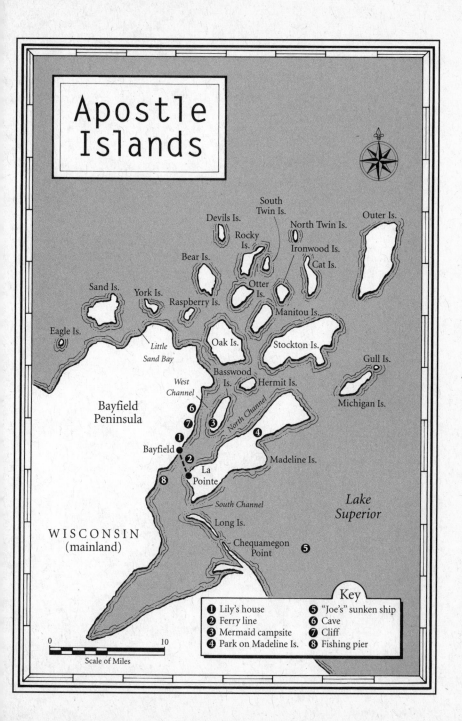

Apostle Islands

Devils Is.

South Twin Is.

Rocky Is.

North Twin Is.

Ironwood Is.

Outer Is.

Bear Is.

Cat Is.

Sand Is.

York Is.

Otter Is.

Raspberry Is.

Manitou Is.

Eagle Is.

Little Sand Bay

Oak Is.

Stockton Is.

Gull Is.

Basswood Is.

West Channel

Hermit Is.

Michigan Is.

Bayfield Peninsula

❻

❼

North Channel

❸

❶

❹

Bayfield ●

❷

Madeline Is.

La Pointe

❽

South Channel

Lake Superior

Long Is.

WISCONSIN (mainland)

Chequamegon Point

❺

Key

❶ Lily's house
❷ Ferry line
❸ Mermaid campsite
❹ Park on Madeline Is.
❺ "Joe's" sunken ship
❻ Cave
❼ Cliff
❽ Fishing pier

0   10

Scale of Miles

Mother, may I go out to swim?
Yes, my darling daughter.
Fold your clothes up neat and trim,
But don't go near the water.

—Anonymous

1

CALLED HOME

I hadn't killed anyone all winter, and I have to say I felt pretty good about that. Sure, I'd wanted to, but too many suspicious drownings got people talking. Fearful townspeople were the last thing I needed. Besides, I was getting a sick thrill out of denying my body what it craved. Self-control was my latest obsession. I doubted my sisters could say the same thing.

Rising through the Caribbean waters, I walked my fingers up the bank of dead coral until I found the pattern of cracks I was looking for. I followed it to the surface, coming up at the spot where I'd stashed my pile of human clothes. My cell phone was ringing somewhere in the pile. *Maris,* I thought, gritting my teeth. I'd lost count of how many times she'd called today. I'd let all her attempts go to voice mail.

A splashing sound pulled my attention from my sister's ringtone, and I jerked around to face the ocean. An easy hundred yards away, a girl lay on an inflatable raft. A yellow light outlined her body. She wasn't ripe yet. Maybe, if I waited, the yellow light would grow into something more brilliant— more satisfying—more worth breaking my hard-won self-control over.

Against my will, the memory of my last kill teased the corners of my brain. It tempted me, mocked me for ever thinking I could rise above my nature. My fingers twitched at the months-old memory: the grabbing, the diving, the guise of human legs giving way to tail and fin, the tingling sensation heating my core as I pinned my prey to the ocean floor, absorbing that intoxicating light, drawing the brilliant emotion out of her body until I felt almost . . .

Oh, what the hell.

But before I dove after the unsuspecting girl, my cell went off again. For a second I considered chucking it into the ocean; it was the disposable kind, after all. But that was a little extreme. Even for me. I let it go to voice mail. I mean, it wasn't like I didn't know why Maris was calling. The old, familiar pull was back. That pull—somewhere behind my rib cage, between my heart and my lungs—that told me it was almost time to leave Bahamian warmth and return to my family in the cold, bleak waters of Lake Superior. It was time to migrate.

A shiver rippled down my arms. *Get a grip, Calder,* I told

myself. *Ignore it. You don't have to leave quite yet.* I could hear the memory of my mother's voice telling me the same thing, just as she had before my first migration. *Focus, son,* she'd said, rumpling my curly hair. *Timing is everything.*

Thirty years might have passed, but the loss of my mother still gripped my stomach. It hurt to remember. And the great lake only made the memories more painful. No, there was no good reason to go back to the States. Except that I had no choice.

The urge to migrate was irresistible. Far more powerful than the urge to kill. With each rise and fall of the moon, with each turn of the tide, it grew more impossible to ignore. Experience told me there were only a few more weeks before I had to rejoin my sisters. By the end of May, I'd be shooting through the water on a missile's course. God help anyone who got in my way.

My cell went off again. With a resigned curse, I pulled myself halfway out of the water and dug through my clothes until I found it and hit Send.

"Nice of you to take my call," Maris said.

"What do you want?"

"It's time. Get home. Now." Her voice, originally sarcastic, now rang with her usual fanaticism. I could hear my other sisters, Pavati and Tallulah, in the background, echoing her enthusiasm.

"Why now?" I asked, my voice flat. "It's still April."

"Why are you being such a pain?"

"It's nothing." There was a long pause on the other end. I closed my eyes and waited for her to figure it out. It didn't take more than a few seconds.

"How long?"

"Five months."

"Damn it, Calder, why do you always have to be such a masochist? God, you must be a mess."

"I'm pacing myself. Mind your own business, Maris." There was no point in trying to explain my abstinence to her. I could barely explain it to myself. I watched mournfully as the yellow-lit raft girl paddled safely toward shore.

"Your mental health *is* my business. Do you think you could take better care of it? One kill, Calder. Just one. It would make you feel so much better."

"I'm. Fine," I spit through my teeth.

"You're an ass, but that's beside the point. I've got something to improve your mood."

I rolled my eyes and waited for her to give it a shot. *Good luck,* I thought.

"We've found Jason Hancock."

My heart lurched at the sound of the name, but I kept quiet rather than give in to her assurance. I'd heard this all before. My silence prompted something on the other end. Panic? Tallulah's voice was now ringing through the receiver, a fluid stream of words almost too quick for me to catch.

I let my gaze drift up to the thin lace of clouds above me. My sisters sounded sure of themselves. Perhaps this time they'd gotten it right. "Fine. I'll start off tomorrow."

"No," Maris said. "There's no time for you to swim. Take a plane."

She hung up before I could protest.

I tipped my head back as far as my neck would bend and soaked up the last bit of ultraviolet rays. My fingertips dug

4

into the coral as I imagined them around Jason Hancock's neck, dragging him down into the water, watching the last bubbles rise from his mouth.

A trill of girlish voices jerked me out of my fantasy. I looked past the bank of hibiscus bushes and, as expected, saw the glow of pure emotion pulsing out of their happy forms. I diverted my eyes from their orange-sherbet-colored auras and tried once more to ignore the temptation to kill. Maris's words echoed in my head: *Just one. It would make you feel so much better.*

The ancient legends had it all backward about merpeople. We didn't lure humans' ships onto the rocks. Human beings were the happy, shiny lures that caught our attention. They had what we craved: Optimism. Excitement. Joy. Any positive emotion could whip us into a frenzy, compel us to charge, to grab, to absorb the joy from their hearts into our own. Even an ounce of good feeling could provide at least a brief reprieve from the natural bleakness of our minds. And the approaching girls promised much more than an ounce.

Besides, how far did I want to push this attempt at abstinence? I'd heard stories of merpeople emotionally starved for human light, languishing in misery, going crazy in the end. Was that what I wanted to become?

My hands trembled as I imagined what it would feel like to snatch not just one girl but all of them, to dive, to drown, and then to absorb their vibrant auras into my skin— the warmth, the effervescent buoyancy of their collective emotion. I wanted it. It would be easy to take. It could all be mine. And it had been such a long, long time. . . .

I shook my head and waited for the girls to pass. It wasn't

their fault I'd let myself get so low. They didn't deserve to be wrung out, their empty husks stashed under rocks, simply because they'd crossed my path. Their laughing faded as they moved inland.

When I knew I had a few minutes of privacy, I pulled myself completely out of the turquoise water and onto the black rock. The transformation began before I could catch my breath. First the tightening—and then the ripping as my body strained and pulled against itself. Bones split and stretched, popping into joints that seconds ago hadn't existed. I thrashed silently on the dead coral, cutting my shoulder and gritting my teeth against the pain, until I eventually flopped onto my back, gasping and bleeding on the rock.

I staggered to my feet and dressed quickly. God, I hoped Maris wasn't pulling me back early for nothing. If this Jason Hancock was *the* Jason Hancock, it wouldn't be our typical kill. I wouldn't want to absorb anything his body had to offer. He wouldn't even count against my experiment in self-control. No. This time it would be nothing more than revenge.

With that word heavy on my tongue, I lowered my Ray-Bans over my eyes and turned away from the ocean. I was trapped by the inevitable: it was time to head back north.

2

THE RELUCTANT BROTHER

Minneapolis sprawled below me as I circled the airport in a DC-9. My quads cramped with dehydration, and I groaned involuntarily. It was a good thing I wasn't looking for sympathy. It wasn't like anyone could have heard me over the roar of the engines.

A businessman shimmied down the narrow aisle, bumping his beer belly on people's shoulders as he passed. "Excuse me, excuse me," he said. A little boy dropped his Mad Libs into the aisle, and his pencil rolled toward me. I unbuckled my seat belt and leaned over the armrest to scoop it up for him.

"Mad Libs. Cool." I reached across the aisle to set the pencil on his tray.

The boy nodded. "I need an adjective."

Miserable. Anxious. Freakin' pissed. "Try 'reluctant,'" I said with a wry smile. I straightened my legs and brushed the pretzel salt off my pants.

"How do you spell that?"

I wrote it out for him, then dragged a deep breath in through my nose. Dry, stale air laced with people's breath and body odor filtered through my lungs. The insides of my cheeks constricted against my tongue. I dug a plastic bottle out of my backpack and shook the last drops of water into my wasted mouth. According to my watch, I'd been dry nineteen hours. Twenty-four was as far as I'd pushed it before. Maris always warned us that that was the limit. I'd never felt the need to challenge her. On that point, at least.

The flight attendant stood a few rows ahead of me, checking to see if everyone was prepared for landing. I raised my empty bottle and shook it to flag her down. When she glanced at me, I raised my eyebrows sarcastically. *Hello, sweetheart. Yeah, you. A little quicker, please.*

"Can I help you, sir?"

"Bottle of water."

"I'm sorry, but our beverage service is over. We're starting our descent." She pointed toward the window to convince me.

Outside, traces of dirty, late-season snow lay crusted and clinging to the Minnesota cornfields and roadside ditches. I clenched my teeth. *Maris better be right about this or so help me. . . .* There had been false alarms before.

I combed my fingers through my dark hair—jerking them through the snarled ends—then quickly gripped the armrests as the plane touched down and took on that out-of-control feel before finally slowing to a stop. Everyone jumped up from their seats before the seat belt sign was turned off.

I retrieved my tattered baseball cap from the seat back. It bore the logo of the resort where I'd stayed all winter. I ran my thumb along the frayed brim, then pulled the cap down low over my eyes. Powering up my cell phone, I hit Send. Maris picked up on the first ring.

"We've landed," I said. "Come get me. And damn it, Maris, there's still snow on the ground."

"No, there isn't. Now relax, little brother. We didn't pull you out of bikini wonderland for nothing. It will be worth your trouble."

"You're sure you're not wrong about this one?"

"Absolutely sure. And we wouldn't have called you if we thought we could do it alone. As much as I hate to admit it, you're *superior* to us in many ways."

I grimaced. It wasn't true. And it wasn't even false flattery. Maris chose her words like a surgeon chose a scalpel; despite the time we spent apart, she always knew how to cut me. At her mere mention of *Superior,* the urge to migrate tugged more desperately at my heart, like a hook caught in my flesh.

Yeah, yeah. I'm coming, I thought, answering the urge as much as my sister.

I shoved my cell in my pocket and stood up, ducking under the overhead compartment. I gestured for the little boy to go ahead. He dragged and bumped his backpack behind him as he made his way up the aisle. The flight attendants flashed bleached smiles at me as I passed. I would have looked away to avoid the attraction they might pose, but there were no colors radiating off them; there was no true emotion behind their smiles.

I stepped onto the Jetway and felt a sharp wind cutting through the thin, collapsible walls. It might as well have been January. I cursed Maris as I made my way through the airport and went to wait on the sidewalk outside the Lindbergh terminal. There was no reason to stop at baggage claim. Everything I owned was either on my body or in my backpack: pants, shorts, ratty sandals, sweatshirt, two worn-out T-shirts, a scuba watch, cell phone, and baseball cap. My sisters had a bit more, but not much. We all traveled light.

I stiffened my arms at my sides and bounced from foot to foot, trying to keep warm. Every thirty seconds I checked my watch. I didn't know what they'd be driving, but I knew it was them when I saw an old Chevy Impala fishtailing through the barely rolling traffic. I wondered, ruefully, where they'd snagged this one. It looked to be in pretty good shape—far better than the Dodge Omni from last summer. The owner was probably somewhere scratching his head, the victim of my sisters' hypnotic gifts. He'd know he lost something. But what was it again?

Tallulah and Pavati had their windows down, and they hung their heads out, beaming at me. Pavati's long dark hair blew around her face in loose waves; Tallulah's shorter hair hung straight like a thick golden curtain. I shook my head in mock disgust at their taste in stolen property and got in the backseat with Tallulah. She kissed me hard on the cheek.

"I couldn't wait another minute," she said. "I've really, really missed you."

"Me too, Lulah," I said. It was almost the truth.

Maris flipped her white-blond hair over her shoulder. "Yeah, yeah. Kiss, kiss. Now get your head on straight. We've got business to discuss, and I need coffee."

3

THE WHITE SISTERS

Tallulah turned away from the barista at the Daily Grind and glided toward our table, balancing four paper coffee cups between her long fingers. She set the cups down, and we all reached for one. Maris leaned toward me, her smooth forearms resting on the table, her hands clasped, the knuckles white. She scrutinized my face. My jaw muscles flexed in response.

"You need to eat something, Calder. You look skinny."

"I'm good."

"Did you work much this winter?"

"Some. Plane ticket tapped me out."

"We've got you covered," said Tallulah. "Pav waitressed in New Orleans this winter. She saved all her tips."

I nodded. It wasn't that we needed much, but now and then money was handy. Pavati probably had a small treasure trove amassed in the trunk of the stolen Impala. Humans tipped her as if she were serving the secrets of the universe on a blue plate special. She winked at me, popped the plastic cover off her latte, and dipped her finger to scoop out the foam.

A man sitting at a nearby table stared at her mouth.

I couldn't blame him. For better or worse, nature had designed us all to attract the human eye, but Pavati was a particularly gorgeous specimen as monsters went. Unlike Maris's and Tallulah's pale complexions, Pavati's was caramel and melted chocolate. Like a Bollywood superstar, she had square shoulders, a narrow waist, and dark-lashed eyes that glowed lavender. She was, as Maris called her, "The Perfect Bait."

Even I, her own brother, could fall into her hypnotic trap and find myself fantasizing about her in unhealthy ways. It was a disgusting and humiliating experience, even when I knew she was doing it to me on purpose. "Just for laughs," she'd say.

Pavati, I groaned mentally. Maybe I wasn't totally innocent when it came to toying with my victims before the kill, but at least I did it to ease their fears. Pavati could be downright devastating in her allure. If this Jason Hancock was the one we'd been searching for, he didn't stand a chance.

Pavati studied my gloomy disposition and chuckled to

herself. Maris was less amused by the depression I'd allowed myself to fall into. She narrowed her eyes at me. "We *are* right this time," she said.

"I'm keeping an open mind."

"He's moving his family to Bayfield—to the old house. What are the chances? This *is* the right family, Calder. It's him."

Now she had my attention, but I tried to hide my excitement just to piss her off. "Let's say, just for kicks, you're right, and you've found him," I said. "How do you plan to do this?"

A smile slowly spread across Maris's face. Pavati looked up quickly.

Tallulah slid her chair closer to me and linked her arm through mine. "Isn't it good to have him back?" she asked the other two. She kissed my cheek and squeezed my hand; I squeezed hers back twice before slipping my hand away. This outward image of family harmony was like manna to Tallulah. If it were just the two of us, maybe this family would actually work. But there was no use hypothesizing. We'd never be rid of Maris.

Tallulah turned toward her. "Tell him," she said.

Maris nodded once, happy to have the floor. "We've been watching the family for a while," she said; her eyes glowed silver.

"I assumed as much." I rocked back in my chair again.

"He has two daughters."

"They're close to their father," said Pavati.

"And?" I asked.

"*They*"—Maris paused for dramatic effect—"are our ticket. To *him*."

I rocked forward, slapping the chair legs onto the floor. "Geez, Maris, isn't that a little . . . sick?"

She smiled and sat back in her chair. "Thanks."

"Seriously?" I glanced hopefully at Tallulah. Was she in on this? "Do we have to make this more complicated than necessary? Why involve children? If he is who you think he is, why not let Pavati just do her thing?"

"Sounds good to me," Pavati said, perking up.

Maris rolled her eyes. "He's married."

"So?"

"*Very* married. I don't think he's the type to fall for the beautiful-girl-in-the-water routine."

I shook my head. "Obviously you don't know men."

Maris leaned in. "He killed our mother, Calder."

"No. *He* didn't. *Tom* Hancock was the debtor. His son is only the collateral."

"You know what I mean."

"What makes you think Jason Hancock knows anything about his father's promise? Or what breaking that promise did to Mother? Or to us?"

"What are you saying?" Maris asked, her voice wild and incredulous. "You don't want to collect on the debt?"

I leaned in, encouraging her to whisper. "Of course I do. I want Jason Hancock as much as you do. I'm just saying . . . if this Jason Hancock is really Tom Hancock's son . . . there's no reason to make this more dramatic than necessary. Let Pavati lure him in. Once he's in the water, we can all take part in dragging him down. We can all get our justice that way. Short and sweet. Done. Then we each go our own way."

"Why don't you want to stay with us, Calder?" asked

15

Pavati. Her full bottom lip thrust out in a seductive pout. The man at the neighboring table licked his lips reflexively.

"Have you three looked in the mirror lately?" But I was only looking at Maris. Summers were bad enough. The thought of wintering in New Orleans with my sisters was beyond imagination. "A solidarity of vengeful mermaids? It's charming."

Maris's eyes flashed with an electricity that made the overhead lighting fizz and blink. A pimply-faced boy who got too close stutter-stepped away. The other patrons looked up at the ceiling.

"I'll tell you what, Calder White." She spit my name through her teeth. "You play nice. Do this my way. And when it's over, I promise you can leave without us ever bothering you again."

"Maris," Tallulah pleaded.

Maris waved her off. "What do you say, Calder?"

It was tempting. I'd been with my sisters since I was three. From then on, I'd been tethered to them, our minds connected by an invisible thread I could not sever. When Mother died, Maris became the head of our little family— now only she had the power to cut someone loose. If Maris was suggesting she'd let me go . . . No, it was impossible to imagine. But if she meant it . . . Well, if I ever missed my sisters, I could find them. But it would be on my terms. No more emergency summonses. No more guilt trips. No more physical urge to reconvene each spring. Independence wasn't natural for our kind, but I never claimed to have come to this life naturally. Maris never let me forget *that*.

Tallulah's fingers tightened around my bicep, and Pavati looked back and forth from my face to Maris's.

"Deal." The word was bitter on my tongue. Tallulah made

a softly strangled sound, but I didn't look at her. "What do we do now? Assuming you're right."

"You get close to one of the sisters," said Pavati.

"How?"

"I'm sure you'll figure something out." Maris leaned over the table and ran her fingers through my thick curls. "You're not entirely hideous."

Tallulah fidgeted as Maris touched me.

Laughing, Pavati tossed her hair, and her necklace jangled. Beads of sweat popped up on the upper lip of the man to her left. My eyes darted to him, and he quickly looked away.

Pavati drew closer, putting her arm around my shoulders. "Get invited to the house, Cal." Her breath was still warm from the Mississippi Delta, and her full lips brushed my ear as she said, "*Meet* the parents. *Be* the boyfriend."

I nodded. The proposed seduction played out in my mind like a movie—the fake smiles, the deceitful kiss . . .

"Get Jason Hancock to trust you," Pavati continued. "Tell him you've never been fishing. Let him invite you out on the lake."

I closed my eyes.

"Then we'll just show up," she said brightly.

I pictured the three of them transformed, circling the boat like sharks, their lithe bodies cutting through the water, then slinking over the rail.

"Then what?"

"He'll beg for mercy. He'll ask us why," Tallulah said, her voice ringing.

"We'll take our time," whispered Pavati.

"We'll tell Jason Hancock about his father's boat accident," said Maris. "We'll tell him how our mother saved his father."

"For a price," chimed in Tallulah.

"We'll tell him that his father was weak. That he promised his infant son in exchange for his own miserable life. We'll tell him that our mother agreed. We'll tell him," Maris said, spitting through her teeth, "that Tom Hancock may have broken his promise, but he, *Jason Hancock,* still belongs to us."

"And then we'll take him down." Tallulah leaned her head against my shoulder.

· "Slowly," Maris added. "We'll let him come up for air, and then we'll drag him down again."

I shook my head.

"And then do it again," said Pavati. Her light giggle raised goose bumps on my smooth arms.

"He'll be screaming," I said. "It will call unnecessary attention."

"Trust me, little brother," said Maris. "By the time anyone comes, we'll be long, long gone."

4

LILY HANCOCK

Maris pulled down a quiet street in South Minneapolis, made a U-turn, and parked on the side of the road, a few houses down from a Tudor two-story with a For Sale sign in the yard and a moving van parked out front. My eyes focused on the name stenciled on the mailbox.

HANCOCK

"Go on," said Maris. "See what you think."
I hesitated. Breaking and entering wasn't really my style.

"Listen, little brother. If you don't find out for yourself, I'll have to listen to you bitch all the way up north. Get in there. Check them out. If you aren't convinced it's the right man, well . . . we'll cross that bridge later."

I gave her a jerky nod and got out of the car. Budding sugar maples lined the street. Other than the bustle of activity surrounding the moving van, it was quiet.

I crept along the neighbor's privacy fence and climbed over the top, dropping silently into the Hancocks' backyard. The yellow grass crunched under my feet as I edged my way to the rear door. Barely opening it, I slipped inside. I couldn't remember the last time I'd been in an actual house, but the kitchen—even stripped bare of its appliances—was strangely familiar, what with the yellow walls and silver sink. But as I struggled to pull a memory out of the darkness, the smell of bleach overtook me, and I crinkled my nose against the fumes.

I slunk through the empty rooms, looking for any clues that Maris had found the right Hancocks, but there wasn't much left inside. A few cardboard boxes marked *Mom's Paints and Supplies* stood stacked by the front door. Another box, labeled *Photo Albums,* gave me pause. I opened it carefully and paged through the album at the top of the stack. Three sheets in, I found a family photo. The father stared up at me from the happy composition. Could this be Tom Hancock's son?

I closed the box and watched through the front windows as one of the moving crew carried a wheelchair up the ramp into the van. Another man pointed and gave instructions about its placement. Before I could give any consideration to the second man, floorboards creaked above my head. I knew I was pushing my luck, but my curiosity was piqued.

Stealing along the wall, I crept up the stairs, controlling each footstep, avoiding squeaky treads, until I got to the first bedroom, where a hand-painted sign still hung on the door. *Lily*, it said. Someone was moving around inside, making clinking sounds and dropping things onto a hard surface.

I slipped through the door and into the bedroom closet, positioning myself so as not to jostle the wire hangers, and adjusted the slats in the door with my finger. My eyes darted around the room as I peered through the gap. Deep indentations marked the spot where a bed had been. Rectangles of darker paint and bits of tape marred the walls.

The en suite bathroom door stood ajar, and a teenage girl bent over the white counter, leaning into the mirror. *This must be Lily,* I thought as I assessed her: average height, with dark auburn curls that tumbled down her back.

She readied the sharp point of a charcoal pencil by the corner of her eye and drew a thick line along her lashes. She smirked at some private thought and drew the line thicker, shifting her weight. My eyes settled on her backside, round and nubile in a black miniskirt, and my stomach twisted like a snake in a jar.

The girl returned to her bedroom and was now just several feet from where I hid. She dropped a green velvet bag on the floor and sat down to lace her tattered combat boots, worn over plum-colored tights. In her richly textured colors and auburn hair, she reminded me of a classical oil painting. I memorized her every detail, wondering if she should be my target, wanting her to be my mark.

A circle of skin showed through a hole in the knee of her tights. It mesmerized me. Just the size of a quarter, like a bright pink petal floating on dark water . . . The flow of electricity bounced from my fingers to the wire hangers, making a tiny snapping sound. Then there was a flash, and I spun toward the movement. Still jumpy as hell. God, what was I doing in here? I re-adjusted the closet door slats to get a better view.

A smaller girl—her sister?—was standing in the doorway. She was younger than I expected. Small with blond ringlets. Her pink backpack, partially unzipped, bulged with books and dolls. She twisted up her mouth and eyed her older sister.

"What are you wearing? You look weird."

The older girl flinched but didn't respond.

The smaller one leaned against the bedroom doorframe. "Did you hear me? I said, 'You look weird.' Why do you have to dress like that?"

I thought I saw the older sister stifle a smile.

"Y'know what? 'Weird' was kinda the look I was going for. Thanks, Sophie."

"If you ruin my chance to make new friends, I *will* kill you."

The older girl finished tying her right boot, and this time she did smile. I did, too. There was something about a little girl handing out death threats that appealed to my twisted, darker side.

"Then I'll try not to make you the social outcast of the North Woods," she said.

The younger girl made an exasperated sound while the older one leaned forward to grab a book off the floor. Her blouse rode up, exposing her lower back.

"Oh my gosh, Lily! Is that a tattoo? I'm telling Mom and Dad."

The girl called Lily pulled her shirt down and stood up. Turning toward her sister, she said, "No, you're not."

"Why not?"

She put her hands on her sister's shoulders. "Because you wouldn't do that to me, and I would never do something like that to you."

Sophie Hancock lowered her chin and looked at the floor. I waited for her to laugh and run to tell her parents. But she didn't move. I couldn't understand. Any one of my sisters would have jumped at the chance to make me miserable. Even Tallulah on a bad day.

"Fine. I won't tell. But they *are* going to find out."

Lily Hancock nodded. "By then I'll have figured out a way to soften the blow."

Sophie turned away, and I watched her leave, analyzing her from a strategic standpoint. She was smaller, probably easy to manipulate. It wouldn't be a seduction with her. Too young. I'd have to think of a new tactic.

The room was now empty save for Lily Hancock, and me in her closet. She reached again for the book on the ground. It was old, oversized, its binding loose and its cover cracked. It flopped open, exposing a page that was blank except for a smudged inscription written in a large, looping hand:

An insignificant sacrifice for one so loved as you.

I doubted the inscription was for her. Probably written before she was born. She couldn't be more than seventeen.

The girl let her fingers caress the inscription before

gently closing the cover and cradling the spine. I caught the title before she slipped it into her bag: *An Anthology of Victorian Poets*. Geez, the book was ancient. What did she like about the old thing? My curiosity was interrupted by a woman calling up the stairwell, and I jumped again, almost giving myself away.

"Lily honey?" she asked. "Are you still up there? It's time. We're all waiting."

"Coming, Mom." Lily Hancock divided her ponytail and pulled it tight. She buttoned a black brocade vest that accentuated her hourglass figure, then slung the velvet bag across her chest and shoulder. Taking one last look around her room, she headed for the door. A car horn beeped just as her feet crossed the threshold.

"I said I'm coming, you guys. Geez."

When Lily's combat boots hit the stairs, I made my move from the closet. But I had to dodge back into my hiding spot when she unexpectedly returned to grab the *Lily* sign off the nail on her door. She stared at the closet handle for too many seconds before clomping down the stairs. After that, I don't know what was louder: the front door slamming or my heart pounding through my chest.

I went to the window and leaned my forehead against the glass. Below me, the Hancocks threw their last small items into the family SUV. The father assisted the mother into the passenger seat, making sure she was comfortable, and he handed her a wooden cane.

They weren't exactly happy about the move. I could tell that much. Their auras were all wrong. Anxious, maybe? That was my best guess, judging by the muddy green light that hovered around the car. I wondered if they knew what their family was going toward. Did they know their Hancock family history? If Maris was right, did these girls know their dad was in danger?

I slunk down the stairs and slipped out the back door. A neighbor's dog followed me, a growl rumbling deep in his chest. I met his eyes and thought, *Beat it.* The dog yelped and ran away, leaving me to find a place to spy.

"And we're off," said the man behind the wheel, but he didn't put the car in gear. "I can't believe it. I'm finally going." I flinched at the sound of his voice, muffled because the car windows were closed but still clear enough for me to hear.

From behind a tree, I listened to their conversation. How many times had I imagined Jason Hancock—his image changing with each passing year as he turned from baby to boy to man? His face, his hair . . . his voice. Never had I imagined the sound to be gentle.

"This is going to be good for all of us," he said. I wasn't sure whom he was trying to convince. "Nothing but blue sky, fresh air, clean water . . ." He paused then, and the family waited silently for something more. When he didn't say anything, Lily Hancock leaned forward and put her chin on his seat back.

"We have water here, too, Dad. Minneapolis, City of Lakes, ever heard of it?"

"Don't get smart," said her mother.

"But it's not the same," Jason Hancock said, shaking his head. "Lake Superior is more like an ocean. You'll see."

"I know," Lily said, forcing a smile. "I'm sorry." She put her hand on her father's seat. "It's going to be great, you guys."

Mrs. Hancock tapped the girl's hand reassuringly.

Lily turned toward her window, and her gray eyes aligned with mine. For a second, I thought she saw me.

I retreated behind the tree and counted to five before leaning around the trunk again. When I did, she wasn't looking in my direction; she was flipping through the songs on an MP3 player and pushing earbuds into her ears, a look of patient surrender on her face.

Jason Hancock backed the SUV into the street. When he looked forward, I scrutinized his features, narrowing my eyes to focus. There was definitely something about him that looked familiar. I had never met the older Hancock, but I'd seen his face in my mother's dying thoughts: *Tom Hancock running away with his family, depriving her of the young life he'd promised; she, racing along the shore, following his car as the road traced the lake.*

All the pieces fit. This man, unlike the others my sisters had brought me to see, was in fact Tom Hancock's son. I was sure of it. My fingers flexed, then curled into fists.

The SUV pulled past the mailbox and headed up the street. Hancock flipped on his blinker at the stop sign, then turned right.

Maris honked twice. I gave her a two-fingered salute and jogged back to the car. Tallulah threw open the door for me, and I slid in beside her.

"Well?" asked Pavati. She twisted a lock of dark hair around her index finger, her lavender eyes keen and nervous in the visor mirror.

"Well?" repeated Tallulah.

I watched Maris's lips press into a long straight line. Her

26

eyes were silver, soulless things. As eager as I was to end this Hancock obsession for myself, she was the most fanatical of all of us. I considered dragging out her anxiety, toying with her nerves, but had an unexpected flicker of mercy. "Okay, I'm convinced."

The girls erupted into peals of laughter that made me wince. I was on board when it came to the end result we all desired, but I still couldn't embrace their methods. Sure, I fantasized about killing Hancock, but it wasn't in me to prolong the torture. Particularly if he knew nothing of his father's promise. Of course, even if he was ignorant, we'd still have to kill him. But he didn't have to suffer. And the more I thought about it, the more convinced I was that Hancock knew nothing. Why else would he move his whole family back to the lake?

"He's oblivious," Maris sneered. I nodded. His ignorance would make things easier. In fact, it all seemed a little too easy. Maybe that was what had me nervous. If we got too relaxed, if we assumed too much, we'd make stupid mistakes.

Maris shifted the car into drive and revved the engine; the tires squealed, leaving long black marks on the otherwise quiet street.

5

ROAD TRIP

Light and shadow flashed like fire through my eyelids as I dozed in the backseat of the Impala. I wasn't curious where Maris was driving us. We were creatures of habit. We'd be at the Mississippi River Gorge below the old Pillsbury Mill in a matter of minutes. We'd ditch the car and follow the Mississippi south to the St. Croix River hookup, then north up the St. Croix as far as we could go. We'd make the last twenty miles to Lake Superior on foot.

I breathed sleepily and let Tallulah sink into my side, but minutes later Maris interrupted the moment of satisfaction by throwing the car into park. I crashed into the back of her headrest.

Tallulah sat up, and for a second, we all just stared out the window. Across the river, the city of Minneapolis shone with cold steel and glass, its buildings seemingly huddled together for warmth.

I pulled myself out of the car and followed my sisters down the winding path and over the wobbly footbridges. Maris carried our bag and led our line. When we got to the bottom, my feet sank into the sated ground. A blue heron was wading tentatively in the shallows at the base of the Stone Arch Bridge. The river was so high from the winter runoff that it climbed the tree trunks along the bank. Other than the birds, there was no one around. That was good. It was impossible to strip down with an audience—not to mention let the metamorphosis take over.

Maris pulled our bag over her head and set it on the ground beside her. She waded in. The water lapped at her ankles. She pushed her shoulders back and arched. Pavati's long skirt dragged in the water. In the middle of the river, a duck stretched its neck and shook off the cold. That caught my attention. If ducks were complaining . . .

"You know what? Forget it," I said. "I'm not doing it. Not this early. No way." Tallulah startled, and Maris and Pavati turned around slowly to stare at me. "If you'd only waited. Would a few more weeks kill you?" I hated sounding like a baby about this, but I hated the cold. I mean, I *really* hated the cold. Maris raised her eyebrows to suggest that big boys didn't act like this.

"It's always cold," she said.

"Really? Have you ever swum the river this time of year?" I gesticulated wildly at the swollen waterway.

Maris looked at me as if I were a petulant child.

"I'll do whatever you say when it comes to Hancock. But I'm not getting in that river, Maris. You can *drive* my ass north."

Tallulah leaned toward me, her hand on my lower back. "Come on," she said to Maris. "I think compromise might be a good thing right now. And it might be useful to keep the car."

Pavati looked to Maris for direction, and Maris considered Tallulah's pleading expression. She conceded with a quick nod, and Pavati shrugged. She wrung the water out of her long skirt and picked up our bag.

We retraced our steps back to the car, and when Maris put it into gear with a rough jerk, Tallulah laid her head against the window, saying, "Play nice," though I wasn't sure whom she was admonishing.

A stream of obscenities flowed steadily under Maris's breath. I would have never won this battle without Tallulah, and it put Maris in a sour mood. Fortunately, she was opting to give me the silent treatment. That was good. It gave me room to think.

Pavati passed me a box of saltines and a bottle of water, and I mouthed *Thank you*. It had now been twenty-three hours since I'd last submerged, and I needed to retain as much moisture as I could. Already my skin stretched taut across my cheekbones. I put the box between my knees, dug into it absentmindedly, and powered down the water.

The first decision: Which Hancock sister would be easier to get at? Which one had the closer bond to the father? The younger one was small, possibly weak. I remembered her words to her sister—she was looking to make friends. *I* could be a friend. Or maybe I looked too old for that. The goal was to get closer—not to repel.

I'd reached eighteen years by human standards, so I looked nearer in age to the other sister. *Lily,* I thought, picturing the sign on her door. That might make better sense, and she was definitely the more appealing of the two. Plus, she was old enough for me to use my more practiced skills on. I imagined my fingers trailing her neck, over her shoulder, down her arm, my arm encircling her soft waist. I swallowed down the lump rising in my throat. But was she close enough to her father that she would bring me to him?

Personal preferences had to take a backseat to practicalities. I decided on the younger sister. My money was on her being the daddy's girl. She'd be easier to manipulate, too.

I smirked. I had nothing on Pavati and her way with human beings, but I had a few tricks. I'd take the big brother tack. Find a common interest. Barbies? I snorted and Tallulah sat up quickly to see what was wrong.

"Nothing," I told her. A second later, my phone vibrated in my pocket. I pulled it out and saw a text from Tallulah. She wiggled her eyebrows at me as I shot her a puzzled look.

LU: Wanna talk?

I looked at her again, and she tipped her head suggestively toward Maris. Oh. So that was what this was about. I really didn't want to get into my bargain with Maris. Tallulah would only want to talk me out of it.

CALDER: ur not gonna change my mind
LU: You won't even let me try?
CALDER: u don't know what it's like
LU: Want to bet?
CALDER: it's diff for u—I'M diffrent
LU: You know I never saw you as different. That's
   just Maris. You got to stop thinking like that.
CALDER: too late. besides, doesn't mattr. she's
   giving me a way out. i'm taking it.

Tallulah turned back toward her window and laid her
head against the glass. The road jogged north through sleepy
Wisconsin towns—some barely more than the sign their
names were written on—past plowed-over cornfields, hunting-
supply stores, and cheese chalets. My phone vibrated again.

LU: You shouldn't let Maris affect you like that.
   There's no way you can make it on your own.
CALDER: watch me
LU: So . . . what . . . ???? After this summer
   you're gonna stay in the Bahamas year round?
CALDER: got a better idea?
LU: Yes. One. Stay with us. :)
CALDER: Drop it. >: (

Tallulah bent over and held her phone between her
knees. Her thumbs flew over the keyboard.

LU: You'd never come back?
CALDER: that's the idea

LU: WHAT ABOUT ME?????
CALDER: ????????
LU: Screw you, Calder.
CALDER: u could visit

Tallulah sat up, scowling, and pinched my chest. Hard. I knew I wasn't being fair. She would always be compelled to follow Maris on the migration north, just as I was (for now). Call it the school mentality so common in fish. Call it whatever you wanted. Didn't really matter to me. Bottom line: It just plain sucked.

Five hours after leaving Minneapolis, we caught our first glimpse of Lake Superior, what the ancients called the Great Gitche Gumee, and the first island in the Apostle Islands chain. Despite my earlier reluctance, I had to admit there was a relief in having arrived—a sense of coming-home completion that no other body of water could provide. My sisters' faces expressed the same eager expectancy. Pavati trembled in her seat with her palm pressed against the glass; Maris's knuckles whitened on the steering wheel. Tallulah rolled down her window and leaned out into the wind.

Only a few hours of daylight remained when we pulled into Bayfield. Nearly every front yard was a yellow smear of daffodils, and many of the small storefronts were still closed for the season. Maris parked our car by the town playground at the end of Dock Road. The sun hung like a ripe orange over the trees.

Inhaling, I took in the familiar smells of my new environment—rotting fish, charcoal grills, and pine sap. It didn't smell like the channel had frozen solid this winter, but it would still be cold—even colder than the Mississippi. The wind off the lake promised me as much. I didn't have to look at Maris to know she was enjoying my discomfort. I'd run out of excuses.

The Madeline Island ferry was halfway across the channel on its five-thirty run. It was early in the season and there were only a few people making the crossing, their cars topped with kayaks and luggage racks. They stood along the rail on the upper deck bundled in down parkas.

We watched from the car, fighting the ubiquitous lure of the humans' happy expressions and the raspberry-colored glow that outlined the ferry.

"Patience," Maris said. "Maintain focus on Hancock. We'll need to pace ourselves this summer. I don't want anything to put him on alert."

We nodded. There was work to be done. Maintaining focus on our target was Job One.

I regretted not having made a kill when I was still in the Bahamas. It was a stupid experiment—seeing how long I could go—and what did it get me? Nothing in the end. The too-familiar threads of depression were already pulling through my veins. I could have used the emotional fix that a human life would provide—particularly now that I was stuck with Maris 24/7. I closed my eyes to the ferry riders and repeated the mantra: *Focus, focus, focus.*

6

TRANSFORMATIONS

For over two hours we sat in our parked car, staring out the windows, barely speaking. Occasionally one of us would glance at Maris to see if she thought it safe to go. My muscles tensed in preparation for the shock, but by this point my body craved the water—whatever its temperature. Thirty hours had passed since my last submersion. This was new territory for me, and Maris studied me curiously in the rearview mirror. A dozen empty water bottles lay at my feet. I'd only drunk half of them; the rest I'd poured directly on my skin.

Outside my window, shrouded sailboats stood in dry dock. I stared at the name on one of the uncovered sterns. *Kismet.* Was that the one? Since falling out of my parents' sailboat as a toddler, I'd struggled to remember the name of the vessel. Not knowing how to read at the time made it harder to remember now. My only memory was a vague shape of letters. Maybe a *K*? Or an *R*? Unlike me, my sisters had been born to this life. I envied their easy minds, never fighting against nature, never wondering *what if.*

When the sky finally darkened, Maris gave a short nod and we all scrambled out of the car. It was late on a school night, and the park was finally deserted. Still, I couldn't help but look behind me to make sure we were alone. The girls didn't bother. They were stripping down and shoving their street clothes and cell phones under the seat of the car. Maris grabbed the canvas bag and slung it across her bare chest.

"You'll adjust, Cal," Tallulah said, the bitter remnants of our last text messages lingering in her tone. "You always do."

Pavati winked. "Just swim fast. You'll warm up."

We were all naked now. The wind raised goose bumps on my arms. "Try and catch me," I said. I ran across the grass to the fishing pier, jumped onto the railing, and dove, my sisters a half second behind.

As my hands pierced the surface, the icy temperature sliced through my skin, upward and outward, like a thousand razors. My heart constricted, and my mouth contorted with pain. White blossoms of clean bright light bloomed in my field of vision. Water filled my ears with a tinny ringing. The freezing water rushed into my lungs, and I took my first deep breath in what felt like days, luxuriating in the fullness of it. Despite the night sky, underneath the surface, light still bounced and played between my fingers and around my arms. I barely noticed as my body temperature dropped to match the water's.

Surrendering to the inevitable, I relaxed my muscles and dolphin-kicked my legs as one unit, propelling myself with a fluid thrust, reveling in the liquefying feeling that hummed and pulsed as the ripple of change washed through my body. My thighs tingled, then burned, as the metamorphosis took over—first knitting my bones, then breaking through the skin with scales and fin.

As usual, Pavati changed quickest and burst forward with admirable speed. Her cobalt-blue tail flashed by my face. *"Showoff!"* I teased, and heard a trickle of a laugh in response.

Tallulah swam beside me, waiting for me to finish the change. A metallic silver ring appeared around her throat, as I knew it eventually would around mine. Her lower half was already covered in rows of scales, like silver sequins.

Maris tore by without a backward glance; her sleek onyx-colored tail nothing more than a shadow. The girls always changed quicker than I did. They were born to this life, plus they never went as far south as I did. Their bodies didn't take as long to acclimate.

My body heaved and—*Ah*—with one big whip of my legs, my tail was fully embodied. I relished the freedom—as close to happy as I ever was—and shot through the deepening water like a torpedo.

Tallulah and I coasted along the sandy bottom and searched ahead for any danger. It was still too early for there to be much vegetation, so we stayed clear of the ferry's path. It would only take one person peering over the rail to start a scandal. Usually that meant more trouble for the witness than for us. The general public tended to frown on mermaid reports. But we didn't need Hancock to hear that kind of noise—particularly on the off chance he'd heard his father's story and believed it was true.

As I cut through the dark water, constellations of tiny particles streamed by me. My ears welcomed the familiar squeaks of lake trout and the low vibration of far-off ore boats. I shot over sunken timbers and chased a sturgeon. Its rough skin reminded me of the sand sharks I'd played with only the day before. I dragged my fingers across its flat head and down the row of spiny bumps on its back. It was young, only half my size.

Tallulah grabbed my arm and tugged me in a different direction. I looked away from the fish and saw why: a row of nets along the shore. I whipped my tail, stirring the sand and scaring the sturgeon, and tore off perpendicularly to my original path. Tallulah never left my side.

We followed Madeline Island's far shoreline and rounded its northern tip. Tallulah looked at me playfully, challenging me to a race. We circled Madeline twice before she tore off in the direction of our usual campsite on Basswood Island. I would have liked to swim another hour—*hell,* as parched as my body had been, I could have swum all night—but I followed in the plowed path of Tallulah's wake, because if we were launching Operation Hancock tomorrow, I was going to need my sleep.

Within a few minutes Basswood's familiar rocky ground came up to meet us, welcoming us home. When it became too shallow to swim, we searched for a break in the rocks and a sandy spot to make the change. For the first time, Tallulah moved away from me, giving us both the room we needed. Forcing our bodies back into human shapes sucked big-time. As kids, we rarely left the water; the transformation usually left us puking in the sand. These days, the worst I got was the dry heaves.

When the bones began to split, I arched my back and braced against the pain. Twisting in the sand, I bit down on my lip until I tasted blood, then gasped with ragged breaths that burned my lungs. A minute later the last of the tremors rippled past my toes as I sputtered and coughed at the dry air.

Tallulah looked down as she walked past me. She winked at my vulnerability, the inevitable result of being naked and unable to run. I rolled my eyes to watch the water run off her in little rivers that trickled down her arms and dripped off her middle fingers. The backs of her bare legs were red from the recent trauma.

After another minute my breathing fell into a rhythm, and I clawed my way onto dry sand, finding my legs and pushing myself to standing. My sisters sat on the beach, wearing the yellowed cotton rags they'd pulled from Maris's canvas bag. The silver rings were already fading around their throats. Pavati tossed me a pair of tattered shorts as she fed driftwood into a small campfire. Maris had my sturgeon friend skewered on a spit.

7

MOVING

The next morning, I woke before the girls. For a few minutes I lay quiet and unmoving in the sand, my back pressed up against a boulder, my skin cool in the shadow of the oak trees, my brain trying to remember where I was. The previous day's conversations trickled back into my consciousness. Maris turned over sleepily and mumbled something unintelligible. I got up, and she rolled into the empty spot I left in the sand. She murmured again, "He was supposed to come home."

I kicked at the sand, dusting her legs. "I *did* come home.

Get off it, Maris." She groaned in response and curled into a ball.

The sun was just rising, and it cast pink beams of light on the spires and gingerbread details of Bayfield's oldest buildings. I set my teeth in preparation for the job ahead of me. I knew what I needed to do. But as eager as I was to earn my freedom from Maris and the family, my first priority was going to have to be food—and lots of it. Even at this distance I could smell yeast and bacon grease wafting through the air from Bayfield's breakfast joints.

I tossed my shorts in the bushes and wrote a note for my sisters in the sand: *On it.*

Three long strides and I splashed into the lake, diving into the sunlit path when I could no longer stand. I counted out the seconds in my head as the transformation took place. It was quicker than the night before but crap, I had a lot of work to do on my timing.

A fishing boat passed overhead, and I took advantage of its hull for cover. Its shadow was wide and deep, and I was able to follow it all the way into Bayfield. When it veered south along the shore, I swam under the pier and crawled up onto the jagged rocks. My breath came out in gray, frosty huffs, and I closed my eyes to the wisps of old spiderwebs that laced the underside of the pier. Twisting and writhing, I reopened the newest cut on my shoulder, which had barely begun to heal. The smell of cinnamon rolls was the only distraction from the pain.

When it was over, I crept up the bank, listening for voices, then flung open the door of the Impala and slid inside. My khakis and T-shirt were tucked under the seat, right where I'd left them the night before. I wrestled them over my wet body and scrubbed my fingers across my head until my hair settled into a look of precise dishevelment. Meeting the Hancocks meant looking presentable, or in other words, two-legged, well groomed, and—most of all—benign.

I turned the key, and the Impala coughed and wheezed before agreeing to move. I followed a direct path to the Blue Moon Café and the strong smell of melted butter and coffee that wafted through the screen in its bright blue door. A motherly-looking woman appeared in the front window; she taped a Help Wanted sign to the glass. When she retreated, I stole inside and loaded my arms with day-old muffins from a basket on the marble countertop. Just as I turned, the woman came back. *Busted.*

"Oho. And who do we have here?" She laid two white cardboard boxes on the counter and appraised me with an amused smile.

The name Hancock was written on the top box in black marker. I dropped my stolen goods back into the basket and said, "Sorry."

She laughed and glanced at a clipboard hanging on the wall. There seemed to be some kind of to-do list with not much crossed off. "It's nice to meet you, Mr. Sorry. I'm Mrs. Boyd."

"Actually, it's Calder White, ma'am, and I really am sorry." I lowered my voice and locked my eyes on hers, staring into them, twisting my will into her mind, making my thoughts her own. I tried to come up with images that would make me seem trustworthy: me in one of her blue aprons, working behind the cash register.

"I don't have any money," I said, "but it smelled so un-believable in here I couldn't resist."

Her pupils dilated, and she chuckled warmly. "I just popped a slew of muffins out of the oven." She rested her hand on the boxes. "I'm bringing them up to the old Hancock place."

"You don't say."

"My husband Bill's up there right now, moving in some of the heavy stuff. I was just about to head up there with the goodies. I'll tell you what. Run these up to the Hancocks and I'll throw in a couple extra just for you."

"Deal."

"Let me write down the directions." She picked up a pen and tore a sheet out of the receipt book.

"I got it."

She looked up, her eyes still wide. "You know where you're going?"

"Actually, I do." I picked up the boxes and turned for the door. Too bad Maris hadn't seen me in action. It might have bought me a nag-free night.

I'd downed two muffins before reaching the north end of town, pushing the speed limit as much as I dared. When I'd gone about a mile, I dropped the Impala down to a crawl and counted the clumps of birch trees . . . three, four, five . . . until the familiar driveway came into view. It was just as I remembered it from some forty years earlier, but more overgrown. Matted yellow weeds and leftover snow clung to the edge of the driveway. Potholes gaped in the tire tracks.

I rolled slowly over the natural speed bumps until I reached the Hancock house—two stories of weathered clapboard, with a peaked roof and a small, darkened porch that sagged in the middle. A square window was centered under the peak and above the porch. A dormer window on the right side of the house faced the lake. Plywood covered the first-floor windows. Shingles lay in the yard rather than over the black hole in the roof. Time had not been good to it.

Ahead of me, Hancock was laughing and slapping men on the back, throwing apologetic looks at his wife, who leaned on a cane. When it came to killing Jason Hancock, his wife looked like she might beat me to it.

I parked the car on the far shoulder, scraping the passenger side with the tree branches.

A parade of men, women, and a few kids carried boxes into the house and then returned empty-handed, only to grab another load and repeat the trip. Several of the people wore Northland College sweatshirts even though they were clearly past their college years. Colleagues? Was Hancock a professor? I'd never considered him anything other than prey. Someone had already worked hard enough to shed his sweatshirt and leave it draped over the back of his tailgate. I snagged it up and, though it was a little tight, managed to wrangle it over my chest.

The little Hancock girl stepped primly down the porch steps, avoiding a hazard I couldn't see. Perhaps a loose board? She looked even younger than I remembered. What role could I play for her? Teacher? Hero? Maybe hero would work. I could lure her into the woods, where she'd get conveniently lost. After a failed search party, I could appear with her in my arms. That had to be worth *some* show of gratitude. Like a fishing trip out on the lake. How could Jason Hancock refuse me?

Lily Hancock came out next, wearing the same black corduroy miniskirt from the day before, a rose-colored cardigan, and a yellow beret. I smirked at the thought of her little sister's reaction to this outfit. Lily stopped on the porch and laid her palm against the banister. She tested its strength, and it wobbled under her hand. Her eyes drifted to the porch roof.

I strolled up the driveway toward the house, carrying the boxes of muffins. A cool breeze blew off the lake. Lily wiped her hands on her skirt and pulled her sweater low over her hips. *Still hasn't confessed the tattoo,* I guessed. Sophie noticed me first and smiled. She ran up to greet me while Lily stood frozen on the steps. For a second I thought she might have recognized me from before.

"Are you here to help?" Sophie asked, her voice high and hopeful.

In my peripheral vision, I noticed Lily's mouth hanging open while she watched my exchange with her younger sister. Another girl met Lily on the steps, and I listened to their conversation while having my own with Sophie.

"I'm delivering muffins," I said, "but I'm happy to help."

"Who is that, Gabrielle?" asked Lily.

"Good. I'll take 'em inside. You can grab something out of the van," said Sophie. She took the muffins and headed toward the house.

The girl next to Lily whispered, *"Never seen him before, but if that's the kind of guy waiting for me at college, I can't wait to get there. Check out his hair. And, oh my God, check out his arms— even through that sweatshirt. I bet he works out."*

"Okay, I'll get to work," I called after Sophie.

"You think he's good-looking? I guess. But he didn't get that tan around here," said Lily. *"I wonder where he's from."*

45

Jason Hancock appeared from the other side of the moving van. He looked up at Lily, then followed her gaze to me. My eyes locked with Hancock's, and I clenched my teeth. I had to force my jaw to relax so I could speak.

"Hi," I said with feigned enthusiasm. "Mrs. Boyd sent me up here with some breakfast for all the movers. She thought maybe I could lend a hand, too?" My voice faltered, and I cleared my throat to regain control. A second later Mrs. Hancock rounded the van, stepping cautiously on the uneven ground, leaning on her cane.

"Thanks so much," Hancock said. "I'm Jason Hancock. This is my wife, Carolyn."

Hancock reached out to shake my hand, but fortunately I'd already picked up a box. I didn't think I could handle any physical contact. I was pushed to my limit as it was.

"Calder White," I said.

"Good to meet you, Calder," Mrs. Hancock said. "It's so nice of you to help. God knows we need it." And then she laughed, her voice light and lilting. I would have liked to shake *her* hand.

"Have you met our daughters?" Hancock asked. "Lily's our oldest." He waved toward the porch and Lily raised a tentative hand. "And Sophie just ran inside. This is my parents' old place."

I nodded and forced a smile.

"I guess I didn't realize it was so run-down." He put his hand on his wife's shoulder and gave it an apologetic squeeze. "Carolyn's right. We've got a lot of work ahead of us."

I barely heard anything he said. My mind was speeding forward, trying to ignore Mrs. Hancock's sympathetic tug on my heart and strategizing my best options for getting her husband onto the dock. But if I took Hancock down alone, without letting my sisters have their own share in his end, I'd pay for it. Still, it would only take a second to grab him . . . I needed to get my mind on something else. Maris wanted to drag this out.

"Do you fish?" I asked. *What the hell?* I groaned mentally; I was already slipping. It was no good being so close. I couldn't think straight. The air stretched into a thin trickle of oxygen. Was my tongue always so thick?

Jason Hancock chuckled. "Nope. Not at all."

I walked quickly toward the house and Hancock followed. He kicked at a pile of shingles, and they shattered like shale. When we passed Lily on the porch, I stole a sideways glance at her. The girl named Gabrielle rocked back and forth on her heels, clearly amused by something.

"But of course, we do have a lot of fishing and hunting gear here at the house," Hancock continued. We stepped through the doorway, and he gestured to an impressive-looking gun cabinet by the fireplace. "This was all my dad's stuff. I'm more of a book guy. I'll be teaching at Northland starting fall semester."

I put my box down on the dining table and looked around: to the left, a small living room with green shag carpeting, knotty pine paneling, and a stone fireplace; to the right, a tiny kitchen featuring cracked linoleum and peeling wallpaper with images of sheaths of wheat. There appeared to be a bedroom beyond the living room. A narrow wooden staircase, open on one side, rose like a ladder out of the middle of the house.

At the foot of the stairs, a few black-and-white photographs hung crookedly on the wall. I walked over, fixated on one face. I took the photograph off the nail and wiped away a thick layer of dust.

"My parents," Jason Hancock said, clearing his throat. "They lived here when they were first married. I was just a baby."

"Tom Hancock."

"Right," he said, surprised. "Did your grandparents know him?"

Before I could answer, the floorboards creaked and we both looked toward the door. Lily was there along with the other girl, who fidgeted with her shorts. Lily pushed a strand of auburn hair behind her ear. My eyes followed the long, pale line of her neck, now exposed.

"Hi," she said, and then she bit her bottom lip. "I'm Lily Hancock." The other girl jabbed Lily, hard, in the ribs. "Right. And this is Gabrielle Pettit."

"Gabrielle's dad is a carpenter and handyman. He's going to help me fix the roof," Hancock explained as he swiped a small tube of lip balm across his chapped lips. Then he headed back to the van.

"Mrs. Boyd sent me up with muffins," I said. "Thought I'd stay and see if you needed any help."

"My brother's out back," said the Pettit girl. "He's helping, too."

"So, you live around here?" asked Lily.

"Yeah, sure, just over there." I gestured vaguely and hoped she'd be satisfied with the ambiguous suggestion. Sophie Hancock came in behind Lily and smiled shyly at me. "So . . .

I guess I'll go grab a couple more boxes, then?" No one said no, so I trotted out the door.

"God be praised," the Pettit girl whispered, giggling.

I passed off a laugh as a cough and stopped to help a group of men wrestling with a mattress. The girls moved back onto the porch, and I could feel their eyes on my back.

"Do you think I should go talk to him?" Gabrielle asked. *"We could double."*

"Double what?" Lily asked.

"You and my brother. Me and him."

"Yeah, I don't think so. Besides, we're supposed to be helping my dad, not playing matchmaker."

"Your dad's got plenty of help."

When I finally reached the moving van, a guy emerged from the back, balancing an impressive tower of cardboard boxes. Judging by his resemblance to Gabrielle, I guessed him to be her brother. His muscles flexed under the weight he carried.

"Quit showing off, Jack," Gabrielle called. "You don't want to break anything."

"Don't worry, I got it," he yelled back. I picked up a few boxes of my own and followed Jack Pettit to the house. As he passed through the doorway, I thought I saw him wink at Lily, but it might have been my imagination.

He set his boxes down on the orange kitchen counter, knocking a huge tub of Vaseline onto the floor. I set my load down on the table and returned the Vaseline to its place.

"Hey, thanks," Jack said. "Didn't see it there."

"No problem," I said.

"Are you one of the Hancocks?" he asked.

"Hardly." I almost laughed.

"I'm going to be working with my dad," Jack said. "We're going to turn this hellhole back into a dump." He rolled his eyes. "Should make for a fascinating summer."

I looked past his shoulder to Lily and Gabrielle, who were helping Mrs. Hancock stock a linen closet. Gabrielle caught me looking. She tapped Lily on the shoulder and dragged her toward me and Jack.

"Yeah," I said. "Maybe I'll see you around." Jack and I headed back for more boxes, reaching the front door simultaneously, with Lily and Gabrielle right behind. As Jack and I did the "after you; no, after you" dance in the doorway, our chests bumped. Jack sucked in a surprised lungful of air. His nostrils flared, and his eyes widened. He snapped his head around to look at Lily, then at me, then back at Lily. Sadness tugged at the corners of his eyes before a darkness clouded his face. He inhaled again, holding his breath.

"Okay there, buddy?" I asked, all the while thinking, *He knows. How could he know?* But then I had to laugh at myself. I guess paranoia was a fallout symptom of my abstinence. I'd stretched this little experiment out so far, I was now in uncharted waters. I wondered what would go next.

8

HYPOCRITE

All the boxes were moved into their appropriate rooms. I carried the last of Sophie's things upstairs to her bedroom, which faced the lake. Judging by the pale blue walls, I assumed it had been Jason Hancock's nursery years ago. There was a lingering fragrance in the walls that was strangely familiar. I struggled to place it but eventually had to give up the effort. I tore open a box and started placing Sophie's books on her bookshelf.

Downstairs, several men were moving the bigger pieces of furniture into the living room. From the next upstairs bedroom,

I could hear the Pettit brother and sister talking with Lily. It was hard to tune everyone out and focus on Sophie, particularly because the Pettits were talking about me.

"Are you sure you should let that guy hang out in your little sister's room?" Jack asked. His voice held a mixture of concern and distrust.

"C'mon. Don't be gross. He's not hanging out. He's helping us move just like everyone else."

"Well, I wouldn't let him near my sister."

Gabrielle laughed. *"He can get near me anytime he wants. I like danger."*

I grinned to myself and placed the last of the Baby Sitter's Club series on the shelf.

"Calder, can you help me with this?" Sophie asked. "There's too much tape. I can't open it." I got up and took my car key out of my pocket. I sliced through the tape and gestured like a magician's assistant at the contents—mostly nappy stuffed animals.

"I seriously doubt he's dangerous," said Lily. The sound of pulling and cutting tape followed her words.

"Wouldn't matter," Jack said. *"I could take him."*

"Neither one of us needs your protection, Jack," said Gabrielle.

"What are you taping on your walls?" Jack asked. I heard the faint rush of air as someone ripped something out of someone else's hands.

"What do you like better, Calder? Pandas or frogs?" Sophie asked.

"Hmm? What? Oh, frogs, I guess."

She handed me a green stuffed animal. "You can have that one, then."

"They're pictures of famous poets," Lily said.

"Looks like a bunch of old dead guys," Jack said.

"Dude, don't be such a philistine," Gabrielle said. There was the sound of someone, probably Jack, pounding his chest like a gorilla.

"Besides," Gabrielle continued, *"how is this any weirder than the crap on your walls?"*

"That's art," Jack said. *"And my paintings aren't crap."*

"Right," Gabrielle said. *"They're inspired."*

Light footsteps fell in the hallway, and I looked up to see Lily standing outside Sophie's door. She'd lost the beret, and her hair was messed up. She stole a nervous glance at me. "Everything okay in here?" she asked.

I wondered if maybe Jack Pettit was right. Was I acting too familiar too soon? I always had a hard time gauging normal human behavior. *Pace yourself,* I told myself. *Time to back off.*

Hancock called up the stairs to the Pettits. "Gabrielle, Jack, your dad's ready to go."

Jack was immediately beside Lily, his eyes doing little to mask his disapproval of me or his disappointment in leaving. His chest inflated with air and his earlier look of confusion returned. This time I was sure I wasn't imagining it.

I stood up, dropping the frog onto Sophie's bed. "Well, I guess that's it," I said a little louder than necessary. I stepped into the hallway. "Hope to see you all soon." *Some of you more than others,* I added mentally, throwing Sophie a parting wave. Lily frowned.

"You're leaving?" Sophie asked, clutching a matted bear to her chest. "Already?" Her eyes grew round, and her bottom lip projected. "Don't you want the frog?" She reminded me of a smaller, human version of Pavati.

"Oh, sorry," I said, retrieving her gift. "Of course I do."

The Pettits' van passed me as I walked to my car. So did the rest of the movers, looking weary. One of them massaged his own shoulder before climbing into his vehicle. One guy looked under his truck for his missing sweatshirt.

I drove down the road a half mile and parked at a nearby boat launch before doubling back on foot. I had strict instructions from Maris to learn as much as I could as quickly as I could, so I prepared to study the Hancocks for the rest of the afternoon, to see what they did when they thought no one was watching.

I sat in the pine branches, spying through the newly uncovered windows. Hopefully, I'd learn something of value that would keep Maris off my back for the night. Maybe she'd actually let me sleep.

The late-afternoon sun drew long shadows across the Hancocks' front yard. It was cold in the trees. And quiet. The Hancocks were settled in. Mrs. Hancock was in the kitchen, unpacking boxes. Through another window, I could see Hancock assembling a bookshelf.

Lily lay belly-down on the living room floor, her knees bent and her feet crossed in the air. She was reading a book but not turning the pages. She seemed to be reading the same lines over and over, mouthing the words as she read them. Memorizing them?

Sophie played nearby. She had her Barbie and Ken dolls in bathing suits, swimming through the green shag carpeting like they were crossing the channel. When her shaggy lake came to the base of the gun cabinet, Ken and Barbie turned into rock climbers and scaled its mahogany doors.

On the other side of the glass panes, the Hancocks lived their lives, oblivious to the danger I posed. Somewhere in my history, in some distant memory, I remembered what it meant to be a family. Or at least something close. It bothered me that I'd have to disrupt this peaceful picture. Doubt gnawed at my gut. Maybe I couldn't do this. Maybe I didn't have it in me. But if I couldn't complete my assignment, Maris would never release me.

I was such a hypocrite. Why was it okay to destroy a family when I knew what it meant to be destroyed? *Because this is justice,* I reminded myself. *And it's justice deserved.*

I squirmed in my hiding spot. *Do something, people,* I urged. *Say something.* The silence dragged on. I imagined my first report to Maris: "We have underestimated our enemy. They are lethal. We are in serious danger of the Hancocks boring us to death. Abort, abort, abort." I was just about to laugh at my own self-entertainment when a clatter of dishes shattered the silence. I jumped and pulled farther back into the branches.

"Carolyn! Are you all right?" Jason Hancock was on his feet. The girls stared at each other for a second before running after him. I climbed higher to get a better view. Carolyn Hancock sat on the kitchen floor, curled into a ball in the center of a debris field. An empty box marked *Everyday Dishes* lay on the floor beside her.

"I thought this was supposed to be one of my good days," she whimpered into her knees. Lily knelt beside her mother and helped Hancock pull his wife to her feet.

"It's okay, Carolyn."

"How is this okay?" she asked.

"It's only dishes, Mom."

"Stupid dishes." She picked up a plate that had managed to survive and smashed it against the floor. "Stupid house. Stupid body."

"Carolyn honey . . . Shhhhh, baby, it's okay."

Sophie let out a sob and ran for the stairs. Lily followed, calling after her. Mrs. Hancock cried into her husband's shoulder. "Don't ever leave me," she said, and she laid her head against his chest.

He supported her as they walked to the couch. He grabbed her cane as they passed through the kitchen door.

"As if I could."

"Jason, what are we doing here?"

"You know what we're doing here. It's going to be good for all of us, Carolyn. You'll see."

"Restful climate," she said with disgust. "We could have gone anywhere. Why here? Why now? How is this supposed to make things better?"

Hancock's gaze drifted to the ceiling. From the upstairs bedroom, Sophie's wailing cry filled me with shame.

9

INDECISION

My sisters and I surfaced one at a time, fifty yards from the Hancocks' shoreline. Behind the house, treetop silhouettes pierced the pink and purple sky. We'd been repeating this scene every summer for over forty years: swimming back and forth in front of the house, watching the windows, hoping for some sign of the family's return. It felt strangely dreamlike to be seeing light in the long-darkened windows.

Our bodies bobbed in the inky water, nothing more than shadows. We had no concerns of detection. Tallulah broke the silence.

"What have you decided, Cal?"

"The little one."

Tallulah looked pleased with my choice. Relieved, maybe. Pavati, not so much.

Maris nodded. "She's smaller. Weaker. How will you do it?"

I grimaced. "She likes pretty things. Pavati?"

She turned at the sound of her name, but I kept my eyes straight ahead.

"She'll follow you," I said.

"Of course she will."

"I want you to play with her. Be nice. Show her things. Let her have a good time. Keep her out past dinner."

"I can do that."

"Tallulah, can you be gentle?"

A worried look crossed her face. "How gentle?"

"You'll need to knock her out. But you can't kill her. Can you do that?" Of the three of my sisters, she was the most likely to pull it off. I stared into her eyes as her mind processed my request. I could imagine her hands around Sophie's neck, slowly cutting off her oxygen, while Pavati smiled into the little girl's face, telling her she looked sleepy and didn't she just want to take a nap?

"I think so. If I'm careful."

"What about me?" asked Maris.

"I don't want you to do anything."

She feigned offense, but then added, "You're probably right."

"When she's unconscious, carry her to the rocks. They'll search for her. I'll join the search party."

The girls nodded.

"When she wakes up," I continued, "you can tell her she fell. I'll carry her home."

"You'll be their hero," said Pavati.

"That's what I'm thinking," I said. "It'll also give me reason to go back and check on her. Hopefully, they'll want to thank me. That's where your fishing trip will come in, Maris."

A slow, thin smile spread across her lips. Her hair floated on the surface of the water like spilled cream.

"I'll take over from there," she said.

I shrugged. "Whatever."

The light in the dormer window lit a path across the side yard toward the water. We could see Sophie's face. She was brushing her hair.

"Is that the one?" Pavati asked, a look of adoration filling her eyes.

"Yes."

"Such a pretty little girl."

"I guess so." My voice fell flat.

"If I had a daughter," said Pavati, "I'd want her to look just like that." She put her hand on my shoulder. "Don't worry. I know just what to do. I'll find her tomorrow." She pressed down on me and pushed herself upward, rising from the water. Then she dipped her head and dove into the lake. Maris and Tallulah followed without the slightest splash.

I remained behind, watching Sophie in the window. She stood up and walked out of sight, then flipped off the light. I was just about to follow my sisters when the front door slammed and another figure stepped off the porch and started walking toward the water. I was transfixed. Was Jason Hancock going to come to the water's edge? Could it be this easy? I felt like a crocodile lurking at the shore, watching a zebra come down for a drink.

Involuntarily, I floated closer.

But it wasn't Jason Hancock. It was Lily coming down to the boat dock. She kicked off her sandals and hitched up her skirt before sitting at the end, letting her legs dangle off the edge of the dock and into the freezing water. Was that normal?

I dropped beneath the surface like a weighted line and searched for her scent. It was sweet, with a spicy edge like oranges or pine needles. When I resurfaced, I only let my eyes and nose break the waterline. I didn't realize how close to shore I'd come, and my first instinct was panic. I dropped an inch.

"You don't have to be so sneaky. I know you're there," she said.

Shit. My heart hit my stomach like a fist. *Flash!* I was gone. I swam north twenty yards to a willow branch that hung low over the water like a bench.

Jason Hancock was walking the length of the dock toward his daughter. He was rubbing some kind of balm into his bare arms, and it made his skin glisten even in the fading light. "Sorry, hon," he said. "You just looked peaceful sitting there. I didn't want to disturb you."

He sat down beside her and put his arm around her shoulders while I, lurking in the shadows, worked to lower my heart rate. I peered over the willow branch at them.

"Y'know Mom's pissed about the house," said Lily.

"She'll get over it."

"It's a pit, Dad. The whole place is falling apart, and you're not exactly a handyman."

He smiled. "I've got help, remember? You've always been too much of a worrier. Your mom will be fine."

"I heard what she asked you," Lily said. "How is this move supposed to make things better for *her*?"

"What's that supposed to mean?"

"I'll give you that Bayfield's more quiet than Minneapolis, but is it really going to improve her health? I'm just wondering if moving here is more about your curiosity than anything else."

"Lily Anne Hancock, your mother has always been my number one priority. All I've ever wanted is to make sure she's taken care of."

"Easy, Dad. I'm just wondering about Grandpa's stories. Maybe you just wanted to—"

"How do you like your room?" Hancock asked.

"Don't avoid the conversation, Dad."

"This *is* a conversation. It's a question."

"Fine," said Lily. She bobbed her head slowly, considering her words. "It's nice, I guess. Cozy."

Hancock tested the water with his fingertips and groaned softly. "So maybe you're a little bit right. This move is for your mom, but I can't deny that it feels good to be here. I don't know what it is, Lil, but it's like this lake is calling me. Sometimes I really regret not having learned to swim."

"If we were back in Minneapolis, you could take lessons at the Y."

Hancock smirked and kissed his daughter's cheek. "You've

been a good sport. I know you miss the city, but thanks for giving this a shot. Leave the worrying to me, Lily. I'll take care of your mom. You try and have some fun."

"Fun. Sure," Lily said. "Did you know Bayfield is, like, the apple capital of the upper Midwest?"

Hancock chuckled and withdrew his arm. "Maybe you and Sophie should go exploring tomorrow. Check out the town, the woods."

I perked up at his suggestion and ventured out from under cover.

"Yeah. Sounds great, Dad. I'm sure Sophie would *love* a hike in the woods."

Ah, sarcasm. This girl was more my style.

Jason Hancock threw his head back and laughed. "Yeah, maybe not," he said. "She's never been the outdoorsy type."

Lily lay against her father's shoulder. "I love you, Dad."

I dove for the bottom and took a course toward Basswood. Someone might have argued I was meant to witness this father-daughter moment—that it was a sign Hancock and Lily had a stronger bond than I'd originally thought. But even though the older girl was more my type of target, I couldn't abandon our plan just for personal preferences. Sophie was the girl. Besides, I didn't really believe in signs.

10

BEST-LAID PLANS

All night I worked on the details of my plan. Synchronicity would be important. Our art of persuasion would have to be spot-on perfect. What I hadn't factored in was the weather, and that was one thing I couldn't control. Well, one of many.

The new day brought with it a change in atmospheric pressure that prickled my skin and squeezed my temples. There was an electrical charge buzzing between the tree branches, and the animals in the woods had all gone silent. How long could the rain hold off?

It was three o'clock when the Hancock sisters finally set

off on their forced-march expedition into the woods. They stepped out their door just as the *Pettit's Handyman & Cabinetry* van pulled into the driveway. Jason Hancock followed his daughters out and greeted Mr. Pettit. Gabrielle and Jack climbed out of the passenger-side door. They jogged around the front to say hello to Lily.

As for me and my sisters, we'd only been on land for a few minutes. They were somewhere north of the Hancocks' house, while I lurked in the trees just outside their front door. My leg muscles, still newly morphed, trembled beneath me. I leaned against a tree for support and strained to listen to the Hancocks' and Pettits' conversation.

Waves crashed against the shoreline, making it harder to catch everything. Something about fixing the roof, obviously. The Pettit man gestured at his kids. He nodded at Sophie. Gabrielle Pettit didn't seem to be saying much. The men talked and pointed at the house. There was a moment of unexpected silence from the lake, and Lily said, "We were going to explore the woods."

My back straightened, and I leaned forward.

Jack Pettit shook his head. He braced his hands on the toolbelt around his hips and pointed up at the sky. It had been overcast all morning, but now the clouds were less of a gray canvas and more like churning ashes. I looked anxiously at the Hancock girls to see what they'd decide.

Lily shrugged, and I rallied. She obviously didn't like being told what to do. If she was anything like me, she'd storm off into the woods. Of course, that stubborn streak could pose a problem for me, too, if she refused to follow my lead and separate herself from her sister. Right on cue,

Lily kissed her dad's cheek and stomped off, dragging Sophie behind her.

I hit the Send button on my cell. "They've left.... Yes, both of them.... Due west.... I don't know. You'll have to think of something.... Wait, let me see." I closed my eyes and inhaled. The familiar scent of oranges filled my nostrils, only more diluted by the air than it had been in the water. "Oranges," I said, then searched past that scent for Sophie's. I choked on the sudden dryness of the air. "And talcum powder.... Yes, I'll follow for a while, but I don't want to get too close. Where are you? ... I'll call if they change direction, but you should pick up the scent in fifteen minutes."

Lily still had her little sister by the hand. Sophie didn't seem to be sharing any of Lily's enthusiasm for adventure. She was complaining about something and gesturing at her sandals.

They followed a worn deer path until it intersected with something man-made. The new path was lined with timbers stripped of their bark. Wood chips filled the borders. Sophie's ankles turned on the soft path and she stopped with a stamp of her foot. She folded her arms across her chest. I marveled at Lily's patience.

"Here, take this," said Lily. She removed her cardigan and handed it to her sister, leaving herself in only a lacy tank top. "Better?"

Sophie nodded and Lily's mouth slipped into a smile I didn't recognize. Was it mockery? No, it didn't seem to be that, because she slipped her arm around her sister's shoulders and squeezed. It was something softer. I paused and rummaged through the catalog of human expressions I kept in my mind. But it wasn't a human expression I landed on. It was my mermaid mother's. I could almost hear her saying, *There, there, now, Calder, isn't that better? You know, if you spent more time swimming and less time visiting the shipwrecks, you'd stay warmer.*

I shook my head to clear the image and fixed my eyes on Lily's face. Soaked it up. Memorized it. Her auburn hair captured the scarce bits of sunlight that broke through the trees. Each strand was a slightly different color, reflecting light like little rainbow beads. It cascaded down her back in loose curls. Her arms and legs were long and limber. She was surefooted. Her voice . . .

I snapped out of my reverie when I realized they'd moved too far for me to hear them anymore. They trudged on until the path stopped, as did the dense understory. The deciduous forest gave way to pines, now sparsely spaced in the silty soil.

I dug my cell out of my pocket and waited for Pavati to pick up. "Listen. Slight change of plans."

Pavati's voice came shrill through the phone.

"Let me talk to them first," I said. The new plan was taking shape as I spoke. "I don't want the older one to be unnecessarily nervous when you separate them. Give me five minutes and then show up. The younger one wants to turn back anyway. Use that opportunity. I'll distract the older sister. You offer to walk the younger one back to the house. Tallulah can knock her out as soon as you get her out of her sister's sight."

I clicked the phone off and shoved it into my pocket.

The Hancock sisters stopped to admire the lake from the

higher vantage point—or at least, one of them did. Sophie was picking bark off a pine tree, looking bored.

I made a little noise so as not to scare them with my sudden appearance. Still, Lily whirled around with a yelp. I put up my hands, palms forward, to calm her down.

"Whoa. Sorry. Didn't mean to scare you," I said. *That will come later.*

A huge smile spread across Sophie's face, but Lily looked less certain.

"Hi, Calder," said Sophie. "What are you doing out here?"

"Same thing as you," I said. "Taking a walk. What do you think of the view? Pretty spectacular, isn't it?"

Lily agreed, and she turned back toward the lake. "I heard they have sailboat races around Madeline Island sometimes."

"Not till summer." I thought about her reaction to Jack Pettit's warning back at the house and said, "Hey, it's getting kind of cold." Hopefully I'd get the same defiant reaction from her. That would keep her from wanting to go back with Sophie once Pavati showed up. "For a girl," I added.

Lily's chin pulled up and her mouth tightened.

Bingo.

A familiar laugh broke out of the woods, and Pavati and Tallulah sauntered up the path toward us, heading in the direction the Hancock girls had just come from. Tallulah feigned surprise when she saw us standing there.

"Oh," said Pavati. "Hello there, sweetheart." She fixed her hypnotic eyes on Sophie, and I could feel the electricity in the air. I stole a look at Sophie, and she was—just as I knew she would be—getting that glassed-over look our prey assumed seconds before we dragged them under. Having been on the receiving end of Pavati's gift, I knew what Sophie was feeling. The spell acted as a sedative; she didn't feel much. Humans rarely fought back. Tom Hancock had been one of the few. I hoped resistance wasn't a family trait.

"Oh, I didn't expect to see you here. These are my sisters," I explained to Lily. She would never let Sophie go with strangers. I still wasn't much more than that myself, but I hoped my introduction would ease her concerns.

Tallulah looked at me, surprised. We hadn't talked about this kind of personal approach.

Pavati didn't seem to notice. She was still smiling intently at Sophie. "You're cold," she suggested, and Sophie nodded, instinctively pulling Lily's cardigan closer around her.

"Listen, Lily," I said, summoning as much charm as I could. "If you'd like to keep exploring, I can show you something. It's just a little farther up the path."

"Sure," she said. Her pupils dilated, and I gave a short nod, which Tallulah picked up.

Tallulah said, "Well, how about we walk your sister back home, then?"

"That sounds great," I answered for Lily, and although I was looking only at her, I heard her little sister repeat the word *great*.

And just like that, they were gone, and I was alone with Lily. A wave of nausea rolled over me. There was something about her that terrified me, and I broke eye contact. Lily shook her head and looked back over the lake.

"So, what did you want to show me?" she asked.

"Um. It's a rock formation. Just up ahead. Follow me." I walked past her, and my hand brushed against hers. Electricity hummed on my fingers, and I was sure she felt it, too. She lifted her hand to her face and examined it.

"Something wrong?" I asked.

"No," she said. "Unless I'm about to have a seizure."

"You're not having a seizure," I said, laughing. I dialed back my emotions to mitigate the electrical impulses that flowed naturally through my body. Fear, anger, any intense feeling—in this case, a raging bout of nerves—always had to be kept on low. If I let my emotions take over my body, I could make a tree spontaneously combust just by leaning against it. It was my least favorite aspect of my makeup. Any resemblance to eels disgusted me. I preferred to think of Maris as the only slithery one of the four of us.

We stepped through the trees and up to the edge of the cliff. Basswood Island was at its closest point here, and I could still see the remains of our campfire from the night before. A trickle of gray ash caught in the wind and licked up from the spot.

The water and sky were now the same charcoal gray, turning Basswood into a dark, woodsy spaceship hovering in the air. I hoped Lily wouldn't notice how stormy the sky was getting so I could stretch this out a few more minutes.

Paper birch and aspen fringed the edge of the cliff, their gray-green bark a thin skin compared to the shingled bark of the pines. The aspens grew haphazardly, clinging to the bank, often shooting out in precarious angles over the water. I crept to the edge and started to climb down the bank, using an aspen as a railing.

"What are you doing?" Lily asked.

I could hear the alarm in her voice. I took as deep a

breath as my lungs would allow and exhaled all the emotion out of my body. "Take my hand," I said. "I'll help you down."

Lily looked at it hesitantly, then slowly slipped her hand into mine. It was unexpectedly warm. I wrapped my fingers around hers, which sent a strange electricity shooting up my arm. I glanced at Lily, but she didn't seem to feel it.

"Watch your step," I said. She found her footing and we eased our way down about eight feet to an iron-colored rock that jutted out into the lake, about ten feet above the water level. The rock was pockmarked with natural indentations that were full of old rainwater now warm from days of sun. Microscopic insects skated across the surface of the pools.

"Oh, this is so cool," she said. "It's so wild . . . and primal. . . ."

"Definitely wild," I said, "but it gets cooler. Lie down and look over the edge. There are sand martins roosting in holes in the sandstone."

I wasn't trying to be hypnotic in any way, yet she followed my lead. Was she responding to me or the scenery? She gripped the edge of the rock with her fingertips and brought her chin past its edge.

"I can't see anything," she said.

"You can't?" I lay down beside her, my shoulders extending past the edge of the rock, and curled around the edge to see. "You probably have to lean out more." Lily pushed herself out farther and bent her head. She wriggled forward a little more, and then there was an intake of breath and her back muscles tensed. Before I realized what was happening, she was toppling over the edge and falling into the freezing water below.

I looked up, and Maris stood over me, peering down into the concentric circles that marked the spot where Lily had disappeared.

11

CHANGING PLANS

"What the hell?" I jumped to my feet. "You pushed her?" I looked desperately around for something to reach down to Lily. But there was nothing long enough. Panic gripped my thighs. "What do I do?"

"Do?" Maris looked at me with incredulity. "What are you talking about? You were looking to make a rescue . . . so rescue her."

"Geez, Maris. In the freaking water? Are you insane? We had a plan. Sophie is our girl, remember?"

The lake was onyx, with patches of flinty gray where the

sun hit it. We peered over the edge of the cliff, looking down into the black chops. Directly below us, the water churned into a butter-colored froth against the cliff edge.

Lily came up with an audible gasp. I could feel the cold piercing her skin. She reached behind her head with one shaking hand and came away with blood. Maris and I took a big step back from the edge so she wouldn't see us.

"H-help! S-s-someone! Calder!" Lily called.

My muscles tightened in response. "I can't get in the water with her." Maris knew that. I growled with frustration, "I haven't had the chance to build up any tolerance to the lake yet. I won't be able to hold back the change."

"Fine. We'll wait it out." Maris looked up at the clouds. "She'll be dead in a few minutes anyway." Maris sat down on the rock. "Maybe this will be even better. You can carry both of his children home—one dead, the other clinging to life." She seemed to play the scene out in her mind, and I could see she liked it.

A trawler sped by, close to shore but not seeing the girl in the water. It created an onslaught of waves that battered Lily against the jagged edge of the rock. She was pinned to it, then sucked back, only to be slammed into the rock again. Another wave lifted her up and smashed her right cheek against the cliff.

There was nothing for her to grab. There was nothing to put her foot on. Clouds roiled overhead.

A half second later my phone was at my ear. "Pavati, has Tallulah done anything yet?" I exhaled. "Well, don't. . . . You heard me. We've got a big problem. *I've* got a big problem," I corrected. "Just bring the little girl straight home. I'll explain later. . . . Pavati? Are you listening to me?"

There was a "Yes" on the other end just as my phone beeped. Out of minutes. I chucked it into the woods.

There were no more screams from the water. I peered over the edge. Lily was vertical in the water, her arms extended, head tipped back. Her face went under, then resurfaced, only to dip under the waterline again. She exhaled and inhaled quickly with each resurfacing.

"Oh, man, I can't believe I'm doing this." I said, stripping off my clothes.

"You're going in, then?" Maris asked, her voice bored.

"What choice do I have?"

We could both hear the "he-he-heh" of Lily's desperate intakes and exhales. She couldn't get the oxygen necessary for an effective plea. She didn't have much time. I desperately hoped there would be no one else on the path this close to a storm. The last thing I needed was spectators.

I stood naked at the edge of the cliff and closed my eyes, my lips rolled inward. I wasn't sure what I was waiting for— maybe something to convince me this was the stupidest thing I'd ever done. I'd never transformed in the water near a human I intended to release. As far as I knew, none of us had. If this was going to work, she couldn't see me, and Lake Superior was notoriously clear.

The anticipatory tingling crept through my body, starting in my toes, then spreading upward and inward. It rode roughshod over my carefully cultivated self-control until my internal organs rammed around like bumper cars at a fair. The electrical flow was so strong my hair stood up on my head.

"Get it together, Calder," Maris said as she examined her fingernails. "You hit the water with that many volts and you're going to zap every fish within a hundred feet. It'll be fish floats all over the place, and it probably won't help the girl, either."

I took one last look over the edge. Lily was gone.

I exhaled, blowing all the electricity out of me and into the air. It fizzed in the humidity. When I felt only a dull numbness, I dove.

A strangely smooth feeling came over me as I soared through the air. When I hit the black water, it was with such precision that it was like being threaded through a needle.

Down, down, at least three fathoms, until my hands touched sand. I opened my eyes and swam back toward the rock. I thrashed as the change happened, then beat my tail even more to stir up the sandy bottom. If I couldn't resist the change, I had to make it more difficult for her to see me, but clouding the water made it harder for *me* to find *her*. I followed her scent, turning in a circle, my head meeting my tail. I crisscrossed my arms in front of me, feeling for something that didn't belong.

When I struck something long but soft—not a branch, but an arm—I turned her around to face me. Her eyes were closed, her mouth slack. Pallid yellow particles floated in the water that filled her mouth. She was already gone.

I rocketed toward the surface, leaping twelve feet out of the water and landing on the rock better than any trick whale at SeaWorld.

Maris looked over without expression.

Grit from the rock stuck to Lily's face and bare shoulders.

I pressed my lips to hers and blew. Nothing happened. I blew again. And then again. She gagged and choked, then spewed a fountain of water. My silver tail thrashed violently against the rock. Maris stepped over me and threw her jacket over Lily's face. She didn't need to see the monster convulsing beside her.

I rolled onto my back as my heart beat out a syncopated, lurching rhythm. Gritting my teeth while my skin tightened and ripped, I groaned in agony, trembling like an epileptic and sucking blood off my lip as my tail split and morphed into human legs.

Maris didn't watch as I stood up and yanked on my pants. She stood coolly over the girl, who was still motionless on the rock.

"Lily." I whipped the jacket off her face and shook her. "Are you okay? Oh, man. Lily."

Her skin was as pale and translucent as her ivory tank top. A red line trickled from a gash on her cheekbone, and her lips, slightly parted, were the color of lilacs. Grains of sand clung to her eyelashes. She could have been a rag doll, flopping around in my shaking hands.

"Lily," I called again. I rolled her onto her side. Her tank top rode up, exposing the tattoo on the small of her back: five words in elegant black script—*No Coward Soul Is Mine*.

She gasped, dragging in another ragged breath. "I-I'm o-okay," she said. Her body shook in spasms.

"You're not." I balled up my shirt and scrubbed her arms with it, trying to rub color back into her skin. I didn't want to touch her directly. Not yet.

"S-sorry," she said. What was she apologizing for? Was

she delirious? Had I waited too long? Had she lost some brain cells?

I kept scrubbing the warmth back into her limbs. I barely noticed Maris stalking away.

"H-h-how?" Her jaw convulsed and her teeth chattered so hard I feared they might shatter. She rolled onto one side.

"Don't get up," I said, ignoring the tightening sensation that was still going on inside me.

She sat up and vomited over the edge of the rock. That was just what I needed to calm myself down. I laughed so loud I startled her.

"Don't worry. I've got you," I said as I lifted Lily from the rock and climbed up the embankment. Cradled in my arms, she dipped her head into my shoulder. It was nearly the same rescue scene I'd planned for her younger sister. The sky darkened like ink spreading through a shirt pocket as the first raindrops hit my bare shoulders. Lily's face was soft and relaxed. I curled my body around her to shield her from the rain and strummed her cheek with my thumb. I worried over the blue tinge that still lingered around her lips. I took a breath and realized I'd been holding it.

Slowly the house came into view. Jason Hancock was in the yard, helping the Pettit man throw tools into his truck. When Hancock saw me, he pushed off Pettit's chest and came running. I stole one more look into Lily's face. If Maris had any idea how I was feeling, she'd be all over my ass like a shark on a seal.

12

I MAKE HER NERVOUS

Two days later I followed Lily to the Blue Moon Café and sat on the park bench across the street, waiting for her to come out, shoving french fries in my mouth as if they were linked together. I checked my watch. She'd been in there for twenty minutes. My knee bounced up and down. *Let's go, let's go, let's go. What are you doing?* She wasn't sitting at a table—I could tell that much—but she was taking too long to be ordering coffee to go. I glanced at my watch again.

A girl slid onto the bench beside me and smiled. My lips twitched in response. She was wearing a bikini top and soccer shorts, bobbing a flip-flop that dangled from her foot.

When I didn't say anything, she stuck out her hand. "Katie," she said.

Sometimes I really wished we didn't have this effect on humans. It could be more irritating than flattering, and right now her timing sucked.

"Calder," I said, wiping the salt off my fingers and shaking her hand. She made her hand go light and limp in mine.

"I don't remember seeing you around here before, Calder," she said. It was almost a purr, and I turned to look at her more closely. She didn't take her hand back, so I had to let go first.

"My family has a sailboat down in the marina," she said. "She's called *Ragtime*. You should come by and check her out sometime. Maybe go for a sail?"

"I don't know," I said, fighting back a smirk. "I'm not much of a water person."

"Well, maybe a movie?"

This was getting ridiculous; I wasn't even turning on the juice.

Lily stepped out of the Blue Moon and stopped on the sidewalk, facing us. She looked at me, her gray eyes wide, and then at the girl beside me. Her mouth popped open in a small o.

"Sorry," I said, not looking the Katie girl in the face. "Gotta go."

I stood up, tossed the fry box in the garbage, and jogged across the street. Lily looked around nervously and pulled at what appeared to be a pair of striped socks she was wearing on her arms. As I got closer, I saw she had cut holes in the socks for her hands; she clutched a piece of paper in her right.

"Well, you've clearly recovered," I said, keeping my tone low, my cadence slow, in that comforting way I knew put humans at ease. I locked my eyes on hers, preparing to bend her will to mine, but was only able to hold her gaze for a second.

"Um. Yeah. I took a dozen hot showers, y'know? And Mom about drowned me in chamomile tea."

I smiled and tried to think of something clever to say, but my mind turned to pudding.

"I'm not sure I really thanked you properly the other day," she said, looking at her shoes.

Is she purposely avoiding eye contact? "Oh, sure you did. You said something that sounded like it, anyway. You were kind of mumbling the whole way back."

She looked up at me then. "Did you really carry me home?"

I blinked. "No big deal."

She shook her head and stared past my shoulder. "It was just the weirdest thing ever. One minute I was on the rock, and the next minute I thought I was going to drown, and then it was like I was flying."

"I'm not surprised," I said. Electricity seared my veins, and I instinctively took a step back as the first little hairs rose off the back of my neck. "You hit your head really hard on that rock. Did you have to get stitches?"

She didn't seem to be listening to me.

"It was just so bizarre." Her voice was barely above a whisper. It sounded like she'd been repeating that line to herself for quite a while. Even now I wasn't sure she was talking to me. "It was just like . . . Never mind." She shook her head again.

"No, tell me. You've made me curious." Terrified was more like it. Did she know she'd been pushed?

"Well, this is going to sound weird, but, there aren't, like, any dolphins in Lake Superior, are there?"

I forced my face to stay controlled. "Dolphins? Don't be crazy. This is a freshwater lake. It was probably just the cold affecting your brain."

She scowled at me. "I know, it's just that I . . ."

"So, what's the paper you got there?" I asked, pointing to the most convenient distraction I could find.

She looked down at her hand as if she'd forgotten she was holding something. She pulled one of the socks up over her elbow.

"Oh. This. I need to get a job."

"Don't you have to start your new school on Monday?"

"No. It's so late in the year, my mom arranged to home-school us for the last couple months. This way I get to gradu-ate with my class back home."

"So how's it going?"

"Just got started, but okay, I guess. I've got to do a com-parative essay on Keats's 'Ode on a Grecian Urn' versus Yeats's 'Sailing to Byzantium,' but Mom's given me a little more time because of my near drowning and all."

"The advantages of having a parent as a teacher."

"Were you homeschooled?" she asked.

I shrugged. "I guess you could call it that. I had a very . . . *practical* upbringing."

"Exactly. That's what I've been saying. All you really need to know is how to survive. I love the poetry. At least that's useful. But where's advanced calculus going to get me?"

"I wouldn't know about that," I said. There was so much I wanted to ask her. Hundreds of questions, really, but for now I could only pick one. The rest would have to wait.

"How come you've never come to Bayfield before? I mean, I am right about that, aren't I?"

"You're right." She paused. "I guess my dad was never ready until now." She looked down at her job application and rolled the paper into a tube. She held it up to her eye like a spyglass and looked at me through it.

"What does that mean?"

She dropped her spyglass and put one hand on her hip. "Y'know, you ask a lot of personal questions."

"Well, I figure having saved your life and all, I'm entitled to know something about you." A strand of hair blew across her face, and I hooked it back behind her ear. She slapped at my hand.

"Okay," she said. "How 'bout this? I'm going to the U of M in September, and I need to make some serious money before then." She looked back at the Blue Moon doubtfully. "And I like coffee."

Nodding appreciatively, I wished her good luck on the job search and then stood there, stupidly, with nothing more to say. It was an awkward moment; she was presumably wondering why I didn't go and I was wondering what she was waiting for.

"I'm supposed to meet some people here," she said finally.

"You've made friends already?" Surprisingly, the words came out angry, and Lily flinched.

"Just Gabrielle and Jack Pettit," she said in a small voice. "You met them the other day at our house. They said they'd show me around town."

"I could do that." Still too angry. I relaxed my shoulders to suppress the bleakness roiling in my brain. "Ditch them. Come with me. It would be more fun, I can promise you that. Besides, you owe me."

"Y'know . . . thanks, but no thanks. I already said I'd meet them, and, well, this is going to sound bad but, I mean, I'm *so* thankful you pulled me out of the lake, but seriously, Calder, you make me a little nervous."

This wasn't working. She was supposed to be drawing nearer to me, not backing away. Maybe she had good instincts, but it felt like I was on the fritz or something. That other girl back on the bench hadn't been repelled. Far from it. *What is wrong with this Hancock girl?* I wondered. *Why didn't Maris just let me go with my gut? Sophie wouldn't have been nearly so much trouble.*

"Sorry," I said. I took a step back. Maybe I'd moved too close to her. "I didn't mean to make you nervous. I just wanted to check up on you. Make sure you're safe and feeling better. All that stuff. Anyway, I'll be off now. Places to go, people to see." *Lame.*

I raised my hand to wave, but she'd already turned away. I didn't get it. Not that I wanted human girls to fawn all over me—truly, I didn't—but they could at least have the decency to do so when I wanted them to. When I needed them to. I walked away, my head hanging, my hands shoved

in my pockets. She was a puzzler. And probably not worth the effort. It might not be too late to resurrect the original Sophie plan. I glanced over my shoulder and caught Lily watching me. Blood rushed into her cheeks and she spun around.

Okay. All's not lost yet. You'll just have to be patient with this one. . . .

Jack and Gabrielle Pettit pulled up in a pea-green Pinto. The engine died with a sputter, and they climbed out. Gabrielle looped her arm through Lily's, laughed at her sock-sleeves, and started walking her away. I followed them with my eyes right up until I felt Pavati watching me from the opposite corner.

Her face and hair blended in with the chocolate-colored paint on the front of the burger joint; I hadn't noticed her. She skipped kitty-corner across the intersection and took my hand.

"Cal-der," she drawled. "Whatcha doin'?"

"You know what I'm doing," I snapped. "I'm getting close to the girl. Like we planned."

"Really? Then why is she walking away from you?"

"Ha, ha. You're a riot, Pavati."

"What's bugging you? You're awfully unobservant, and you didn't come out to the island last night."

"So?"

"So, I know you, Calder. You always want to be alone when something's on your mind."

"Geez, maybe I just like to be alone."

"Hey, I get it, you not wanting to be around Maris all the time. She's a little . . ."

I looked at her knowingly, daring her to fill in the blank.

"Intense," she said. "It can get exhausting feeding off that kind of energy all day. But I don't think that's it." Worry flashed in her lavender eyes. "You don't see something going wrong with the plan, do you? Do you think we should just make this one a quick hit?"

"No!"

She stopped with her mouth open.

"No. I mean, I don't think there's anything wrong with the plan. It's just going to take a little longer with this girl than I originally thought." A small part of me lit up at the thought of getting to spend more time with Lily.

"So? What's her name again?" Pavati finally asked with an exhale. She smelled like smoked fish and . . . pipe tobacco.

"Where've you been, Pav?"

"Never mind."

I leaned in and gave her a good sniff. "Damn it, you took an old man? You heard Maris. We're supposed to pace ourselves. It's a long summer, Pavati. We just got here."

"Take it easy, Calder. It was only one."

"And we've got a priority target." The remnants of the old man's happiness still lit up the corners of Pavati's mouth. Irritated by her lack of self-control but envious of her catch, I reached up with one finger toward her lips. Perhaps I could scoop just a little bit of the light for myself. She smiled and gently lowered my hand.

"So, what's the girl's name, Cal?"

I pulled my gaze from her mouth to her eyes. This time it was my turn to feel sheepish. "Lily."

"Is she going to pose a problem?"

I furrowed my brow. "What's that supposed to mean?"

"Listen, Calder. As a rule, falling in love with your prey is a mistake."

I smiled broadly. Out of all of us, Pavati was the only one who had any experience in this department. I knew nothing of love; all I knew was that none of Pavati's lovers survived to see a second date. "Is that right, Pav? It's a rule?"

"Yeah, that's right."

I crossed my arms over my chest and rocked back to get a fuller view of her. "And you think I'm falling in love? With her? Is that even possible?"

She linked her arm through mine. "I'm not sure yet. But you'll have to be careful. Trust me on this one."

"You shouldn't project your own romantic tendencies onto me." I pulled my arm out. "She's just a girl."

"Uh-uh. She's not *just* a girl," Pavati said, shaking her head. "If you fall for her, you'll ruin everything."

"I don't follow. Anyway, just drop it. This is a ridiculous conversation. I have everything under control."

"Have it your way, but I will be watching."

I shrugged. "Watch all you want." We stared after Lily Hancock, who was now almost out of view. "She's just a means to an end."

"Whatever you say."

I sighed. Pavati was going to believe what she wanted to believe. Nothing could change that.

"So don't you think you should follow her? Maybe start gaining valuable information? Maris will be quizzing you later."

She pushed me off with a shove on the shoulder. I thrust my hands back into my pockets and strode off in the direction Lily and her new friends had taken. I turned and walked backward a few steps. "See you later at the island, then?"

"Looking forward to it," Pavati said with a wave, her gold bracelets jangling.

13

LEGEND

I followed the scent of orange blossoms up the street to where it teed and then trailed it to the same playground where we kept our car. Lily and the Pettit kids were sitting on the swings. They weren't swinging but were simply hanging in the rubber slings, letting their feet drag in the dirt until little tawny dust clouds floated around their ankles.

I ducked behind a sailboat still up in dry dock, then followed a line of bike racks to a large green garbage bin. Dropping to the ground, I pulled my knees up to my chin.

An older couple walked by and looked at me questioningly. There was no good reason to be sitting here on the ground, by the garbage. I nodded to them, and the woman raised a hand to wave tentatively. The old man frowned at me and took his wife's hand. They walked away, arms swinging happily, apparently satisfied that I wasn't some juvenile delinquent. Their satisfaction in each other was palpable. It drew a yellow halo around their bodies that tasted like lemon drops.

I thanked God I wasn't running into them out on the water. My sisters were bad enough in their hunger for that level of emotion. Pavati's impulsiveness today was just one example. I eyed the old couple. If I came across that kind of love out on the water—well, as thin as I was stretched, they wouldn't stand a chance.

Lily's voice rose on the other side of the garbage bin and reminded me why I was there. Gabrielle Pettit was laughing uproariously. It irritated me that she seemed to be mocking Lily.

"You must have hit your head pretty hard," she said, laughing again.

"Don't be a jerk," said Jack. "You don't know what she saw."

"I'm sure she didn't see a dolphin. In fact, I'd bet my life on it. Even if one could find a way to get here."

So she was still on that stupid dolphin.

"What do you think it was, you guys?" asked Lily. "It was really big."

"Some sturgeon can get huge," said Gabrielle. "They've been reported at seven feet." She turned around and around until the chains were twisted all the way to the top of the swing set.

Jack nodded. "These days more like three. Five tops."

"No, it was bigger than that," said Lily. "Bigger than me."

I closed my eyes and let the whole scene play out in my head. I'd thought Lily had been unconscious. What had I done? What had she seen?

"It grabbed me, and we flew out of the water. I mean, I fell, like, *way* far down. And we flew out of the water and landed on the rock. It was like being shot out of a cannon."

"Dude," Gabrielle said, "that definitely sounds like a hallucination."

"And then Calder carried me home."

"That hot guy who helped move you in?" Gabrielle picked up her feet and let herself untwist, spinning into a blur of long dark hair. "You didn't say you'd been hiking with him."

"I wasn't really hiking *with* him. I was hiking with Sophie. He just sort of showed up."

"See, I don't like the sound of that," said Jack. "I've lived here my whole life and I've never heard of him before. Besides, if he was with you, why didn't he rescue you?"

"He *did*. He pulled me out," said Lily. "I mean, he *said* he pulled me out." She shook her head. "I just swear I saw something else there, too. Something big . . . with a silver ring around its neck."

"Oh, man," Jack said. The words came out in a long breath.

Gabrielle looked at him and frowned. "Dude, shut up. Don't feed her that bullshit."

"A silver ring?" Jack asked, ignoring his sister.

"Right," said Lily. "I can't stop thinking about it."

"Come on, I've got to show you something."

"No, Jack. Don't," Gabrielle said. "The girl's messed up enough."

Jack grabbed Lily's hand and they were running. Gabrielle jogged behind, looking entirely pissed off. I got up and stalked after them, dodging between dry-docked boats, a three-tiered rack of dinghies, and a few parked cars.

They got back to the Pinto, and I figured I'd lost them. Once they were in the car, I wouldn't be able to keep up. But they didn't get in. Jack popped open the trunk. He pulled out a square frame and flipped it around for Lily to see. It was an oil painting. Crude. Little talent. But clear enough. It was Pavati. Or something like her. Dark brown hair looping and spiraling across her shoulders. Almond-shaped lavender eyes rimmed in thick lashes. Brown skin, shimmering from some unseen light source. The arms, the cobalt-blue tail . . . the silver ring around her neck. This wasn't the product of imagination, but if he knew Pavati, how was it he was still alive?

Lily looked from the painting to Jack. "You've got to be kidding."

"You said she had a silver ring around her neck."

"Yeah," Lily said, focusing on the painting again. Her voice came out barely audible. "A mermaid?" Clearly her imagination hadn't gone to this extreme.

"I did this for my art class," said Jack. "We had to do an artistic rendition of an American legend."

"You guys think there are mermaids in Lake Superior?"

"No," said Gabrielle, and Jack grimaced. "No, we don't think that. Jack's painting is based on a legend from way up in Maine. Tell her, Jack."

"Sure," Jack said reluctantly. "There's a Passamaquoddy legend. The story is that a long time ago there was an Indian, with his wife and two daughters. They lived by a big lake."

"No. Not a lake," corrected Gabrielle, "the Atlantic Ocean."

"Yeah, right. The ocean. So the mom told her daughters never to go into the water because if they did, something terrible would happen. But the girls snuck out. They wanted to swim to an island they could see from their house."

"Then what happened?" asked Lily.

"They didn't come home."

"Geez, Jack." Gabrielle put her arm around Lily's shoulders.

Jack continued. "Everyone looked for the girls, but no one could find them. The dad went out in a canoe to search the lake, and he saw the girls swimming, but they didn't look like his daughters anymore. They were like black snakes, and they were caught in some kind of slime.

"The dad tried to get close to them, but the closer he got, the deeper the girls sank into the slime. The farther they sank, the more beautiful they became. But *get this*. They had silver rings around their necks.

"After that, whenever the Indians got into their canoes, the girls would sing and carry them. The Indians never needed to paddle. The mermaids were like the guardian angels of the tribe. But then someone wanted to try and catch one of them."

"And he cut off her hair, blah, blah, blah," said Gabrielle. It sounded like she'd heard Jack's recitation a few times already. She rolled her eyes, which I hoped would persuade Lily to drop the whole thing. Jack Pettit was being far too convincing.

"He cut her hair?" Lily repeated, her eyes wide.

"Yep," said Jack. "He tried to catch her, but she was too slimy. All he was able to do was catch her by her hair, and when he cut it, she capsized his canoe and drowned him."

"Freaky," said Lily.

"Yeah, but remember," said Gabrielle, "there are no legends of mermaids around here."

"Not exactly," Jack said. "The Anishinabe have legends about water gods. They call them manitous. You really shouldn't rule anything out."

"There's a water way from Maine to here," said Lily.

Tucked into my hiding spot, I pounded my fist against my forehead. Why was she trying so hard to make this real?

"They could have followed the St. Lawrence Seaway to Lake Superior. That would make sense."

"Are you listening to yourself, Lily? That doesn't make sense at all." Gabrielle had clearly hit her limit. "Come on, I'm hungry. Let's go up to the IGA. I've got a coupon for Twinkies."

"My mermaid wasn't slimy," said Lily. "It wasn't like a snake, either. . . ." She drew her finger along the painting, tracing the tail.

"You don't *have* a mermaid," said Gabrielle. She took the painting from Jack, tossed it into the trunk, and slammed the trunk shut. Then she dragged Lily away from the car and up the sidewalk. Jack followed. "And what about Calder?" Gabrielle asked. "Did you ask him if he saw anything strange?"

"He told me I was stupid to think I saw a dolphin. I guess he was right about that."

"Man," said Jack. "I've said it before, I'm going to say it again. I don't think you should be hanging out with that guy."

I stalked behind them and shot dagger eyes at Jack. I

didn't need him pushing Lily further away from me. I was doing a good enough job on my own.

"I mean, what's he doing telling you to lean over the rock anyway? It's almost like he wanted you to fall in. He sounds like an asshole to me."

"It *is* weird that we've never heard of him before," offered Gabrielle. "What did you say his last name was?"

"Um, White? I think that's what he told my dad."

"Well, there's one way to solve this," said Jack.

They were now by the door of the IGA. An old pay phone mounted on rusted bolts hung on the outside wall between the grocery store and Big Mo's Pizzeria, a phone book tethered to the shelf. Jack flipped the water-warped pages to the back.

"Huh. There is a White. Just a phone number, though. No address."

"Dude, call it," said Gabrielle.

"I'm not wasting my minutes on this guy."

Lily wasn't listening to them. She was still stuck in the original conversation. "Whatever it was, it was amazing. It was the most fantastic thing I've ever seen."

Jack nodded. "I believe you, Lily."

"You do?"

Gabrielle rolled her eyes. "What you saw? It was probably just the endorphins talking. They made you feel all happy because you weren't going to die, so everything looked good. Don't forget, you *do know* who pulled you out, and I'm willing to bet this Calder White doesn't have a ring around his neck. Or a tail, for that matter."

Lily looked uncomfortable. She couldn't deny the fact

that I'd carried her home on two legs. And as far as she knew, I had no ring around my neck. Lily's eyebrows pulled together and the corners of her mouth turned down.

I could see I was going to have to get to know her better, to understand what she was thinking. If she was having serious qualms about me this early, we were going to have to change tactics again.

Lily and the Pettit kids walked into the grocery store, and I emerged from behind a Dumpster, catching my reflection in the window of the Blue Moon Café. My eyes settled on the Help Wanted sign.

14

PROMISE ME

The next day, I found myself pacing in the shadows of a sea cave, peering out on the world through a curtain of ivy. Everything was black. The depression gnawed at my brain, feeding on my fear of failure with Lily, gorging itself on the thought of never being free of Maris. Or was it the aching memories of Lake Superior that pushed me so close to oblivion? Whatever it was, I was teetering on the edge, and watching a most unfortunate kayaker approach.

Holding my breath, I waited for her companion. Kayakers always traveled in pairs. They were like loons. But as she drifted closer, I realized she was alone. I should have known. The woman's aura pulsed with purple ripples: the color of independence and adventure. A companion would have slowed her down.

My insides constricted as she drew closer and I waited for the right moment. If I gave her too much notice, if she saw me too soon, the deliciousness of her high emotion would ferment and then putrefy into fear. Human anxiety was bitter enough on my tongue, but to absorb their fear . . . fear left me retching in the bushes for hours.

An expensive-looking camera hung around her neck. It was heavy enough not to sway as she paddled. The woman rested her paddle across her lap and picked up the camera, holding it to her eye. She aimed it at a rock formation to my right and clicked as she scanned the foliage, lowering it to scan the waves licking at the mouth of the cave.

Then she froze.

And I knew what was centered in her viewfinder.

Lunging, I was at the woman before she dropped the camera. Once the kayak overturned, it was only too easy to pull her out. The camera slipped from her neck and sank to the bottom of the lake, destroying any evidence she might have recorded. I entangled her in my arms, dragging her deeper, waiting for her emotion to seep through my skin. It was taking longer than expected, and I got only a trickle of excitement before the sour taste of panic hit my tongue. My eyes popped open, and I saw Maris watching me smugly from the bottom of the lake. It was her twisted smile that made me release the woman, who scrambled to the surface, only a tiny trickle of bubbles trailing from her nose. I didn't look back to see if she would reclaim the surface. She'd never report a merman attack to the authorities and, really, who would believe her if she did?

Maris shook her head in disgust. *"Follow me,"* she said, her words a telepathic punch to the gut.

We swam toward Manitou Island until she stopped and surfaced. I broke through the watery plane five full seconds behind her.

"Look around, Calder. What do you see?"

"Someone who enjoys my misery," I said.

A small smile tugged at the corners of her mouth. "Touché. But do you recognize this spot?"

I turned in a circle, calculating the distance from Manitou, to the mainland, to the next closest island in the chain. It formed a triangle with me at its center. Yes, I knew this spot. "This is where I fell in."

"Bingo."

The memory of the sailboat rose again, the mystery letters stenciled on the stern, my human parents drifting away, scrambling to drop the sails, to turn back, to throw a life preserver. . . . My lungs burned with the memory; I remembered the sunlight fading into a pinprick of light as the dark waters swallowed my tiny body and my heart slogged to a stop.

"Should Mother have left you for dead, Calder?"

The question snapped me back to the present.

"I've often wondered," Maris went on. "You've never been completely right for this life. If you need any more proof, that woman back there . . ."

"I'm just out of practice."

"That's what I mean, Calder. Why should you be out of practice? It's not normal."

I didn't know what to say to that. But I knew where she was going, and I knew the answer to her next question.

"She was my mother, too, Maris. And I *will* avenge her death."

"Silly boy," she said, her tone patronizing. "I know you want to. The question I'm asking is *can* you."

"Get a grip, Maris. We made a deal. I *can*. And I *will*. And once the deed is done, you'll never have to be bothered with wondering if I'm normal or not."

Before Maris could answer, a 330 Sun Sport came around a bend in the shoreline, its engine churning the water, its driver fixated on the shore, binoculars scanning the rocks. Behind his back, Maris and I made no attempt to submerge ourselves.

"Should I take that one?" I suggested sardonically. "Would that prove something to you?"

"No," she said coolly. "Not that one."

I focused on the figure in the boat. What was so special about him? It surprised me to recognize the lucky boater as Jack Pettit. "Why not him?"

"That one's Pavati's."

I choked on a laugh. "Oh, man, you're telling me she's got dibs?"

"You'll have to ask her."

"Never mind. She can have him. Besides, I'm going to be late for work."

"You have a job?" she asked, amused.

"I'm the newest barista at the Blue Moon Café."

"They hired *you*?" Maris asked.

"Maybe I'm not *completely* lacking in skill, Maris. I can be persuasive. And it's all part of my plan. Like I said, you don't need to worry about me. I've got this."

She raised her eyebrows in an expression of doubt and dove away, leaving me to slump back into the bleakness she'd found me in.

As I swam toward the Bayfield fishing pier, I felt Tallulah trailing several yards behind.

"Calder, wait up."

I looked behind me and saw her arms curled around a newborn baby. My throat tightened in revulsion, and I pulled up quick. *"Aw, geez, Lu. Why?"*

But when she extended the bundle toward me, I realized it wasn't a baby after all. Just a whitefish bloated with roe. She laughed, reading my initial impression in my fading thoughts, and wrapped a long, waxy arm around my neck. She pulled me closer. Chuckling, I pushed her off and examined the catch.

"Where've you been?" she asked, her thoughts revealing her own colorful imagination.

My eyes popped wide at the images. *"Geez, Tallulah, would you quit it? I'm not Pavati. You can stop imagining the worst."* But I couldn't help latching on to the last picture she showed me: Lily in a hammock, pressed underneath me, her fingers in my hair, her heel trailing up the back of my calf.

Tallulah smiled and took my hand. We swam together, the whitefish tucked under her arm, our twin silver tails glistening, matching stroke for stroke. Again, I wondered what it would be like for us to live without Maris. Maybe hook up with the mermaids in Lake Michigan? Then again, maybe not. With our luck, they wouldn't be a trade up. Besides, wasn't it bad enough being tethered to my own sisters? I couldn't imagine making that kind of persistent bond with strangers. Like any school of fish, once it was formed, no individual broke away from the group. Not for very long anyway, and not by choice. As far as I knew, I was the only exception to that rule, and I could only hold on to my winter hiatus for a few sweet months. Hope burst like chrysanthemums of light in my brain. The promise of being released from the group chokehold was too precious to fathom. Lily was sure to deliver Hancock to me. Eventually. It wouldn't be long before I was cashing in.

Tallulah dove seven fathoms and found a seat on a large boulder on the lake floor. I checked my watch, then circled her three times, watching as she pulled her lips back and sank her teeth into the fish, tearing the flesh with a shake of her head. When she finished, she looked up at me balefully and said simply, *"I don't like you spending time with her."* Lily's face flashed across her mind again.

"You don't have to like it," I said.

"If Maris had just stayed out of it . . . The original plan was better." She flashed her teeth at me and looked away, her head instantly full of confusing images: a school of alewives, a restaurant in New Orleans, the backseat of the Impala.

I laughed, recognizing her attempt to keep her true thoughts private. Image scrambling was a trick I often used on my sisters, and I wasn't about to deprive Tallulah of the little bit of privacy she could make for herself. She was always good to repay the favor.

I winked and waved goodbye, but before I left, she grabbed my hand and jerked me back until we were nose to nose.

"I heard what Maris said to you back there."

Of course she did. It wasn't like Maris was subtle about anything.

"I don't think it was a mistake for Mother to reinvigorate you, Calder. I never have. You are a beautiful creature, weird behavior and all. It doesn't matter to me what Maris thinks."

"So you don't think I'm going to fail?"

"No, I don't. I need you to succeed, Calder. And then, when she cuts you loose"—she squeezed my hand harder—*"I want you to take me with you."*

I pulled my fingers free.

"Promise me you'll take me with you." Her eyebrows pulled up into an inverted V.

"I gotta go, Lu. I don't want to be late for my first day." I reached up toward the surface of the water, leaving her underneath a shower of electric-blue sparks with no promise given.

"I won't let you fail," she called after me, the words distorting in my wake.

Later that night, long after my shift at the café had ended, I surfaced outside the Hancock house, all jacked up on caffeine and pacing back and forth in the glass-calm water. Just exactly how was I going to make this work? A breeze blew through the trees, bringing a piney citrus tingle to my nose. When I crossed some invisible line in the water, a low humming filled the air, followed by a loud *ka-chunk,* and floodlights illuminated the lake in a one-hundred-foot radius from the end of the Hancock dock.

I froze, momentarily blinded. The porch light flashed

on and Hancock's voice called out, "What is it? Who's out there? Show yourself."

"It's okay, Dad. It's nothing. Just bats chasing mosquitoes. Must have set off the motion detectors."

I shielded my eyes with my hand and searched for the voice. Sitting on the edge of the dock, her feet in the water, her arms bracing herself, her eyes like saucers, Lily stared into my face. The porch light went off, Hancock muttering something about Lily needing to get back in the house "A-SAP."

"What are you doing out there?" Lily hissed. She clicked off a small flashlight and slammed her book shut.

"Would you believe me if I said I was just passing by?"

She groaned. "You are a terrible liar, Calder White."

My heart did a weird little skip at the sound of my name on her lips, and I worked to keep my tailfin from flashing to the surface. "Sorry if I scared you."

"You didn't scare me."

"I didn't?"

"No. But you still haven't told me what you're doing out there. If you didn't get the memo, no one swims in Lake Superior, especially in April, at midnight. And it's dangerous. There are . . . Never mind."

Avoiding the obvious question, I focused on her eyes, penetrating the darkness. I was confident she couldn't see any more of me than my face, but it didn't do anything to calm my nerves. This girl was too aware. And way too much in control of herself. The best I could do was throw the accusations back at her.

"I could ask *you* what you're doing out here in the middle of the night."

103

"This is my house. I live here. I can do whatever I want."

I exhaled my defeat. "Fine. You win."

"So? Are you going to tell me? Or should I assume the worst?"

The worst? For a second I considered telling her the truth—not that she'd believe it. She'd just chalk it up to sarcastic mockery if I told her I was a serial killer, stalking her family in the night. "If you must know, I'm doing a triathlon this summer, and I'll have to swim a mile in open water. There's too many boats during the day, so I'm training at night."

She snorted. "The boats are still in dry dock."

I scrambled for a response, but she kept talking.

"I hope you're wearing a dive suit."

"Of course."

Lily twisted up her mouth like she wasn't buying any of the crap I was selling. She stood up. "Whatever."

"Where are you going?"

"Inside. It's late." She looked over her shoulder at the house. "And I need to make sure you didn't give my dad a massive coronary or something." She muttered something else under her breath that sounded like *"Crazy,"* but I wasn't sure if she was talking to me or to herself. She switched on her flashlight. The beam of light bobbed in front of her as she stormed up to the house, her old poetry book held tight against her chest.

15

VICTORIANS ON THE GREEN

The next morning, I leaned against the brick exterior of the Harbor Bookstore, one knee pulled up, the brim of my baseball cap low over my eyes. My hair was just starting to dry and curl at the ends. The bookstore was still locked up. I checked my watch. It should have been open a while ago.

A few people passed on the sidewalk, and I nodded at them as they said good morning. One man, newspaper tucked under his arm, walked a basset hound whose belly nearly dragged on the sidewalk. It looked up at me with bloodshot eyes, and his thoughts were all about *How much farther?* as he waddled toward the corner. Behind me, the dead bolt clunked open, and I jumped at the noise.

"Come in, come in," said a woman. Her Apostle Island sweatshirt was new and still unwashed. She folded the cuffs up over her wrists as I walked in.

"Sorry I made you wait," she said. "I had to catch the cat. She snuck out the back when I came in." A calico rubbed up against the woman's denim-sheathed ankles and rumbled a contented purr. I bent down to pet its head, and it lifted its chin, sniffing my fingers. Then it hissed and ran for the back room.

"Sorry about that. She can be so touchy. Anything I can help you find?"

"Poetry," I said, straightening up.

"Hmm, well, we don't have a *huge* selection in that regard. Mostly we carry the bestsellers and some books of regional interest. But . . ." She walked past me and slid a ladder out from behind the counter. "I think . . . ," she said, setting up the ladder and climbing to the third rung.

She looked down at me. "Robert Frost?"

"Actually, I was looking for something on the Victorians."

She grunted a dull "Huh" and fingered through a few books on the topmost shelf. "Ah. How about this? I think it covers the Regency and Victorian periods." She handed it down to me, and I turned it over in my hands. The cover read:

A Time of Elegance

Below the gold-leafed title were the names Brontë, Byron, Keats, Kipling, Rossetti, Tennyson, Wordsworth, Yeats.

"Perfect," I said, smiling up at her.

"Oh, good. Glad that'll work for y'now. So let's see. . . ." She backed her way down the ladder and headed for the cash register.

I pulled a crumpled twenty from my pocket. The smell of New Orleans still lingered in its folds.

"Poetry buff, huh?"

"Not exactly. Not yet, anyway." I handed her the money just as the cat peered around the corner at me. I stared it down and it bared its teeth.

"Mrs. Murphy, no," scolded the woman. "Be nice to the customers."

"No worries," I said, and let myself out the door. Moments later I found a grassy strip of city park that followed the shoreline between the Bayfield marina and the ferry dock. A line of giant boulders buffered the shore from the waves. A crooked white oak grew out of the center of the park. Just outside the edge of its shade is where I found my seat on the grass.

Opening the book, I scanned the table of contents for the Victorians and started with Emily Brontë, searching the poems for something useful, something enticing, something seductive that would draw Lily closer and end this ridiculous repulsion she felt for me. Then my eyes landed on the most obvious weapon. I'd read the first line before—and not on the page of a book, but in Lily's tattoo: *No coward soul is mine.*

Dog-earing the page, I whispered each line aloud until it was etched into my memory, then moved on to Tennyson's "Charge of the Light Brigade" and its "Half a league onward, /

All in the valley of Death." Another poem was all about "blue isles"; a third about the Lady of Shalott.

Who were these people? Every one of them asked the same question I did: How to escape a life where everything good was fleeting? But when I got to Yeats, my heart nearly stopped.

"A mermaid found a swimming lad, / Picked him for her own, / Pressed her body to his body. . . ."

I snapped the book shut and pressed my eyes against my knees. What did Yeats know about anything?

Despite the sunny day, a shadow passed over me, cooling my skin as drops of water hit my bare toes. There hadn't been any clouds that I noticed before. I reached to protect my new book from the rain and startled to find Tallulah peering down at me.

She was fully clothed (thank God!), but her hair was still dripping wet from her trip over. Her face eclipsed the sun, creating a halo of light around her head.

"What are you doing here, Lu?"

"Looking for you," she said.

"Well, you found me. Have a seat."

She sat close, and the wet soaked into my right side, calming me, as I ran through the poems in my head. As if she could read my thoughts on land, Tallulah reached over me and grabbed up the book.

"What's this?"

"Homework."

The book opened to the dog-eared page, and Tallulah turned pages, stopping with a snort. "Wow, what's this?"

I didn't have to guess which one she was reading. "Victorian poetry. Lily likes this stuff. Can you believe it?"

"Just coincidence, right?"

"Oh, yeah. I mean, there's plenty of other stuff in there that has nothing to do with us, but definitely weird, right?"

"To say the least."

"Do you think it's a good thing or a bad thing?"

"I suppose it's what you make of it, Calder. Use it to your advantage, without giving us away, of course."

"As if."

"Just make this quick, all right?" She cuddled up to my side and laid her head on my shoulder. "Here. How about this one?" she said, flipping the page to something new. "If you were reading this to me, I'd be putty in your hands."

I slipped the book from her fingers and read aloud:

"First time he kissed me, he but only kissed
The fingers of this hand wherewith I write;
And ever since, it grew more clean and white,
Slow to world-greetings, quick with its 'Oh, list,'
When the angels speak. A ring of amethyst
I could not wear here, plainer to my sight,
Than that first kiss. The second passed in height
The first, and sought the forehead, and half missed,
Half falling on the hair. O beyond meed!
That was the chrism of love, which love's own crown,
With sanctifying sweetness, did precede.
The third, upon my lips, was folded down
In perfect, purple state; since when, indeed,
I have been proud and said, 'My Love, my own.'"

"Putty," she repeated, sighing deeply. "But I think a little of that will go a long way. This book should carry a warning label."

"'Caution: Use Sparingly'?" I suggested.

She nodded. "Or 'Keep Away from Open Flame.'"

"Roger that," I said, giving her a little salute.

16

LIKE A BOOK

Two days later, I had just finished wiping down the multi-colored tables and chairs in the Blue Moon Café and had started polishing the black marble countertop. I looked up as the bell rang out and Lily walked through the door in a blue velvet jacket and felt fedora. She took two steps, then skittered to a stop when she saw me grinning.

"Oh, c'mon. You again?" Her arms stood out from her body at an odd angle. I knew she'd react that way. I'd anticipated it. It was even funnier than I imagined.

"Me again," I said, shrugging and giving the counter another swipe.

She looked around nervously as if she were wondering whether she should leave, but then she squared her shoulders and set her jaw. She walked quickly across the black-and-white checkered floor and put her hands on her hips. "What are you doing here?"

"I work here," I said matter-of-factly, folding up the wet towel. "The more appropriate question is, what are *you* doing here?" I suppressed a smile. I knew the answer, but it was still fun to ask. Maris had given me lots of crappy jobs in the past. At least this one was turning out to be fun. It was embarrassing how much satisfaction I got out of teasing Lily.

"I work here now," she said. "This is my first day."

"You don't say. Well, in that case, grab an apron. They're under the counter." I bent over to replenish the bakery case with cream cheese Danishes. She leaned over the counter and peered down at me.

"Are you stalking me?" she asked.

"I was here first."

"You knew I was applying for a job here."

I stood up and faced her accusation head-on. "Did it ever occur to you that maybe I already worked here when you told me that?"

She paused for a second, considering the possibility, balancing embarrassment against persisting doubt. "Is that true?"

"No."

She sighed and rolled her eyes. Her aggravated expression made me smile. This whole thing was aggravating. She was supposed to be malleable, persuadable. Easy pickings. That was what was supposed to be happening here. *Don't fail, Calder. I won't let you fail.*

112

She blew all the air out of her lungs and gave me the full force of her glare. "So you *are* following me."

There was no point in lying. "Yes. I am following you."

Her carefully controlled exterior faltered. *"Why?"*

I leaned across the counter, clasping my hands together and bringing my face closer to hers. We locked eyes once more, but this time I refused to let her look away. "Because I like you. I'm sorry if that makes you nervous."

All the color drained from her face. "I thought *you* thought I was crazy."

"I like crazy."

"You're unbelievable," she grumbled.

"So I've been told."

She slid her velvet jacket off her shoulders and hung it on a hook screwed into the wall. Her lace blouse barely met the top of her skirt, exposing a sliver of pale skin. I pulled an apron out and tossed it to her. She came around the counter as she tied the bright blue apron around her waist.

Mrs. Boyd walked out of the back, checking things off a list she had clamped to a clipboard. Her pink-and-blue-flowered skirt waved as she walked. She wasn't watching where she was going, and she nearly bumped into Lily.

"Oh. Lily Hancock, is it? Good. Punctual. I like that. I've got to pick up some more milk at the store. Calder, there's supposed to be a delivery soon, so if the driver needs you to sign, just go ahead and do that.

"Lily, Calder can show you around. He just started the other day, but he picked things up really fast. You're in good hands." She folded her list and put it in her purse, slipping the clipboard behind the register. "Back soon," she said. The bell over the door jingled.

Lily spun to accost me. "*You're* training me?"

I shrugged. "There's not much to it. The cash register has each of the menu items on a separate button. Push what they order, hit Total. Make change. I'll teach you how to run the espresso machine as the orders come in."

"Is it going to get busy?"

"Highly doubtful. It'll be busier this summer when the tourists start coming, but it'll be dead slow until Memorial Day. You won't have much to do except talk to me."

"Great." She dragged the word out to let me know just how little she was looking forward to it.

Her eyes met mine for a second. I stared into their clear gray, the sky before a storm, almost the same color as the aura fuzzing around the curves of her body. It reminded me of the color kids put off when they're feeling put upon, but for Lily the vibration was different, more silvery, like resigned martyrdom or a willingness to sacrifice.

"What are you doing?" she asked.

"Looking at you. Do you find that odious?"

"Odious? Who says that?"

"Hmm. I guess I do." I reached toward her, and she slapped my hand.

"Well, don't stare at me like that. I don't like it," she said.

"What would you say if I said I couldn't help it?"

"I'd say you were being odious."

"Why don't you like me, Lily Hancock?" I didn't know why I asked so directly. Probably because it was driving me crazy not knowing. If I was doing something wrong, I needed to change my strategy. Or was it something else? Regardless of Maris's plan, did I *want* Lily to like me? I pushed the thought out of my head. It was ridiculous.

Lily folded her arms across her chest. "Fine. Here it is. Why did you wait so long to save me?"

"That's what all this hostility is about? So unnecessary. Lily, I got there as quickly as I could."

She stared at my neck, and my Adam's apple bobbed. I knew the silver ring didn't show, but she seemed to be looking straight through me. She stepped closer, and I took a quick step back, suddenly . . . nervous, like she presented some unknown danger. Pavati's accusation lurked somewhere in the back of my head.

"I guess," she said.

"And you're clearly fine."

"Whatever." She looked around the café. "Is there something I should be doing?"

"Come with me." I led her to the back room and showed her where Mrs. Boyd stored the bags of coffee. "Bring a couple bags up to the front each morning. One for the bin. Put one underneath. The napkins and paper towels are here on this shelf." I grabbed a big handful of paper napkins. "Make sure the holders are stuffed tight."

"Got it," she said, laboring under the weight of the coffee bag.

"So," I said, choking back a laugh. *Make this light. Keep the conversation going.* "Are you enjoying Bayfield so far?"

She exhaled an exasperated sigh. "Well, as you know, it got off to an interesting start. *Uff da.*" She dropped the bag on the counter.

"True, but I'm still waiting for you to tell me why you've never come before."

"Mom and Dad just announced one morning we were moving."

There was something more she wasn't telling me, but I nodded. "Spontaneity is a good thing. The best things in life happen when you just let events . . . unfold. When you try to control things too much, you do yourself a disservice."

"I know what you mean." She headed back for the second bag, and I followed close behind.

"So, your dad teaches at the college?"

"Yeah. He's going to teach in the Humanity and Nature Studies department starting next term. But enough about me," she added quickly. "How 'bout you?"

"Um. What do you want to know?" I asked, disappointed she was no longer willing to be the subject of conversation. "I'm an open book."

"Then tell me everything," she said. She looked around for something to cut the bag, and I handed her a scissors.

"How about the abridged version?"

"You can start there. Right here?" she asked, opening the bin. I nodded.

"Okay, let's see, I like . . . wool socks and cotton T-shirts."

"Duly noted. What else?" She combed her fingers through her hair and pulled it into a loose bun. I wondered what it would feel like to run my fingers through her hair like that, and I let myself get distracted in the fantasy until my skin burned under her patient gaze.

"I like the color of the Caribbean." I paused and absorbed the warmth of her smile before adding, "Dogs, not cats.

Boxers, not briefs. Redheads over brunettes . . ." I glanced sideways at her, and she met my gaze. "I have a penchant for girls in velvet jackets . . . and I think you're the most beautiful girl I've ever seen."

She choked in surprise, sputtered, and shook her head. "You see? This is what I mean."

"What?"

"Nobody talks like that. I barely know you."

I was genuinely confused. Didn't girls like to hear this stuff? Besides, it was, conveniently enough, the truth. "Well, *I* talk like this. And you should be used to people telling you you're beautiful."

"Well, I'm not," she said, and she sounded like she was getting irritated with me again. The feeling was mutual.

I leaned against the wall and pulled up one knee. "Okay. I take it back. You are completely average. Dull, dull, dull. Unremarkable in every way."

"Much better," she said, mollified. She flicked her finger against my shoulder.

A woman came in and bought six chocolate croissants. I showed Lily how to ring up the order, and she put them into a bag. "Thank you. Please come again," she said, waving to the woman as she walked out the door.

"So . . . ," I pressed, "back to you. Your family. What's your dad like? He must be a complete bore to sire someone as banal as you."

She exhaled an exasperated sigh. "He's funny." Then she smiled like she was remembering a joke. "He loves my mom a lot, and he's not totally embarrassing in public." Another smile.

"Really? No lame jokes? No embarrassing pants?"

She dropped into a bright purple chair and stuffed a stack of napkins into the stainless steel holder. "Nope. He's cool. He had a tough time as a kid with the whole parent thing, so I think he works extra hard to be a good dad. He's wanted to come back here forever, but I think he was afraid to."

"What's there to be afraid of?"

Lily hesitated, as if she hadn't planned on getting so personal so quickly. Her mouth hung open and blood rushed into her cheeks. "I guess you could say this place tore his family apart."

I was fascinated by the irony. Wasn't it my family that had been destroyed? I couldn't let her stop there. I stared into her eyes and willed her to share more information. Thoughts spun out of me—images of the two of us whispering in confidence—and I pushed them into her mind, compelling her to trust me. She fought against it. She was stronger than I'd expected, maybe stronger than any human I'd ever encountered. But right when I thought I couldn't get through, right when I thought I was a bigger failure than even Maris had guessed, Lily's resistance gave way.

She drew up her chin and said, "The story is that this place made my grandpa go crazy."

I leaned against the counter, the marble cool under my palms, and braced myself against what was coming next. She pushed her chair back hard, making it screech across the floor.

"He said he saw a monster in the lake." She watched me closely. "Sorry you asked?"

"No," I said.

"He dragged the whole family away from here without

118

any warning. Everyone said he was crazy. After that, my dad was never allowed in the water—*anywhere*—and they for sure never came back here. Even when my dad was old enough to come alone, he stayed away out of respect for his dad."

"So why the change of heart?"

"Partly because of my mom's health. And Grandpa died in January. I think this move is a meet-your-demons-head-on kind of thing for my dad."

I swallowed hard. Fortunately, she had no way of knowing the demon was inches from her, steaming a carafe of milk into a perfect froth.

"The whole monster obsession broke up my grandparents' marriage. Grandpa was even medicated for a while. I don't know. Maybe he was crazy, but—aside from the weird stories—he always seemed pretty normal to me. Why are you looking at me like that?"

"Like what?"

"Like you're in pain or something." She frowned. "You've been around here a long time, right? Have you ever seen—"

I winced. I don't know what she saw in my face, but whatever it was made her suck in her breath.

"Oh my gosh, you know. You've heard the stories! You have, haven't you?"

I pretended to be distracted by the thermometer on the steamer and rebuffed her accusation. "Get a grip, Lily. I'm just thinking that's quite a family history you've got there. Did your grandfather ever say what the monster looked like?" I cranked off the steamer.

"Y'know what? Just forget it."

The way she shook her head when she said that, the way

her face took on the same expression as when she looked at Jack Pettit's painting . . . I could tell she knew exactly what kind of demon the old man warned them about. Of course, they all thought he was nuts, but his son wasn't as oblivious as we originally thought.

No wonder she was pissed at me for telling her she was crazy. She probably thought it was genetic. Maybe my little rescue stunt had her worried she was going to end up in a mental hospital. That was why I made her nervous. I was going to have to put a stop to this right away.

"Listen, Lily. Just because your grandpa went off the deep end doesn't mean you're crazy, too. Seeing dolphins in Lake Superior does not make you certifiable."

"Yeah? What does it make me?"

"Well, I'm still sticking to my hypothermia-induced hallucination theory, but how about we go with it makes you imaginative. There's nothing wrong with that. In fact, I'd call it an asset."

She smiled, and I could see she liked that. Time to play my trump card.

I held up one finger and went to the back room, returning with my new poetry book. I flipped the cover around for her to read the title. Her eyes brightened. The expression *hook, line, and sinker* came to mind.

"Imagination is at the root of all creative efforts, Lily— painting, poetry . . . Look at Mary Shelley. If she hadn't seen the monster in her head, she would have never written *Frankenstein*. Or, come to think of it, isn't Tennyson's 'Lady of Shalott' about a girl gone crazy?"

"Cursed, more like it."

"Still, it's a beautiful poem."

"Okay," Lily said. "I get what you're trying to say. I didn't know you liked poetry. I don't think I know *any* guys who do."

I winked at her and she blushed, looking away as the bell rang over the front door. My back stiffened as my sisters walked into the café in a triangular formation with Maris at the head. Her hair hung behind her shoulders like a white cape over a plain white tee. Her silver irises were flashing.

Pavati winked at me. Her pink peasant blouse slipped off one bare shoulder. Tallulah eyed the book as I tucked it under the counter; then her eyes drifted up, pretending to read the menu board.

"What can I get you?" Lily asked brightly.

I yearned to put myself between her and Maris but had to satisfy myself with standing rigidly at her side. Lily didn't show any signs of recognizing Pav and Lulah from the woods (or from Jack's painting, for that matter). I hoped she wouldn't. I just wanted to get them their drinks and push them out the door.

"Hi," said Pavati. "Remember me?"

I groaned.

"Calder's sisters," Lily confirmed.

"Maris White," Maris said, sticking out her hand. "We haven't met yet."

I held my breath.

"Lily Hancock," Lily said, taking Maris's hand casually in hers. She didn't seem to register any sign of pain.

I exhaled as the espresso machine hissed and squealed. I hurried to make the drinks and get them into to-go cups.

Maris gave me a patronizing smile. They took their cups to a table by the window and turned the colorful chairs in an unnatural formation, their backs to the window, all facing the counter in a straight line. They raised their cups in choreographed unison, sipping slowly. Not showing any sign of leaving. Not talking. Just watching me. *Very subtle, guys. The least you can do is blink.*

"Maybe you should go get another bag of French roast," I said quietly to Lily.

She started to protest, but then her eyebrows rose, and she stole a sideways glance at my sisters. She didn't say anything more, just turned and walked to the back.

"What do you think you're doing?" I demanded of Maris.

"We're just seeing how things are going. Nothing wrong with that, is there?"

"You don't have to follow me around."

"Pavati seemed to think we should check in."

I glared at Pavati, and she shrugged.

"Quit worrying. Everything is going great." *Except that Jason Hancock's already on guard against monsters in the lake, and Lily thinks she saw a mermaid.* "I just need a few more weeks."

"Ten days, Calder. I'm giving you ten days. I want to end this."

Hesitantly, Lily came back out front, carrying another bag of beans. There was no good place to put it. My sisters stood up, their chairs scraping the floor.

"It was nice to meet you, Lily Hancock," said Maris.

Pavati waved, and Tallulah shot me a nervous look. She came up to me under the pretense of throwing her cup away and leaned in to peck me on the cheek. She whispered in my ear, "Careful, Calder."

I rolled my eyes and tried to put her at ease. "I told you, Lulah. I've got this. I'll see you tonight."

She pulled away, the words *We'll see* expressed with her eyebrows.

Even after the door closed, Lily stared after them, spellbound, then shook her head as if to clear the clouds. Why couldn't she react to me like that?

"Your sisters are very beautiful."

"They're pains in the ass, that's what they are," I said, trying to dissolve her memory of them. Pavati looked remarkably like Jack Pettit's oil painting. I didn't need that kind of reinforcement in Lily's mind. "Isn't that how you feel about your sister?"

"Sophie? No, not at all."

"Really? I got the impression you two weren't much alike."

"Well, we're not, but that doesn't mean I think she's a pain. Sophie just needs a lot of looking after. I don't mind doing it. She's a sweet kid."

A surge of self-disgust rushed through me. Lily was good and honest and loving, and here I was trying to exploit that. I repulsed myself. I ground my teeth together and gripped the edge of the counter as an electric heat bristled at the back of my neck.

"Are you all right?"

"Yeah, yeah. I'm okay," I whispered, backing away from her. I touched the espresso machine, and a white spark jumped from my fingers to the machine.

"Whoa. Are you sure you're okay?" She reached out

123

and touched the back of her hand to my forehead. "You're really hot."

I flinched, then laughed at her unintended double entendre. Lily Hancock seemed to have some kind of switch hooked up to my brain. Right now she was flipping me back and forth so quickly my mind was a strobe light.

"I thought you said you didn't like me," I joked.

She rolled her eyes. "I was talking about your temperature, jerk. But just to be clear, I never said you weren't good-looking. If you remember, I said you made me nervous."

"Right. So, you think I'm good-looking?"

She swatted me over the head with her fedora, then went back to the cash register, saying, "You're really annoying. If your sisters are pains in the ass, I'm thinking they learned it from you."

17

NO COWARD SOUL

Mrs. Boyd pointed to the clock. "Good first shift, you kids. You'll make a good crew this summer." She wrapped up some day-old muffins and handed them to Lily. "Take these home to your family. Tell them to come down to the café sometime."

"Will do. And thanks." Lily retrieved her bag from under the counter and pulled out her cell phone.

"Oh, don't bother your folks," said Mrs. Boyd. "I bet Calder here would be happy to drive you home." She winked at me. I could have kissed her. "I've got you both on the early schedule tomorrow. Be here at six?"

"I'll be here," Lily said. She looked at me to see if Mrs. Boyd's offer was legit. I nodded and led her out the door to my car. Lily climbed into the passenger seat, and we headed up Manypenny Avenue toward the county road. It felt incredible having her in the car, sitting next to me, like two normal people out for a ride. She slipped out of her sandals and put her feet up on the dash. She pushed her seat back as Bob Marley blared from the speakers.

"But I did not shoot the dep-u-ty," sang Lily. Then she reached forward and groaned, rubbing the balls of her feet. "Ugh. My feet are killing me. It's hard just standing like that all day."

My eyes went back and forth between the road and the shiny turquoise paint on Lily's toes, around the arch of her foot, back to the road, and then along the curve of her calf up to her knee, exposed by the fact her long skirt had slid up around her thighs. I caught myself before the fantasy distracted me from the job at hand.

She leaned over to change the station; then her hand stopped in midair. She reached under the seat, pulling out Pavati's skirt—the same one she'd been wearing earlier.

"What's this?" Lily held it up to show me.

Oh, shit. "I don't know. Looks like a skirt to me."

"Isn't this your sister's?" She bent over and dug out the matching pink blouse and Maris's white T-shirt and jeans. "Why'd they ditch their clothes in your car?"

I shrugged, trying to think of a reasonable explanation. Better to stay as close to the truth as possible. "Out for a swim, I guess."

"Won't they be mad that you drove away with their clothes?"

I sighed. So much for a normal ride home. "Why don't you let me worry about my sisters." Lily faced forward and crossed her arms over her chest.

A few minutes later, I pulled into her driveway, and Hancock came out to meet us. I put the car in park as Hancock put his hands on the edge of the doorframe and leaned in the open window toward me. My jaw flexed, and my mouth ran dry.

"Bringing her home again, I see." His voice was friendly, but there was an edge to it. A fatherly warning, perhaps? I smirked at the thought of *Jason Hancock* having to warn *me*.

"Yes, sir. We're both working down at the Blue Moon."

"Are you, now?"

"Thanks for the ride, Calder. I guess I'll see you later," Lily said, and even though she hurried to get out of my car, she didn't seem entirely put off by the thought.

"Right. Have a good night, Lily."

"No," said Hancock, "why don't you stay for a while? I could use some help moving a pile of lumber closer to the house, and we're going to have a bonfire and cook hot dogs down by the lake later on."

Lily froze, but there was a hint of anticipation in her eyes. I decided I wouldn't be pushing my self-control too much to accept the invitation. Besides, Maris would like this.

"Sure thing." I unbuckled my seat belt and climbed out. Hancock signaled for me to follow. Lily trailed nervously behind.

"So, you said you live north of Bayfield?" Hancock asked, looking over his shoulder at me.

Ah. This wasn't about moving lumber. Hancock wanted to know what type of boy his daughter was hanging out with. I hid a smile behind my hand. No matter how bad Hancock might imagine me to be, no matter what story he'd heard about his father, I was pretty sure *possible serial killer* still hadn't made his list of concerns. I prepared myself for the string of well-rehearsed lies I was going to have to un-leash on them for the rest of the afternoon.

"We did, sir."

"Did?"

"We had a summer house up toward Cornucopia. But my parents sold it and bought a sailboat."

Hancock stopped and turned around to face me. "You're a sailor?"

"So-so. My dad's really more into it. At first it was part of the leasing fleet over on Madeline Island. Now when we come up for the summer, we stay on the boat."

"This early in the season? What's the boat called?"

Lily came up alongside her dad. She kissed his cheek, and I swallowed hard. "You're giving him the third degree, Dad."

"That's my job, Lil."

We lifted four two-by-fours and started walking back to the house. Lily raised her eyebrows at me and mouthed the word *Sorry*.

"So, how old are you, Calder?"

"Eighteen, sir."

"You going to college?"

"Not yet."

"Going to work for a while?"

"Something like that." I set my end of the boards onto the stack already taking shape by the front porch. We returned to the original pile and picked up another load. That was when I spied Mrs. Hancock. She was sitting in a chair by the lake, a canvas set up on an easel, a crocheted afghan wrapped around her shoulders. Sunshine streamed through the tree branches, casting three clawlike stripes across her body.

"You didn't tell me your mom was an artist."

"Oh, I'm full of secrets like that," Lily said mysteriously. The way she said it, coupled with my own darker secrets, made me laugh out loud. Lily raised her eyebrows to say it wasn't *that* funny.

"How was work, Lily?" Mrs. Hancock called. "Is that Calder, too? Our hero!" She smiled and raised a hand, coaxing us over to her. As we got closer my pulse raced. I didn't know if it was because Mrs. Hancock was sitting in a wheelchair— *Was she* that *hurt when she fell in the kitchen?*—or because there was something about being close to a mother. Any mother.

Carolyn Hancock's face softened when she looked at me. Or was I imagining that? Was wish fulfillment another symptom of prolonged abstinence? Was I becoming delusional?

"Hi, Mom." Lily bent over to kiss her cheek. "Calder and I are working together at the café."

"Well, that's wonderful," she said. "Jason, don't work him too hard. Let them relax. They've already been working all day."

Hancock grunted and dismissed us. Lily signaled for me to follow her. I hesitated, reluctant to leave Mrs. Hancock.

"Go on," Mrs. Hancock said, misreading my hesitation. "Jason'll have plenty of help tomorrow. You go."

I followed Lily down to the dock. Sophie came up beside me and touched my elbow. I jumped at the unexpected contact.

129

"Do you want to come with *me*, Calder? I made a fort this morning on the edge of the woods. I have some of my plainer dolls set up in there like it's a hotel."

"I'd like that, Sophie, but maybe in a little bit?"

She frowned and sulked away.

Lily looked back to see if I was coming. She was already sitting on the edge of the dock, between the two newly installed floodlights. I kept my shoes on, stepping over her discarded sandals and the fedora, and walked the length of the dock. Lily had two beach blankets laid out on the cedar slats, and I lay down prone on one of them. She dangled her bare legs in the water. I imagined the smell of oranges spreading out through the lake.

"Why is your mom in a wheelchair?"

Lily stared down at me. "You're very blunt, aren't you?"

"Is that bad?"

"No." She sighed. "Actually, it's refreshing. Most people are too uncomfortable to ask. They pretend everything's normal, when obviously it's not."

I waited. Lily stood up and stripped off her top. I sat up in shock, at first not realizing she had her bathing suit on under her clothes. She grinned down at me, enjoying my scandalized expression.

"It's good to be prepared," she said. She shimmied out of her skirt and gracefully lowered herself off the dock.

"Wait, don't!" The water only reached her thighs. Under the direct rays of the sun, it was warmer than the open lake, but I'd never seen a human in the water this time of year. At least not voluntarily. Was her skin already turning blue? I wasn't sure.

"What?" Lily asked.

"It can't be more than fifty degrees."

"Really? It doesn't feel that bad."

"Seriously," I said. "Get out. Aren't you the one who said no one swam in April? It's dangerous without . . . a dive suit."

She shrugged. "I guess I'm used to it now." She dropped down under the water and came up chin first, letting her long, wet hair drag in a solid sheet behind her. Goose bumps popped up on her arms and stomach, but she wasn't in a hurry to get out. I chewed on the insides of my mouth.

"To answer your earlier question," she continued, "Mom has MS. Some days are better than others. A couple days ago she was walking with a cane; today she needs her chair. It's frustrating not knowing what each day's going to be like. It's like we're losing her bit by bit. I mean, this will sound weird: she's here, but I really miss my mom."

Lily didn't know how well I understood that. "When did she get sick?"

"When I was twelve. It started out slowly but it's gotten really bad this year. Some days she can barely hold her paintbrushes. Her doctor said living in the city was putting too much stress on her. He said we should get out into a 'more restful climate.' Dad thought it was a good time to try it up here. I don't know. I guess it's a good thing. Not as many people to stare at her, at least."

"Why would they stare?" I asked, watching for any signs of hypothermia.

"Because they don't know what's wrong. So they try and figure it out. Sometimes I wish they'd just come out and ask, like you did."

131

"They probably think that's being rude," I said.

Lily laid her hands flat on the water and turned quickly in a circle, sending droplets scattering off the surface. "It's ruder to stare."

"It's not like it's something to be embarrassed about."

She stopped spinning and raised her chin in the air. "I'm not embarrassed. It would just be nice to have a regular family again." She tipped her head to the side and scrutinized me with a puckered brow. "Aren't you going to come in?"

"Do you paint, too?" I asked, avoiding her question.

"No. Not at all."

"You look artistic. Or at least, your clothes did, before you took them off." I picked through her lace blouse and velvet jacket that lay in a pile by my feet. "You dress like an artist."

"Role-play."

"What do you mean?"

"I want to be a poet, so I try to dress like one—or like how I imagine my favorite ones would dress."

"You like the Victorians, too," I said with confidence.

"How'd you guess?"

"Your tattoo."

She smiled broadly and signaled for me to keep my voice down. "You know that poem?"

"Some." I let my mind wind itself backward to my recent study sessions and plucked out the words from memory. "No coward soul is mine, / No trembler in the word's storm-troubled sphere: / I see Heaven's glories shine, / And Faith shines equal, arming me from Fear."

She nodded and a honey-colored glow emanated from her shoulders. The light followed the curve of her arms and then intensified into a sugary pinkish orange. I knew the color well. Lily was happy. I could only hope I was the cause.

"That's amazing," she said. "I'm impressed."

"So, how do you decide what a poet should dress like?"

She shrugged. "Simple, really. I look at what everyone else is wearing and do the opposite."

Nonconformity, I mused. *What a luxury.* "So let's hear it, then."

"Hear what?" she asked.

"Some poetry. Your poetry."

Despite the cold, a rush of blood heated her face. "I can't just spout something off."

"Why not?" I asked.

She sputtered, clearly off balance. "I have to be . . . inspired. I have to be looking at something beautiful . . . or, or amazing."

I gestured at myself as if to say, *What am I?*

She answered the question as if I'd spoken it. "*You* are an annoying guy who has no problem asking questions but won't share any answers." She cupped her hand and flung water at my chest.

I leaned to my side, dodging the spray. "Let me get you started," I said. "How 'bout a limerick? There once was a guy most amazing."

She shook her head.

So I continued. "Who thought that his girl had gone crazy."

She raised her eyebrows at me. I was definitely pushing it with the "his girl" line, but she picked up where I left off.

"The girl he annoyed," she said.

"But she couldn't avoid," I added.

She smiled confidently and finished strong: "His stalking and silence so puzzling."

"Ha. You're right, Lily Hancock. You are a poet."

"Oh, shut up. Why don't you come in? It's not too bad in the sun."

"You're lying. But even if that were true, I didn't bring a suit," I said, waving her off.

"Swim in your shorts."

"No thanks."

"Your loss."

She enjoyed teasing me. A trail of happy satisfaction burned like pink fire, then spun out of her like a pinwheel. It was a magnet that lured me to her. My hand involuntarily reached forward. She came closer, not realizing the motivation behind my gesture, and shocked me by weaving her fingers through mine. I watched—horrified, spellbound—as the pink shimmer crept from her fingertips, across the top of my hand and over my wrist. My forearm hummed and heated until the warmth pushed up my arm and broke across my chest, finally bursting through my lips with a sudden, surprising laugh.

"I know you know something," she said in a low voice. "About what my grandpa saw in the lake. I want you to tell me."

"I don't have anything to say."

"Calder, you say more with your eyes than most people do with their mouths. Right now your eyes are saying you're afraid. A minute ago they were saying it wasn't safe in the lake. You might as well say it plainly, Calder. I know you know something." Then she lowered her eyebrows and faked a terrible Russian accent. "Vee haf vayz uff makeen you talk."

"Yeah, well . . . good luck with that."

"Jason!" called Mrs. Hancock. "I'm losing my sun. Can you move me?"

I dropped Lily's hand, and it splashed into the water in front of her. "I can do it!" I called to Mrs. Hancock.

"Brown-noser," Lily said.

"I don't know why you're so hard to convince," I said, "but I'm really not that bad of a guy."

"Spoken like a true serial killer."

My stomach shrank down to a cold, hard pellet. "You'll see," I said, forcing a smile into my eyes. "One of these days, you might actually like me."

18

THREAT

An hour later a van pulled up and the Pettits piled out, slamming the doors behind them. Jack's eyes were searching. When he found Lily sitting by me around the campfire, he frowned. Gabrielle ran up quickly.

"I invited the Pettits over for the cookout," Hancock said to his wife. "Martin, help yourself to beer in the cooler."

"I should really get going," I said, standing up.

"Already?" Lily asked, taking the bag of chips from me and rolling the top down noisily.

It had been over twelve hours since I'd been in the lake,

which would normally be a piece of cake, but the fire was drying me out to an uncomfortable degree. I really needed to go, but Jack looked too pleased about my announcement, so I changed my mind.

"I guess I could stay for a while," I said, pulling my chair closer to Lily.

Jack grumbled something under his breath and Lily laid her hand lightly on the armrest of my chair.

Hancock poked the fire, sending a spray of sparks into the air. "How are you kids doing? Glad school's winding down?"

Jack looked away from Lily's hand on my chair to her father. Mr. Pettit spoke up. "Jack didn't go to school this year."

"I just took a year off," said Jack. "I'll start college next fall if things work out. For now, I'm taking some art classes at the community college."

"Oh, you're an artist?" Mrs. Hancock asked, her face glowing in the firelight. "You should come over and paint with me sometime."

"I'd like that. Right now I'm taking an art and mythology class. All the Greek classics and then some Celtic and Native American stuff, too. I did an oil painting on the Passamaquoddy legends from up in Maine. I showed it to Lily."

"I'm not familiar with that one," said Hancock.

"It's like the manitou stories from around here," explained Mr. Pettit. He shook a bag of sunflower seeds into his mouth and filled one cheek.

"There are lots of Anishinabe manitous," Jack said while Mr. Pettit spit shells into the fire. "One lay face-up on the bottom of the lake. The Indians offered him tobacco or chunks of copper so he wouldn't capsize their canoes."

Lily sat up and looked anxiously at her father.

Hancock shifted in his seat. "I know about the ancient copper mines," he said. "That's part of my curriculum for next term. But there are no monsters in the lake."

"I didn't say anything about monsters," Jack said as Mr. Pettit roared with laughter.

"Don't get Jack wrong," Mr. Pettit said. "We're not super-stitious, but there was a big resurgence of manitou stories back in 'sixty-seven after . . ."

Hancock got up and retreated toward the house. Lily looked at her mom, who shook her head to silence her.

". . . well, you know . . . ," finished Mr. Pettit, his voice trailing off to nothingness.

"What about 'sixty-seven?" asked Lily. Her question was for Mr. Pettit, but her eyes were fixed on me.

"Just drop it, Dad," said Gabrielle. She pulled her dark hair to one side and began braiding it into a long rope.

Jack moved his lawn chair closer until his knee pressed up against Lily's.

"It didn't take too much for the manitou legends to mu-tate into stories about mermaids. Let's just say some people around here got what you might call mermaid fever," contin-ued Mr. Pettit. He spit through his teeth, shooting sunflower seeds onto the hissing coals. "T-shirt vendors made a small fortune. People were convinced that a lake this big, this deep, had to have something. But it just lasted a summer. People got saner after that. I've still got a T-shirt somewhere."

"So you don't think there's anything in Lake Superior?" asked Lily.

Gabrielle rolled her eyes, and Mr. Pettit chuckled warmly.

"It's the Great Gitche Gumee," he said. "Ancient and unimaginably deep. I wouldn't go so far to say there's *nothing* in the lake."

"It could be true," said Jack. His voice was quiet and unsure and we all turned to look at him. Jack rolled another log into the fire with the toe of his boot.

"What's that, son?"

"I said it could be true. About mermaids. There's the November Witch."

"The November Witch is the name of a *storm*," said Gabrielle.

"The legend," Mr. Pettit said, "is that the November Witch had three sisters who prowled Gitche Gumee."

Lily shivered.

Jack's forehead furrowed. "And I heard another story once," he said, pausing to consider his words.

"That's enough, son," said Mr. Pettit.

Jack went on. "Up at the Peterson fish house. I got talking to an old guy. He told me there were people who were descended from manitous, but they didn't know it. He said they were walking around town, just like you and me."

"I don't think you can quit being a sea monster," I suggested. It was too good to be true, and if it was possible, I would know.

"That's not what I'm saying," Jack said, his voice snapping like a beach towel. "I'm not saying they *quit*. I'm saying they don't *know*."

"Well, *I'm* spooked out," I said with a laugh. "I think I really need to head out this time."

Lily reached toward me and tentatively touched my hand.

"Well, if you've got to go," Hancock said as he returned to the campfire, rubbing Vaseline into his hands. The flickering light of the bonfire reflected off the windows behind him. He didn't sound disappointed about me going, so I was surprised when he added, "But we haven't even broken out the hot dogs. Maybe we could have you and your mom and dad over for dinner some other time?"

I nodded curtly. If I wanted to go before, now it was a necessity. Here it was—the invitation I'd been working toward, coming even sooner than planned—but even the implication of my mother's name on his lips was blasphemous. It stirred up an anger I hadn't felt in years. If I could have killed Hancock on dry land, I might have done it right there. In front of everyone.

"Calder, are you okay?" Lily's voice was alarmed.

I could only imagine the crazed expression on my face. I jogged to my car and jumped behind the wheel. I was vaguely aware of Lily following me. She grabbed the edge of my door and leaned in. "What's your hurry?"

The concern in her eyes tugged at some untested corner of my heart. I wanted to tell her not to worry, that I didn't always act this crazy. Instead, I threw the car into gear and spun my tires on the gravel driveway, covering her in dust. I couldn't afford to be polite. I needed to be prudent; right now, that meant getting far, far away.

But the funny thing was, getting away from Hancock meant getting away from Lily. And the bigger the dust cloud between me and her, the cozier that interloping Jack Pettit would no doubt get. Lily Hancock was tricky enough without having to deal with a testosterone-fueled saboteur.

I hit the brakes hard and staggered out of the car, slamming the door behind me. Squirrels scattered as I stomped through the woods toward the water. I waded into the lake, fully clothed, willing myself not to change. It was still hard to do, but not impossible anymore.

It took all my concentration. My legs trembled beneath me; my lungs burned for the water. I satisfied myself with saturating my body from the outside. I wanted to be ready if she needed me, although I wasn't sure what that need would be. It wasn't like I was going to charge out of the water just to put mustard on her hot dog. I had enough self-control not to do that. Didn't I?

The smell of burning birch led me back. I slogged through the water until I could see the campfire's reflection. The Hancocks' and Pettits' faces glowed with light and heat against the blackness. My heart plunged when my eyes settled on Lily. She was staring intently at the fire. Sparks flew in her direction, but she barely reacted. Gabrielle Pettit sat on her left, Jack on her right. His face was turned toward her, and I could see it clearly. He laid one arm around the back of her chair and leaned to whisper something in her ear. My fists clenched involuntarily. Okay, so I wasn't completely insane yet. I was right. Jack Pettit was a threat.

19

WHAT I WANT FROM YOU

Sometime after midnight I crawled into the hammock the Hancocks had strung between two white pines. It was kelly-green canvas, trimmed in white cotton fringe, and it was the perfect place to hide, to sleep, and to get some time away from my sisters. Tonight it had an added advantage in that Gabrielle Pettit had stayed for a sleepover, and the hammock was a convenient place from which to eavesdrop on her and Lily chattering in Lily's room; they showed no sign of sleeping.

Their voices drifted through the open bedroom window.

They had already covered the requisite subjects of school, fashion, and movies. Gabrielle had given Lily the lowdown on all the popular kids in town—not that Lily seemed much interested or concerned—and now they had moved on to a subject that promised to be more useful to me.

"So," Gabrielle hedged. "Before. When we were moving you in."

"Yeah?" Lily asked.

"You didn't sound interested in getting set up with Jack."

"Oh."

"I was just wondering," Gabrielle continued, "if you have a boyfriend back in Minneapolis."

"No. How 'bout you?"

Gabrielle laughed. "Not the easiest thing to manage when you have Jack as a brother."

"He's protective?"

"I guess *he'd* call it that."

"I always wanted an older brother."

"You mean like someone who'd bring his cute friends around? Trust me. It's not that great. And since all Jack's friends went off to college, there's no one around anyway."

"I meant more like someone to talk to about stuff. I had an imaginary friend when I was younger. I'd tell her everything."

I smirked in the hammock. Seemed Lily and I had at least one thing in common there.

"Like what?" Gabrielle asked.

"I don't know, things I was scared of, things I was excited about, things I didn't want my parents to know."

"I had a dog like that. She was a good listener."

"Exactly," Lily said.

"So, what are you scared of?"

Lily hesitated. "I don't know . . . mainly I worry about things falling apart."

Score two for having things in common. Not that I was worried about "things" falling apart—only myself.

"Are your parents getting divorced?" Gabrielle asked.

Lily laughed. "Hardly. I meant it literally. This house, my mom, me . . . I worry about things literally falling apart."

Gabrielle fell silent—probably wished she hadn't stepped into something so personal. Then a sharp sound escaped the window—*scrape, scrape, scrape*—metal on metal. Orange blossoms billowed on the air. "These are some . . . um . . . interesting outfits you have," said Gabrielle. *Scrape, scrape, scrape.* "This one's kinda cute. Bohemian chic, maybe."

"Thanks? I guess?"

"No, seriously. It's pretty cool." *Scrape, scrape.* "Hmm. So, back to boys. Oh, can I try this one on?"

"Sure," said Lily.

"It was good to see that Calder guy again."

I dropped my foot to the ground and put the brakes on the hammock's gentle swaying. Lily didn't say anything. I wished I could see her face.

"Did you invite him over?" Gabrielle asked.

"No. Not really."

Someone fidgeted and the bedsprings creaked.

"So? He just showed up?"

"We're working together at the café," Lily said.

"No shit?"

Lily laughed nervously. "He brought me home, and Dad asked him to help with some stuff. So, yeah."

144

"And then he just stuck around?"

"I guess."

"He is *so* gorgeous. He's not even *real*-looking. He talks funny, though. Did you notice? It's like his words are liquidy. They run together funny."

Lily didn't respond. Did this mean she agreed? Disagreed? Gabrielle didn't seem to know how to take Lily's silence, either.

"Don't you think so?" she prodded.

"Of course he's beautiful," said Lily with a sigh. "How could I not think so? But he knows it, too."

The smirk dropped off my face.

"Oh," said Gabrielle. "Stuck on himself?"

"More like he knows how to *use* it. He can look at you and . . . well . . ."

Gabrielle giggled. "I'll have to get closer and check that out."

Lily didn't respond at first. I waited through the silence, wondering what they were doing. Eventually Lily asked, "How come Jack didn't want to go to college?"

"You'll have to ask him. He was supposed to go, but something changed last summer, and he just got weirder—moodier—through the fall and winter. I thought maybe having a girlfriend might get him back to his normal self. That's why I was wondering about you. He looks at you funny."

"Funny strange or funny ha-ha?"

"Funny as in I think he's interested in you."

"Sorry, Gabby, that's not going to happen."

"Yeah, I kinda got that feeling after tonight."

"Tonight?"

145

"Well, it's obvious Calder's into you. Bummer for me." She laughed a little.

"I sincerely doubt that," Lily said. "He's not even a good candidate for that older-brother type."

"Not a talker?"

"Oh, he talks," Lily said. "He talks a lot, but he doesn't really ever tell you anything. Y'know what I mean?"

"Mmm," Gabrielle said. "Typical guy."

Lily fell quiet and, again, I wished I had a higher vantage point.

"Calder—" Gabrielle started.

"Are you hungry?" Lily cut her off.

"What? Oh, yeah, sure."

Four feet tiptoed down the stairs toward the kitchen. I rolled out of the hammock and pulled back into the trees. The girls leaned against the kitchen counter, and I got my first look at them in a while. Lily looked paler than usual, except for the dark circles under her eyes. Gabrielle was popping cheese puffs into her mouth.

"So if the thing you have with Calder doesn't work out . . . ," said Gabrielle.

Lily's eyebrows pulled together.

"I'm just saying," said Gabrielle, "if it doesn't, you'd put in a good word for me, right?"

Before Lily could respond, a stick snapped on the driveway. I spun around. Maris? No, she would never mount an attack on dry land. It was beneath her. I squinted through the darkness, my eyes focusing on a familiar silhouette. I wished my first guess had been right.

The beam of Jack Pettit's flashlight bobbed and weaved

on the ground in front of him. Still, he jumped when he saw me charging up on him in the dark.

"Wh-what are you dong here?" he asked.

"I lost my wallet. Came back for it. What about you?"

Jack looked at me skeptically. I guess retrieving wallets in the dark wasn't normal human behavior. Particularly without a flashlight of my own. I'd have to make a note.

"I'm here to break the girls out," said Jack. "There's a party at . . . well, never mind."

"I'm sure they're sleeping. Lily and I are working the early shift tomorrow."

"*Pfff.* What are you, her mother?" asked Jack. "And, besides, how would you know? Even if they *are* sleeping, I bet Lily'd be up for a party. Gabby always is."

I stared him down, and he shifted in his shoes.

"Fine," he snapped. "So what's the deal with you and Lily anyway?"

"'Deal'?"

"Yeah," Jack said, his eyes going to the light in Lily's window. "Have you asked her out?"

"Not yet."

"What are you waiting for?"

Good question, I thought. "Maybe I'm waiting for her to want me to."

"Ah." Jack folded his arms across his chest. "I didn't think she was that into you." He smiled broadly, and I wondered which of his shiny teeth would break the easiest. "Easy, dude," Jack said, holding his hands up, palms out. "Just playin'."

A white moth flew between us and flitted past my hand.

A snap of blue light shot from my middle finger, and the moth dropped to the ground in a charred heap.

"What the hell?" Jack yelled as he staggered back a few steps.

"I think you're going to your party alone," I said, feeling the electric charge pulsing through my fingers. I reached out to turn him around, but he was already running back to his car.

After Jack's taillights disappeared, I returned to the hammock and tried to fall asleep. I might have had fleeting moments of dreams: images of pink awnings and steel drums, a turquoise backdrop. Maris and a sturgeon, my mother's face. But most of the time, I was wide awake and staring through the tree branches at a shattered sky.

I didn't know how much time was passing, or how close we were to morning, or how far I was pushing the chance of Hancock busting me for sleeping in his yard. Rolling out of the hammock, I got to my feet and headed toward the driveway. The loose gravel looked purple in the early morning light, and it crunched under my feet.

"Being the creepy stalker guy again?"

I whirled around. Lily leaned out her bedroom window, Juliet-style, with her hands on the sill.

"Geez, Lily, you scared me. What are you doing up?"

"I think there's a much more interesting question, don't you? Like what the hell are you doing down there?"

"Shhh," I said. "You don't want to wake anyone up."

She looked behind her, then slung one leg out the window and climbed onto the porch roof.

"Careful." I put my hands up, ready to catch her if she fell.

"What is going on with you?" she asked.

Good question. "I just forgot my—" I gestured vaguely toward the fire pit.

She looked at me with a puzzled expression. "Maybe if you hadn't rushed away so quickly, you wouldn't have forgotten something."

"I'm sorry about that."

"It was rude." The roof creaked, and Lily's foot made a scraping sound on the shingles.

"Well, at least I left you in good company." My voice sounded strangely bitter, and her eyebrows arched.

"Are you for real? Is that what this is about? You have something against *Jack Pettit*?"

"Don't be ridiculous."

"Okay, then why are you here? Unless you plan on sticking with another one of your lame excuses." She crept closer to the edge of the roof, and I formed my arms into a basket. "Y'know, you're probably the worst liar I ever met."

"Did Jack Pettit fix that roof?" I asked, cringing.

"Him and his dad."

"You're probably going to fall through."

She laughed and sat down on the edge, dangling her legs over the gutter. Even in the dark, a rosy aura dripped from the ends of her toes like pink candle wax.

"What do you want from me?" I asked. I didn't understand where the question came from. Somehow our roles had reversed without asking permission.

"I told you what I want," she said.

I chuckled low under my breath.

She bent forward and reached down to me. "You have

149

answers to questions I've had since I was little, since I first heard my grandpa tell the story."

"You can think that if you want, but you're wrong. Now will you get off that roof? I'm going to have a nervous breakdown."

"See?" she said. "You're talking with your eyes again, Calder White. You know things. And I intend to know it all, too."

"You're unbelievable," I murmured.

"Ah," she said. "So I've been told."

20

PINK

Mrs. Boyd had the door to the café propped open, and the cool morning air blew in. Lily and I sat at a small circular table with a stack of paper napkins and a bin of freshly washed silverware in front of us. Our hands bumped as we took turns reaching for knives and forks to roll in the napkins. I tried to make it seem accidental, but it was a well-planned maneuver. A half hour later we'd amassed a small pile of table settings between us. Neither of us spoke.

I wondered if she was still irritated with me for leaving the campfire so rudely. That would be fair. I was still pissed that she'd let Jack Pettit get so close. Was she blind? Couldn't she see what he was after? The guy was about as subtle as a harpoon. If she'd been given the choice, would she have gone to that party with him?

Or maybe she was mad because she knew I was lying to her. That would be fair, too.

Lily carried the tray of silverware behind the counter. I scraped my chair back across the floor and followed close behind.

"What are you doing after work today?" I asked.

"Who wants to know?"

"I was thinking maybe we could do something."

Lily turned, dropped the tray on the counter with a clatter, and put her hands on her hips. "Depends. Are you going to run out on me again?"

"I said I was sorry about that."

"And you're not going to tell me anything?"

"No." I reached out, and she didn't object when I dragged my fingers down her arm, shoulder to wrist. She gave a small shiver and turned away from me. "But only because there's nothing to tell."

She pressed her finger to her lips as a bunch of boys came in the door, kicking their skateboards up into their hands. Clustering around a table, they emptied their pockets and pooled their quarters and dimes. Two came up to the counter and ordered a large mint mocha latte.

Mrs. Boyd had a basket of apples on the counter, and I cut one into sections while Lily made their drink. I grabbed a salt shaker and dusted the slices.

"You're salting an apple?" Lily asked with interest. She

snapped a cover onto the paper cup and handed it to the shorter of the boys.

I wiggled my eyebrows at her, and she shook her head. She opened her mouth to say something more, when the door swung open and the bell rang out.

Jack and Gabrielle strolled in as the skateboarders left. The look on Gabrielle's face was priceless—something between surprise and satisfaction. She sucked her teeth and raised her eyebrows at Lily. In contrast, I could smell the testosterone rolling off Jack. The muscle in his jaw bulged as he clenched his teeth.

"Hi, guys," said Lily. I looked at her sharply. Her bright tone confirmed her cluelessness when it came to this guy.

"Hi, Calder," said Gabrielle. She leaned her body over the counter and let her V-neck T-shirt hang open. "You took off too quick last night."

Jack stood behind his sister with his arms crossed. I couldn't tell if his show of machismo was for Lily or for me. My mind instinctively went to thoughts of violence. Jack eyed me up and down and stopped when his scowl landed on my hands. I crossed my arms, matching his posture. Jack dropped his arms when he realized I was mocking him.

I smiled. "Did you have fun last night, Jack?"

"Dude? What the—?"

Lily kicked my foot. "Ignore him. Did you guys want some coffee?"

"No," said Jack. "We just stopped in to tell you we're having a bonfire out at our house tonight. Lots of our friends will be there. You're invited if you want to come, *Lily.*" He glared at me to make his point. I ran through a list of potential responses. I wanted to say that she already had plans. With me. But Lily didn't like to be told what to do.

"Yeah, sure, that sounds fun," said Lily. "Would you be up for that, Calder?"

Jack's expression soured, which was satisfying, but I didn't need to press my luck.

"I've got plans tonight," I said. Lily's eyebrows pulled together in response. Curiosity? Disappointment? I couldn't tell. I turned my back on the Pettits and leaned toward her ear. "But I still want to do something with you this afternoon. Can I take you to Big Bay?"

Her tiny nod was all I needed to sustain me.

A few hours later, I waited impatiently at the pier. The Madeline Island ferry's next run was scheduled to depart Bayfield in seven minutes. Not ten. Seven. Residents set their clocks by the iron monstrosity. *Lily's not coming*, I thought miserably. She was probably just being polite when she agreed to go to Big Bay with me. She probably got a better offer from Gabrielle later, after our shift ended.

Several children dressed in jeans and yellow Windbreakers rushed past me, laughing, casting rainbow beams off their happy faces. I bounced my knee with anxiety, trying to ignore them. It wasn't easy. Their excitement at riding the ferry burned like a neon sign that said *Take Me, Take Me, Take Me*. I closed my eyes to the brightly lit children and sank my teeth into my bottom lip.

Where was Lily? The physical separation ate at my insides. Why couldn't she feel this way? I cursed the abysmal failure I'd become.

Leaning back against a wooden fence, I closed my eyes to

the soft wind that blew across my face. The halyards clanged and clanked against the sailboat masts in the marina.

"Calder!"

I whipped around at the sound of my name and broke into an easy smile. Lily was jogging up to me. She was wearing the most ridiculous skirt, an ankle-length patchwork of velvet and paisley squares. A small backpack hung from her arm. Her hair swung behind her in buoyant curls against a tight navy T-shirt. Her eyes were bright with expectation.

At first I thought she had a pink sweater draped over her shoulders, but as she drew closer I could see the aura emanating off her arms, confessing her enthusiasm. I groaned with desire. It was worse than the little kids. Not that I hadn't seen her like this before, but I didn't have any excuse for escape now. I'd be trapped with her right at my side for the next several hours—her radiating that succulent sweetness into the air. Tingling on my tongue. Begging to be consumed. The familiar bleakness enveloped my mind. Why did I think this would be a good idea?

"You okay?" she asked.

I managed to get out a halfhearted "Perfect" and pushed her toward the ferry, which was already loaded with an old VW van and several cars with kayaks strapped to their roofs. Lily pulled out a card and handed it to the ferry captain. "Season pass," she said to me.

We walked on, weaving between the cars, to a spot along the rail. Once all the cars were in place and their emergency brakes set, the crew flipped the lines off the iron cleats, casting us off from the pier. The captain engaged the throttle, and we set off across the lake to Madeline Island.

Lily leaned over the rail and let the water spray her face. She shivered, and I hesitated for a second before putting my arm around her shoulders. She didn't object.

She gestured to the lake. "It's like bedazzled denim," she said.

I nodded, and my mind raced out, searching for something clever to say. I came up empty. Awkward and off balance, I thanked the ferry engines for being loud enough to excuse my silence. I picked at the peeling paint on the rail.

The wind dissipated the pink glow off Lily's face, shattering her aura and sending pink flecks onto the waves like flower petals. It made it easier to be so close, but I still had to marvel at my self-control. Once or twice I had the urge to scoop her up and dive over the side of the ferry. But there were too many witnesses. Besides, why would I want to end this?

As if she were reading my mind, Lily sighed and leaned closer to me. I looked at her face but she looked straight ahead, making it impossible to interpret her body language. Did she want me to kiss her? Doubtful. I mean, any other girl and that would be the obvious assumption, but there wasn't much obvious about Lily. If she wanted me to kiss her and I did, I'd be making a happy report to Maris tonight. If I kissed her and she *didn't* want me to, I'd lose whatever ground I'd gained in the last twenty-four hours.

I tightened my grip around her shoulders and she leaned more heavily against me. It wasn't like I'd never kissed anyone before. How many times was the kiss just a prelude to the kill? I'd practically invented the move. I pulled my arm back and touched my finger to Lily's chin. Her lips parted, soft and warm, expecting me. But I didn't know how to kiss Lily. When I looked into her eyes, all I could see was my deceit. I cleared my throat and went back to peeling paint.

It didn't take long to cross the channel. Small pale buildings dotted the shoreline. Their docks projected into the lake like little fingers. A few brave children ran along the beach and tested the water with their bare toes while the adults watched in long pants and sweaters.

The ferry turned and backed into the pier. Two seagulls circled a tall wooden pole stained black with creosote, then landed on the railing a few feet from where Lily and I leaned. One of the birds looked at me for a second, accusing me with its yellow eye. *Danger?* it asked. I answered its question, and it was aloft again, soaring to the roof of a long white building.

The captain cut the engine and Lily staggered. I caught her before she fell.

"Nice catch," she said, smiling appreciatively.

I righted her onto her feet. "*I* think so" was my witty response. Innuendo would have to suffice for romance. At least for now.

The moped rental shop was just a block from the ferry landing, on the corner of Main Street and Middle Road. A bearded man in board shorts and a Led Zeppelin T-shirt greeted us. Lily eyed the sign behind his head—*All Minors Must Be Accompanied by a Parent*—and then at me as I stared the man down. Without breaking eye contact, he handed us two helmets.

"Going to Big Bay?" he asked.

I nodded.

"Need a map?"

I shook my head. I signaled to Lily and she ducked out the door.

"What the heck?" she said with amusement. "He didn't even ask for IDs." She twisted her hair up on top of her head and wiggled the helmet over the top.

"Good thing," I said, winking. "I don't have one."

"Did you even pay for these?"

I straddled a blue Honda and revved the engine. Lily hoisted up her skirt and got on behind me. We bounced softly on the tires a few times before taking off up Middle Road. Lily wrapped her arms around my waist, her palms gliding across my sides, her thumbs pressed into my abs, and laid her head against my shoulder blades. I sank back against her heat.

The tiny town gave way to forest, and the trees pressed in on both sides. Long shadows cut across the road. I could hear the thoughts of several deer and a fox, lurking in the woods, just out of sight of human eyes. They watched me pass. Wondering. Worrying. The fox skittered into a hollowed-out log and crouched low.

I kept my eyes straight ahead, waiting for the point where the road would come to the northeastern shore and take a ninety-degree turn to the left, toward the Town Park. I pointed ahead toward the lake, and Lily nodded against my back. The sun hit the water, turning it silver, and I banked the moped into the curve. A few minutes later, the brown Town Park sign was in front of us and we were pulling into the parking lot. I killed the engine and knocked down the kickstand. Lily swung her leg over the back to dismount.

"Do you think it's warm enough to swim?" she asked.

"For you, maybe," I said. "You have a higher tolerance than anyone I've ever met."

"Including you?"

"Definitely including me. I'll be staying on the beach."

"Oh, don't be such a baby."

"We'll see." I took a risk and grabbed her hand. The familiar tingling sensation tickled up my arm to my heart, and the fluorescent pink glow pulsed out of her shoulders, spreading over her body like a perfect outline. I dropped her hand, and the glow dimmed to a rust-colored shadow. *Interesting*. She was happier when I held her hand.

We followed the lichen-crusted boardwalk to the steps that led down to the bridge. Several boards were rotted and broken, so we passed carefully, crossing the ravine and then marching across the sand, through the trees and onto the sun-flooded beach. A few families walked the beach.

Lily ran ahead of me, shedding her clothes. I didn't know what was more appealing, the soft dip of her waist or the orange glow that streamed down her arms and dripped from her fingertips like melted ice cream. The other beachgoers watched incredulously as Lily splashed into the water and then ran back to me, crashing herself against my chest.

Her skin glistened and goose bumps rose all over her body. I reached behind me and pulled my sweatshirt over the top of my head. Lily put her arms in the air, and I pulled the shirt back down over her, inside out.

Maris's voice growled in my ear. *Remember why you're here, Calder.*

I remember, I thought, dragging my finger around Lily's ear to secure a lock of hair.

159

Go too far and I swear I'll . . . , Maris's voice warned.

What's too far? I wondered. Lily shivered. *I can do this,* I thought. *I can straddle this line. I can satisfy Maris and still somehow care for this girl.* I pushed all contradictory thoughts to the back of my mind. What other choice did I have?

A cold wind snapped at my bare chest, and Lily looked at me apologetically. "I should have brought a towel," she said. "What was I thinking?"

"I would have brought one for you if I'd thought you were insane enough to go in." I regretted my choice of words, but she smiled broadly. "I thought you were kidding."

"Insanity. I guess it's in my blood." She pulled out her ponytail and shook her hair.

"Hmm. Right. Your crazy gene pool." I kept my eyes on my feet as I asked the question that had plagued me since I was just a kid. "So, what happened to your grandpa, anyway? After he left here."

I rolled my ankles in the sand, trying to sound oh-so-casual—as if I didn't really care—but my skin prickled with expectation. Over the years, my fantasies had been colorful. The one I'd finally settled on included Tom Hancock hiding in a cave, eating vermin.

"I already told you," Lily said, brushing a dragonfly off my shoulder.

"I mean, how did it end?"

She looked down at the sand and covered my toes with her own. "Alzheimer's. By the end, he didn't even recognize my dad. Every little bit of *normal* just trickled away. The last thing he ever said to my dad was 'Your mother's calling, but don't go home.'"

"What was that supposed to mean?"

"Seeing as my grandma died five years before, not a whole heck of a lot. My dad took it to mean that Grandpa wanted him to stay with him. So of course he did. He held Grandpa's hand while he died. Still going on about the monster . . ." Lily stole a glance at me. "It broke my dad's heart. Mom wouldn't let us stay to watch. I'm not sure I would have wanted to. Have you ever known anyone with Alzheimer's?"

"No."

"It's awful. Watching someone fall apart like that, little by little. I'm not sure I could have watched him go. In the end."

There was a moment of silence and then Lily smiled and shrugged, changing the mood as easily as turning the page of a book. She pulled me to what she declared to be the "perfect spot" and spread out her skirt on the sand like a beach blanket. I lay next to her, wriggling my body until I was form-fitted into the sand. I concentrated on the heat behind me, rather than the coolness of the breeze over my skin. My eyelids burned red and then darkened as a cloud passed over. Lily sat up, but I didn't move. I was thankful for the quiet. A few minutes later I was asleep.

But the monster had never been more awake.

21

DON'T TEMPT ME

Heat. That was the first thing I noticed and the reason I knew I was dreaming. It was the kind of heat that came from being baked from the sun above and the hot sand underneath. In my dream, I opened my eyes, recognizing my surroundings, grateful to be back in the Bahamas. Turquoise and pink replaced the dark browns and greens of the North Woods. A dark-skinned man played a steel drum under a striped awning while vacationers sipped brightly colored drinks through plastic straws. The sand was powder under my skin, and I let it trickle through my fist like an hourglass.

In contrast to the heat on the outside, my heart shook with cold. My mind clouded over, dark and bleak, battling back the threads of despair that were now woven through me like the wefts and warps on a loom. With each passing second, the threads pressed more tightly together, until the despair nearly choked me.

I'd known this feeling before. Way too many times before. It was only a matter of minutes before the depression grew so thick it would overtake any sense of reason I might have left. I wondered what would set me off this time. A smile? A laugh? I just hoped, whoever it was, they wouldn't be too young. Children were harder to get over once the initial high wore off.

And then the dream shifted with the sand as someone stepped closer to me.

A low whisper in my ear: "Remember us?"

An anticipatory tremor ran through my legs.

I looked up, shielding my eyes from the sun. Two silhouetted figures looked down at me, their arms strangely elongated, their heads small.

"From the bar last night," I said groggily, trying to remember their names.

Of course, they couldn't see the danger I presented. They saw me as nothing more than the perfect summer fling: exotic, affectionate, generous with a laugh. I loved them so they wouldn't be afraid—nothing like Pavati, who toyed with her prey like a kitten with its ball of string, letting it roll away before pulling it close again, slowly teasing the emotion out of her victims until they were too numb to fight back. No. I was nothing like Pavati. My victims always died with dignity; at the very least, I made it quick.

"We're going skinny-dipping," one of the girls said, her voice sounding far away, while the other laughed. My eyes darted to her, and my heart lurched with longing.

"We thought you'd like to join us?" she suggested.

One of the girls—I couldn't tell which—grabbed my hand and pulled me up, leading me to a secluded spot, on a high perched rock away from the public beach. I felt her pulling my arm although my vision was tunneling and I couldn't see her anymore.

She stopped. Turned. Kissed me. She laughed in a way that made my insides bubble over. The second girl said, "Kiss me, too, Calder," and her smile flashed like lightning, illuminating the whole scene.

Finding myself naked, I gasped, and in one fluid motion wrapped both of them in my arms. Their joyful shrieks filled my ears as I dove into the ocean, taking them deeper, pressing their bodies to my chest while the metamorphosis took over.

As we went deeper, the increasing pressure of the water helped me squeeze the life from their bodies. Their bright emotions seeped through their skin and into my own.

Like champagne osmosis.

It bubbled through my veins and made me so light I had to struggle not to float to the surface. But I pressed on, spiraling them down toward the sand, wringing them out like dishrags, not looking at their faces, not wanting to see their eyes roll back, their mouths go slack.

It only took a minute.

When I absorbed everything I could, I gave one final squeeze, then discarded their empty shells in my usual spot.

Exalting, I resurfaced, feeling ten times bigger and drunk with triumph.

And then I was conscious of someone watching me.

It was Lily. I was awake. And—*damn it*—I was cold. I gulped back the hunger that now tore with razor sharp teeth at my heart.

"What are you looking at?" I growled. I flung my arm over my eyes.

"Who says I'm looking at anything?" she snapped back.

"I do. I can feel you staring at me." It amazed me how conscious I was of her. I wondered at what distance I could feel her. "What are you doing?"

"Writing."

I pulled my arm back and squinted up at her. She had a notebook balanced on her knees, her backpack open by her feet. Lily bent her head over the page while her pen scritch-scratched across the paper. "What are you writing?"

"I'm writing about you," she said without looking up and without any apology.

I laughed a hard, bitter laugh. "I don't think I want to hear it."

"I'm just trying to describe what you look like. Are you Italian?" This time she looked at me with narrowed eyes.

"No."

"Irish? Armenian?"

"No, why?"

"I've never seen anyone who looks like you before. Black curly hair. Olive skin. But you don't look like you

165

have to shave—not even a little stubble. And you've got green eyes. I mean, who has eyes like that? They probably glow in the dark."

"They don't."

She trailed her finger over my arm, feeling the smoothness. "Do you wax your arms or something?"

"I'm on the swim team," I explained, the corners of my mouth twitching.

"You're lying."

"A little."

"Don't do that."

"I'm sorry," I squinted up at her and she was blushing.

"Okay, so what are you?" she asked, emphasizing the *what* more than I thought was normal. Or was that in my head?

"I'm here. That's what I am."

Her mouth twisted into a smile. "I guess that's enough."

I rolled up on one elbow and leaned closer to her. "So, do I still make you nervous?"

"Abso-freaking-lutely." Lily returned to her notebook. I lay back flat in the sand and allowed my fingers to draw circles over the tattoo on the small of her back. The sun had all but disappeared, and the wind was growing colder.

"Lily?"

"What?"

"Are you sure you're going to Pettits' tonight?"

"Are you sure you're *not*?"

"I'm sure," I said. "I wouldn't want to ruin Jack's party."

"I was hoping you would."

"What? Ruin his party?"

She hit me over the head with her notebook. "No, stupid. I was hoping you'd go."

"We'll see," I said, relieved I was making enough progress to keep *both* me and Maris happy for one more night. "Now let's get you dressed. It's cold. I want my sweatshirt back."

22

BONFIRE

A yellow Lab paced back and forth along the shoreline behind the Pettits' shed. She watched me watching her. Now and then she'd lower herself onto her front legs, then jump to all fours, then down and up again. The bonfire burned behind her. It was built in a ceramic bathtub half buried in the ground, just thirty feet from the shore, and the dry branches piled up inside it burned bright, scattering sparks into the air.

Someone threw an armful of leaves into the fire over the protests of several girls, and a cloud of smoke billowed out of the bathtub. The partygoers backed up into the trees to avoid the toxic smell, and a gray cloud poured over the lake.

The smoke choked off any light the fire created, and I had to work hard to find Lily in the haze. She was—as I had suspected, or maybe feared—standing in the dark next to Jack Pettit. Or maybe *he* was standing next to *her,* because when she sidestepped away, he closed the gap again. He leaned in to whisper something in her ear. She smiled. Her back was pressed up against a tree. I couldn't tell if she was amused or merely being polite, and—*What the hell was she wearing now?* Jack fingered the fringe on a silk scarf she'd wrapped around her head.

The light reflected off something behind her. I squinted through the darkness and realized a garbage bag was hanging from a pine tree. At least a dozen crushed beer cans and plastic cups littered the ground by her feet. A silver keg was half visible behind the tree.

"Who's your friend?" a boy asked Jack.

"Lily Hancock," Jack said, obviously enjoying his familiarity with her. "Lily, this is my buddy Bryce. He's a senior this year."

"I don't remember seeing you around school," Bryce said. "You must not go to Bayfield."

"Just moved here," Lily said. "Plus, I'm homeschooled for now."

"That's too bad." Bryce placed his hand against the tree where Lily stood, and leaned in close. "It'd be nice to have a new face at school. I've known these other girls since kindergarten."

I tried to gauge Lily's reaction but couldn't. Gabrielle came running up and hip-checked Bryce. "Dude, back off," Gabrielle said. "Give the girl some space."

"What's your problem, Gabby?" asked Bryce. "I was just saying hey to New Girl."

"Lily, come with me," Gabby said. She grabbed Lily's hand and dragged her away. "I want to introduce you around." Then she yelled over her shoulder to Bryce, "To some less obnoxious people."

Lily ran off with Gabby. I would have followed to make sure she was okay, but Bryce's leering gaze held my rapt attention. He crushed his empty can and chucked it on the ground under the garbage bag.

"She dresses weird," Bryce said.

"Oh, she's definitely weird," Jack said.

"But cute, right?" asked Bryce.

Jack didn't respond.

"Yeah," said Bryce, "definitely cute. Who'd she come here with?"

Jack folded his arms over his chest and leaned closer, digging the point of his elbow into his buddy's chest. "I invited her. If she's here with anyone, she's here with me."

Without warning, electricity shot from my head down my arms, sending a white flash across the water. The people on shore all jumped. "Was that lightning?" someone asked. "It's not supposed to rain," said a boy. "Better not," said a third. "I won't get another weekend night off until Memorial Day."

A dead fish floated by my outreached hand. "You think she's with you?" I muttered, picking up the fish. I chucked it at Jack and hit him square between the eyes. "You have no idea who's here with you."

"What the hell was that?" Jack yelled.

The dog sniffed along the ground, trailing the mangled fish. When she found her target, she gave it a few good sniffs before sneezing and sitting down on Jack's foot.

"Get outta here, you dumb dog." Jack picked up a stick and tossed it far out in the water. The dog trotted toward the lake, then waded into the darkness. She paddled out forty feet to retrieve it, swimming back with her prize held reverently above the waterline.

She dropped the stick at Jack's feet and shook all the water out of her coat.

"Gah. Get outta here." Jack threw the stick out even farther. It was an impressive throw, and it landed within inches of my hand. If I hadn't known better, I would have said he was aiming for me.

The dog paddled out again. As she got closer, I could detect her white muzzle and tired expression. How well I knew the frustration of her instinctual compulsion. Her nose dropped lower and lower in the water as her thoughts flashed like the images of an old slide show: rabbit . . . food dish . . . someone running their fingers down the groove in her skull . . . and then . . . fatigue . . . PANIC.

Don't turn around, ol' girl. Come to me. I'll help you.

The dog whined and paddled closer.

That's it. A little bit farther. I put my hand under her belly—feeling every rib—and held her up. I delivered her onto the shore, several yards north of the party.

Hiding again, I wished I hadn't left my clothes back at the car. Lurking in the bushes was getting old—not to mention humiliating. Why didn't I just stick with legs and crash the party like any other self-respecting person?

I didn't answer the hundreds of questions that scrambled my brain. Perhaps it was because my head was all messed up, maybe it was because I was listening to the yellow Lab's low, warning growl, but at first I didn't notice the girl climbing into the fishing boat, or the dark figure shoving it off the sand onto the lake. My eyes searched the party for Lily as a thin thread of piney-citrus floated along the rippling waters.

"Have fun," said a voice I recognized as Gabrielle's.

The boat lurched as the darker figure threw one leg over the stern and climbed into the hull. By the silhouette I could tell it was male. The wind off the lake blew his sweatshirt hood off his head, and he took another step, rocking the boat. The girl shrieked, then laughed at herself, saying, "Gabby talked me into this. Do not make me regret it."

"Lily," I whispered.

The boy, still standing in the boat, pulled the starter cord once, twice, until the engine roared to life. He cranked the throttle, and the bow lifted out of the water. Lily faced the center of the boat. She leaned forward, bracing herself on the sides until the engine abruptly killed—just a hundred feet from shore—and she lurched backward.

"Jack, you're a terrible driver," she yelled at the other figure. It was worse than I thought. What was she doing with him out here? There was no light on the bow. I looked around, hoping not to see any other craft. A collision was more than I needed right now. Jack stood up and staggered to the center seat. The boat rocked dangerously, disrupting the water.

"You're drunk. What are you doing?" Lily's voice was panicked.

"What am *I* doing? What are *you* doing?" he asked, teasing.

"You're going to sink us."

"No, I'm not." He moved closer, sitting on the edge of the center seat. "It's nice, isn't it? Getting away from the crowd? I mean, they're okay, I guess, but I couldn't wait to get alone with you."

"I thought we were going for a ride," Lily said.

"Yeah, we will. But I wanted to talk to you first." The words slurred as Jack spoke. "It's not something I can say with just anyone listening. Believe me, I've tried."

"Talk about *what*?"

"About *them*." He laughed nervously. "At first I thought maybe you were one, too. That day you moved in. I could smell them all over your house. Spicy. Like smoke and incense."

He let out a short, hard laugh. "Back when you fell in the lake and you were talking all that crap about dolphins, I actually thought it was some cover story. But then it didn't make sense." He sighed. Disappointed. "You're not one of them. You've just been *near* them. A lot."

Lily leaned away from him. "You're the one not making sense."

"It's okay," he said. "You don't have to pretend for me. I've been near one of them, too. Very near."

"Near one of *what*?"

He smirked. "Quit it. You know what I'm talking about. That thing you called a dolphin." He laughed again and then lowered his voice. *"Mermaids."*

"Mermaids?" asked Lily. "You thought *I* was a mermaid?" Lily smiled, but at this distance, I couldn't tell if she was flattered or amused. "Mermaids smell like incense?"

He nodded and inched closer to her, pulling his knees up to hers. "There's one who came to visit me last summer. Every week. We had a special meeting spot on some flat rocks just south of here."

"Had?"

"I haven't seen her since last fall. But I could smell her on you." He leaned forward hopefully. "I thought maybe you'd seen her? She was supposed to come back for me."

From my hiding spot, I spun in a circle and threw my arms in the air. *"Damn it!"* I swore. So this was what Maris meant? Pavati didn't have dibs on Jack Pettit as prey; he was one of her toys. How come I hadn't seen that before? Maris and Pavati were getting very good at hiding their thoughts.

"Wait. You're telling me I wasn't hallucinating?" asked Lily. "What I saw? Your painting—that was her? My dolphin was the mermaid in your painting?"

Jack wasn't listening. "For the longest time I wished I was one of those people the old fisherman told me about. The ones that don't even know they're manitous . . . or mermaids, or whatever. Just walking around like normal. . . . I thought maybe that's why she came to me. Maybe she knew something I didn't. I tested it out a few times, but nothing happened. I can't even hold my breath for more than seventeen seconds."

Jack pressed his nose against Lily's skin, in the corner where her neck met her shoulder. He inhaled deeply and groaned. "God, you smell good. Just like her."

He put a hand behind Lily's neck. Under any other circumstances it would have been a romantic scene, but it was every horror movie I'd ever heard about. Lily flexed her wrist, and her palm came up flat and rigid against his chest. When it was clear it wasn't just me who wanted to keep Jack Pettit away, I took off for the boat, keeping my eyes above water.

Jack grabbed the ends of Lily's scarf and pulled her hard against him. The boat lurched. Lily screamed as Jack mashed his mouth on hers. She pushed him off and slapped him across the face.

Jack sucked in his breath as if she'd doused him in ice water, and he hit her back—hard. Lily fell over the seat. A vein bulged down the center of Jack's forehead as he pulled Lily back toward him and grabbed her face with both hands.

"Bring me to her," he said. "Tell her I want to see her. Tell her I can't stand it anymore."

Lily cried out, and then her voice was silenced.

Maybe it was because of the darkness, or maybe it was because his eyes were closed, but Jack Pettit never saw the arm come up out of the lake. My arm. My fingers clawing the air, eager for his throat. I grabbed him by the neck and pulled him over the side of the boat so fast he was gone before Lily's eyes popped open.

I almost had Jack pinned to the bottom when I remembered Lily. I rose to the surface, just enough to propel the boat back to shore, and felt the tip of my tail break the surface. Cold night air flashed against my fin.

Lily gasped.

Damn it. What had she seen? As I decided my next move, Jack thrashed and churned the water. He regained the surface and screamed, taking in a mouthful. I gripped him by the back of the neck and drove him back down, pinning him to the sand. I rubbed his face in the grit, then let him up.

"Jack! Jack!" kids yelled from shore. Someone jumped into the lake and pulled Lily and the boat in. I was going to have to remember to thank that guy. I brought Jack down one more time for good measure—just to make sure he'd learned his lesson—and then I was gone.

23

POETRY READING

When I got to work the next day, Mrs. Boyd greeted me as she mopped the floor behind the counter. The morning would be even slower than normal with our few "regulars" at church.

"Isn't Lily working today?" I asked.

"She'll be in by ten," said Mrs. Boyd. She put away the mop and went to her office, closing the door behind her.

I busied myself with the *New York Times* crossword, watching the clock and getting about twenty words filled in before Lily walked through the door. A faint, finger-shaped bruise followed the line of her cheekbone.

She pinched her lips together and put both hands on her hips. "What are you laughing at?"

"Who's laughing?" At the sight of the bruise, I wished I'd finished off Jack Pettit when I had the chance. "I'm just surprised you're working today."

"Why do you say that?"

"Long day in the sun and fresh air, then big night last night." I shrugged, trying to keep things light. I walked behind the counter and tied a blue apron around my waist.

She followed me. "What makes you think I had a big night?"

I turned, and she was right there. Inches from me. I ducked around her and walked to the back to get a few pounds of decaf Colombian. "Didn't you go to the Pettits' party?"

"I did." Her voice was still right behind my ear.

"That's all. That's all I meant." I returned to the front, cut open the bag, and refilled the bin under the espresso machine. The rich smell of coffee billowed up into my face.

"I thought maybe I'd see you there last night," she said.

"I wasn't invited," I reminded her. I touched my finger to her nose as I slid by her again. "And besides, I told you I had plans."

She chewed on her bottom lip, apparently contemplating what to say. "I thought maybe you'd ditch your plans because you'd want to be there with me."

I shuffled my feet and looked for something to clean.

"Was I wrong?" she asked.

"No," I said with a sigh. I gave up and leaned against the wall. My chin dropped to my chest. "I would have liked to have been there with you."

"For a second I thought maybe I *did* see you there?"

I looked up. "Nope. Probably just the smoke playing tricks on your eyes."

She grinned and nodded as if a different question had been answered. Mrs. Boyd came out of her office, locked the door, and headed out the back without another word to either of us. I watched her go, and when I turned back, Lily wrinkled her nose at me. "Y'know, you've been wearing those same clothes for the last three days. Don't you have anything else?"

"Not all of us have the *luxury* of lace and velvet, *Miss Hancock*." The words came out more biting than I intended, but I was happy my lack of laundering was masking any other scent she might have been searching for.

She hung her head. "Sorry. I didn't mean anything. Really." A long silence stretched out between us. Then she said, "If you're interested, I hung out with Gabby most of the night. Jack went to bed early. He had a little boat accident."

"People should be more careful out on the water."

Her eyes narrowed. "Do *I* need to be careful on the water?"

I crossed my arms over my chest and faced her dead on. "What are we talking about, Lily?"

"I'm talking about maybe my grandpa wasn't crazy after all. Jack doesn't think so."

I didn't respond.

"Hey, I'm talking to you," she said, punching my shoulder with the heel of her hand.

I rolled my eyes. "What do you want me to say, Lily? That I think you're right? Well, I don't. You want to know what I think? I think you're spending too much time with Gabrielle Pettit. And while we're on the subject, I don't think

179

much of her brother, either. You want to talk about monsters? Jack is an ass and a half, and if he touches you again he's going to lose a few fingers."

"How do you know he touched me?" She reached out for me, and I stepped backward. My hair bristled on the back of my neck. My eyes flashed to her bruised cheek.

"I don't. I just think you could find better people to spend your time with."

"People?" she asked, her eyebrows rising. "People like you?"

"Sure. People like me. Why not?"

Lily flipped her backpack onto the black marble counter, unzipped the top, and yanked it open, revealing a book with several strips of paper marking favorite pages. I knew the book. It was the one I'd seen her with back in Minneapolis, when I was hiding in her bedroom closet. The memory was shameful, but it was burned into my brain—the book, the green velvet bag, the black miniskirt, her bending over to tie up her boots, the tattoo. It was the moment I decided she was the wrong target, and the moment I knew—subconsciously, I guessed—she was right for me. That was, if we were the same species and I wasn't planning on killing her father by the end of the week.

"I found a couple poems that might interest you. They're some of my favorites. Want to hear them?"

"No."

She gave me a funny look, then cleared her throat, bending over the book. Her hair fell in thick curtains along the sides of her face. "'A mermaid found a swimming lad,'" she read. "'Picked him for her own. / Pressed her body to his body.'"

"I'm not a fan of Yeats," I said curtly.

"Okay." Her stifled smile snuck back into her eyes. "How 'bout Tennyson?"

I shook my head, but she started up anyway.

"I would be a merman bold;
I would sit and sing the whole of the day;
I would fill the sea-halls with a voice of power;
But at night I would roam abroad and play
With the mermaids in and out of the rocks . . ."

She paused, then nervously jumped ahead: "'I would kiss them often under the sea, / And kiss them again till they kiss'd me.'"

"What are you doing?"

"Nothing." She looked at me with huge innocent eyes. Like one of those old Betty Boop cartoons. "You don't like that one, either, do you?"

I glared at her. What did she want me to do? Did she want me to acknowledge her ludicrous assumptions? Did she want me to admit what I was? What would she think when I told her I was more like the monster lying on the bottom of the lake than any of Tennyson's nauseating, narcissistic mermen?

She shivered, but she didn't give up. "Okay. No Tennyson. Do you want to hear something I wrote instead?"

"That might be better." It came out like a growl.

"You won't laugh?" She chewed on her bottom lip as if she wished she could take back the offer.

Now I was intrigued. "I doubt I'll laugh," I assured her.

I was pretty sure it was a promise I could keep. Nothing seemed funny right now.

Lily pulled out a thick spiral notebook with the words *MY SCRIBBLINGS* written in capital letters on its purple cover. She flipped it open and cleared her throat. "I wrote this last night."

"Go ahead."

She took one more anxious look at me. "You promise you won't laugh."

I drew a crisscross over my heart, and she read the words slowly. Cautiously.

> *"Father, when I'm gone from you*
> *Mother, when I die*
> *Do not sit round my little grave*
> *But look in treetops high."*

She stopped and looked at my face to see if she should go on. I nodded, prodding her forward. So far so good. Maybe her little Victorian poetry reading was just an unlucky coincidence. She cleared her throat again.

> *"It's not in flowers planted there*
> *Where you will find me still*
> *But in the soaring heavenward*
> *Of a humble whippoorwill."*

Birds. Good. This was better. Lily looked up at me like she expected me to freak out. She shifted her weight before finishing the last stanza.

"Or down I'll go into the stripèd
sturgeon's slippery lair
Where I'll find myself entangled
in a merman's silken hair."

"Stop."

"Something wrong, Calder?" She looked at me again with the most serene, wide-eyed innocence.

"What's with all the mermaid poetry? This isn't still about your dolphin?" I tried to sound disdainful, but I couldn't disguise the panic in my voice.

"There are no dolphins in the lake, Calder. You know that. You probably know that better than anyone."

"What's that supposed to mean?"

"You know what I mean." She closed her book quietly and slipped it into her backpack. In the same fluid movement, her fingers laced through mine. The flow of electricity from my hand into hers raised goose bumps on her arm, and I watched in horror as the air around our hands turned to raspberry syrup. The sweetness seeped into the spaces between my fingers and pulled color across the back of my hand and then through my wrist. Lily leaned in, and I choked on the sugary heat between us. It burned my lips, and I pulled back with a gasp. My throat swelled shut, and beads of sweat popped up on my forehead.

"Do you smell incense?" she asked.

"I'm not feeling well. I need to go." Before I raced for the door, I thought I saw a satisfied smile pull at the corners of her mouth.

24

TRAPS AND SNARES

I ran to the car, muttering a string of obscenities. The more distance I put between myself and the café, the better. My heart rate lowered with each step. But the farther I got from Lily, the more restless I became. I couldn't put a label on this. The only thing I could compare it to was being caught in a whirlpool. But not in a bad way. It turned me upside down, but I wanted more of it. *And* I wanted to end it. It was a pull as compelling as the urge to migrate.

I jumped into the Impala and slammed the door. No one could see me in the car. The oak trees cast shadows over the parking lot, and Maris had been smart enough to snatch a car with tinted windows. This degree of cover gave me the luxury of time. I needed to regroup. I closed my eyes and banged my forehead on the steering wheel. All I could see was Lily—her ivory face and serious gray eyes, her long red hair curling around her cheek and cascading past her shoulders. The tattoo at the small of her back, her quizzical smile, the feel of her hand in mine . . . the raspberry-pink fire running up the length of my arm.

Stupid. Stupid. Stupid, I all but cried out loud. I shook my head and tried to clear the image, tried to regain some sense of sanity. This was not the plan. *Damn you, Pavati.* It was all her fault for planting the ridiculous idea in my head in the first place. Lily and I as a real pairing . . . I would have never come up with that on my own. Not in a hundred years. But there was no other explanation. I liked her too much. Way too much. I refused to think the bigger word; were merpeople even capable of that? The possibility was too awful to bear.

But it seemed I had fallen for a human—and not just any human, the worst possible human out of all seven billion possibilities. I dissolved into hysterics and lay down on the front seat of the car, holding my sides while my body shook. It was beyond ridiculous. Tears rolled down my cheeks as another round of laughter hissed through my teeth. What would I tell Maris? Nothing, that was what. Nothing at all. So the Hancock girl likes mermaid poems. Big freakin' deal.

I leaned back against the headrest and counted out my breaths, clearing Lily from my brain, envisioning the metamorphosis instead.

Since arriving in Bayfield, I had shortened my time by six seconds, but I was still on a seven-second delay from the girls. It might as well have been an hour. Pavati practically made the switch before her hands hit the water. Maris and Tallulah could have the job done within one or two seconds. The quickest I'd made it this season was nine, but I wasn't consistent with it.

That was where the self-visualization exercise came in. Without it, sometimes I'd have to surface for air before the change occurred. When that happened I usually came up yelling, which made my sisters laugh. There was nothing more eerie than underwater hysterics. Plus, I hated calling unnecessary attention to myself. A few summers ago, a boater thought I was drowning. By the time the man got to me, I was gone. I was reported as another drowning. No one thought it strange that a body was never found. They say Lake Superior doesn't give up its dead.

I stripped off my clothes, not bothering to fold them, and stuffed them under the driver's seat. I waited for the Coast Guard boat to pass; it was pulling a smaller boat with a red UW pennant flying off its stern.

Once it was gone, I set the timer on my watch and flung open the car door. I ran for the shoreline and dove, propelling myself through the air like a javelin before slicing through the water.

For the first two seconds, I was no different than any human swimmer, completely enthralled by the sensation of being encased in water, the cool pressure against my skin. Then the water rushed into my lungs, filling my hungry cells with oxygen. Now I could really breathe.

Still, despite the relief, I braced myself for the metamorphosis. The ripple and gush of cell transformation had a panic quality about it—like a manic roller coaster, or falling down an elevator shaft. The rush of energy raced through my thighs and out my toes, exploding into a great silver tail as fantastic as it was terrifying.

I checked my watch, squinting through the red silt. Twelve seconds. Two seconds worse than last time. I cursed my pathetic lack of focus.

Tallulah must have sensed me hit the water, because she was streaming toward me. Her golden hair waved in the current, barely brushing her shoulders. Her thoughts carried to me underwater.

"I didn't think you'd be coming out to the island."

"Listen, Lu. I don't know what the others are saying, but everything is just fine with me. We're on course. You don't have to worry." The mental gymnastics it took to lie like that were exhausting.

When she got to me, she put her hands up, palms forward, and I pressed my own against hers in greeting. We surfaced together.

Tallulah smiled. Since our mother's death, Tallulah was one of the few comforts in my life. It was the one thing I missed when I was away. She embraced me and kissed my cheek.

My mind flashed to Lily. Wondering what this would feel like if it were *her* arms around my shoulders, her lips at my cheek, my lips . . .

"Raceyoutotheisland," I said, the words rushing out of me; I pushed every thought of Lily out of my head.

Tallulah's face lit up, and she dove out of sight. I made it look good, but I didn't really want to race. I just needed to be alone. Tallulah would think nothing of the fact that she'd beat me once again.

If Maris was going to let me continue with the original plan, I couldn't let my conflicted thoughts betray me. I let images of our mother trapped in a fisherman's net fill my brain. I filled my ears with her strangled calls for help. I filled my heart with our collective grief. I filled my gut with the hatred that only killing Jason Hancock would satisfy, until my inconvenient feelings for Lily were safeguarded in my heart.

When we surfaced at Basswood Island, Tallulah skipped away from me, taking a seat on the sand next to Maris and Pavati, who both sat grinning up at me in a happy stupor. Groaning, I looked around for the cause. Three corpses lay on the shore at the end of shallow drag marks.

"God, Maris, I thought we were pacing ourselves." I knelt down by one of the wasted UW college kids and turned his face out of the water. His vacant expression stared up at the sky.

"We are," Maris said, the words bursting from her lips with a revolting giggle. "This is only our first kill of the summer." Her improved disposition gave me the creeps, and I glanced at Pavati, who raised one eyebrow at me, daring me to rat her out.

"You've gorged yourselves," I said. "What happened to saving ourselves for Hancock?"

"Boys that age," Maris said wistfully, looking at the corpses, "they think they're immortal. In thirty years they would have realized their mistake, and that can make them so gloomy." She sighed with mock compassion. "We were doing them a favor, stripping the life from them now. While they were still young and so deliciously happy."

The corner of my mouth twisted, and I sniffed for any lingering life left in them, but they were just empty husks. Maris misread my expression as judgment rather than pity.

"Listen, little brother, I don't know how you do it. What is this? Six months now? But don't try to push your sick self-denial on us. Although, I have to say, I'm glad to hear how focused you are on Hancock. Pavati seemed to think you were getting distracted."

"Pavati should worry about herself." I closed one of the boys' eyes, dragging my fingers over his lids, and wished Hancock could count on such a quick and easy death.

Tallulah offered me the seat in the sand by her, and there we sat, side by side on the beach—Maris, Pav, Lulah, and me—our bodies so close that I, sitting on the far right, could feel the post-kill heat radiating off Maris.

And the funny thing was, it held no temptation for me. Even the swim from Bayfield to Basswood hadn't chilled the feel of Lily's hand in mine. The more perplexing problem was Hancock. Despite my feelings for Lily, there was still the matter of my mother's revenge and Maris's promise of my freedom.

25

CAUGHT

When I woke the next morning, I sat up like a shot, my heart bashing against my sternum, my head heavy with dreams of pale arms and bubbles rising from a beautiful but dangerous sea creature I couldn't identify. The girls were still asleep, spooned together under a makeshift canopy of vines and bracken, their faces tense even in sleep, their bodies twitching in fits and starts.

I waded into the water, letting it rise to my ankles and then to my knees and waist. My muscles tightened in acclimation to the cold. I took a deep breath and headed out. If someone had asked me where I was going, I might have said "Nowhere." But my subconscious could have answered before the question was out. I was going to the Hancock house—or the waters outside the Hancock house. I needed to hear if Lily was talking about me. If maybe she was confessing her assumptions to her father.

When their dock came into sight, however, I realized it was too early for anyone to be up. Way too early. Only a few lights were twinkling out of the buildings in Bayfield, and the Hancock house, two miles north of town, was dark except for the window over the front porch. Light shone through the panes, throwing four distorted blocks of yellow onto the lawn, but there was no movement behind the glass. Lily must have fallen asleep with the light on. Maybe she was dreaming of a merman. Maybe she was having a nightmare.

The dock was barely visible against the dark water. Someone had turned the floodlights off. I let myself drift closer to shore.

"I can see you, y'know."

Lily's voice pierced the silence—a shot of adrenaline to my heart. I rocketed off to the familiar willow branch and only let my eyes come above the waterline. She was still talking, but she wasn't looking in my direction. Sitting on the end of the dock, she stared at the spot where I'd been.

"Listen, I'm not a big fan of dolphins anyway, so don't think I'm disappointed."

So she was making a joke. She thought this was funny? Was she insane?

"Calder, I don't care that you're creeping around in the

water, following me around town. I don't even care that Jack Pettit will never go swimming again. Would you please just come out and tell me what's really going on?"

"I don't think that's a good idea." The words came out of me without consulting my brain. The sound of my voice surprised me. Lily jumped too when she realized I wasn't where she thought I was. She got to her feet and put her hands on her hips. She turned in my general direction, but she was off by twenty degrees.

"Can't you come over and talk to me?"

"Again, probably a bad idea."

Lily adjusted her sight line, and our eyes met, although I still wasn't sure her eyesight was strong enough to see me in the dark.

"I was just out for a morning swim," I explained, "and . . . skinny-dipping, you know, and . . . I'm modest."

She rolled her eyes and slapped a mosquito that had landed on her knee. "Get off it, Calder. It's me. Lily *Hancock*. I'm not completely clueless about what goes on in this lake."

"If I come closer, will you stay on the dock?"

"Do you want me to stay on the dock?"

I enjoyed the disappointment in her voice. "Very much so."

"Okay then." She sat down.

"Keep your feet out of the water, too."

"Got it." She crossed her legs under her.

I submerged and cursed my bad luck. For now, though, I had nothing to lose. The prospect of being found out excited me. The danger was strangely exhilarating.

I came to a spot twenty feet from the farthest end of the dock and let the water break past my shoulders. Lily's eyes grew large. A red ribbon hung from her hair, across her shoulder.

"It's really deep out there," she said.

I nodded. I could see her gaze drop to my neck. I couldn't tell if she could see the silver ring. There wasn't much moonlight left, and the overhanging trees shadowed the water.

"So, are you going to tell me what you're doing?"

"Checking on you."

"I didn't realize I was in danger." She squinted at me with playful suspicion, and it was obvious her preconceived notions of merpeople were the romantic, fairy-tale variety. That misapprehension was one of our greatest tools, but it sickened me to play on that with her.

"Will you come closer?" she asked.

I propelled myself forward, judging the opaqueness of the water and keeping my torso upright like a buoy, my arms by my sides. Lily nodded, any lingering doubts she might have had apparently resolved by the way I moved. I remembered the last time I'd been next to a girl when I was transformed. It hadn't gone well for the girl. The newspapers reported it as a shark attack. I wouldn't have that excuse here.

"I think this is close enough," I said. Electricity rolled off of me, and a three-foot circle of dead insects floated on the water with me at its center.

She cleared her throat and spoke slowly. "Are you my grandfather's monster?"

I shook my head quickly, happy to be able to deny her question.

This was happening too fast for my mind to keep up. The air dulled my thoughts. All but one, anyway: the image of Lily discovering our secret was going to be too strong for me to hide from Maris. No amount of scrambling could hide this gaffe. When she found out, she'd be furious. She'd expect Lily to warn her father. Maris would need to preempt that. She wouldn't hesitate to kill Lily if that was what it took to salvage her revenge on Hancock.

My breath caught in my throat. Worse yet, Maris's methods were all too familiar to me. I bristled at the idea of her even touching Lily, much less dragging her under. Making her suffer. Enjoying her frantic clawing for the surface. Reveling in the torture.

Bile rose up in my throat when I realized what I had to do. I would have to kill Lily myself. It was the least I could do for her. I could save her the suffering. I could do it quickly. She didn't have to know death was coming. She didn't have to be scared. She didn't have to feel pain. A mercy killing? That would be a first.

"You're not the monster," she said. Relieved.

I closed my eyes. I couldn't do this and look at her at the same time. "Listen, Lily. I'd really rather not talk about this right now. Your family's going to wake up soon, so I've got to get out of here. After breakfast, take one of your kayaks north. You won't have to go too far. There's a cave just north of Red Cliff."

"I didn't think there were any caves until you got to Cornucopia."

I opened my eyes and swam closer to where she sat. "There's one, hidden behind a curtain of vines. I'll be in it." I reached up and pulled the ribbon from her hair. "I'll mark it with this."

"You'll really be there?"

"Yes." I sighed. As if I had any choice now. My reckless-ness had gotten me into this mess; I was going to have to be the one to fix it. "I'll really be there."

26

THE CAVE

The land rose high above the water, and brambles grew on the rocky embankment. I pulled back the veil of ivy, exposing the small cave, and tied Lily's ribbon to the vines. A millennium of black and red sediment lined the rock walls. Over time, water and ice had carved out the small recess. I pulled myself up to sit on a rocky shelf at water's edge and hung my tail down into the surf. This was where I lay in wait.

My innards were tied in so many knots I should have earned a Boy Scout badge. I tried to distract myself from my own misery by thinking of something other than what I was about to do. But no matter how I tried, my mind kept going back to the inevitable. The sun was just breaking over the horizon. Lily would be having breakfast with her family. I imagined her excitement at coming to find me. I wished she were feeling more dread. Maybe her parents would want her to do chores. Maybe she'd figure out on her own that this was dangerous. Would she tell her dad about me? No. I didn't think she would. She wouldn't want him to think she was going crazy like his father had. But if she did tell him, would he pack up his family and tear out of town? Would history repeat itself?

I hoped so. I was losing my taste for this whole thing. If the Hancocks left, I'd be off the hook. For now. But if Jason Hancock took Lily away . . . I didn't like the thought of that, either. It was a ridiculous concern given what I was planning to do.

Two small brown birds chased and squabbled in the air. Their wings beat against each other as they tried to decide if they were well matched. I'd never paid much attention to these springtime rituals before. Lily was putting everything in a different light.

I watched the birds. The female finally gave in to the male's persuasions, and they hid away in a deep crack in the sandstone. Pushing these thoughts of springtime romance from my head, I tried to figure out what would cause Lily to draw nearer to me. Would it be better to remain in the water or to dry off?

My clothes were still in the car, so I'd have to hide in the bushes. What was worse? It was a tough call, but regardless of how sick I was of shadows, I opted for the water and pulled deeper into the dark recesses of the cave. The sun broke through the gaps and holes in the ivy veil, throwing golf ball–sized circles of light on the water; I swam back and forth between the light and dark, moving from cold patches of water to pockets that were merely cool.

It was another hour before the small shape of a kayak came around the bend. The water was a flat mirror, except for the rippled wake of Lily's boat. She looked like she was paddling as fast as she could, but she was still slow.

She'd changed into a white linen dress with a low neckline. The sleeves flowed out behind her as she paddled. Her red hair hung loose down her back. She paddled through the overhanging willow branches, ducking as she went. The breeze blew through the aspens, each newly opened leaf quaking with my heart. I shook my head in disbelief. Always the flair for the dramatic; she'd planned the scene right out of one of her Tennyson poems.

"The Lady of Shalott," I whispered. Then I choked on the dark irony of it: I was no Lancelot, but she would still wind up dead.

I sighed and swam out to meet her, coming up under the kayak and carrying it on my shoulders. At first I wasn't sure she knew it was me who was speeding her up. It could have easily been the wind at her back. But then I heard her gasp, so I knew she saw me.

I carried her to the edge of the cave, then resumed my spot in the shadows. She threw the line of her kayak around a moss-covered birch at the shoreline and turned to stare. Her eyes were intense, and they burned into mine.

"So, you're a mermaid?" She said it like a question because

she refused to look below the water and confirm what she already knew.

My gaze drifted upward. "Merman," I corrected, although I'd always hated the term. It was so Hans Christian Andersen.

We both sat in silence, wondering who would speak next. Lily beat me to it. She fingered the charms on a silver bracelet around her wrist, sliding them back and forth. "Obviously, I've got a lot of questions."

I took a moment to sink under and clear my head. I came up and shook out my hair. "I would be amazed if you didn't."

She smiled broadly as if she'd just won a major award. "So that's okay with you? Will you answer them?"

"I guess that depends on what they are, but I'm feeling generous right now." *Not that any of it matters. You'll be dead in a matter of minutes,* I thought miserably. A lump rose in my throat as I struggled to speak. "Go ahead."

"All right." She turned away, blushing as she spoke. "If you don't mind me asking . . . how is it you've got two legs most days?"

"Evolution," I responded simply. "Survival of the fittest. I can go on land when I need to."

"You're an *evolved* merman?"

"Very." I wiggled my opposable thumbs at her. "But the most primitive traits remain."

"Like?"

Seduction. Murder. Mayhem. "Well, I could give you a pretty nasty electrical shock if I wanted to." I paused to consider that. I'd planned on simply drowning Lily, but a strong enough shock would be quicker, more merciful. . . . "And

I'm telepathic with animals and with my sisters, when we're underwater."

"You can hear them from here?"

"I could, but they're not in the lake today."

"Where are they?"

"At the movies."

She snorted and choked back a laugh. "Sure, why not?" She giggled, then composed herself.

"I've met your sisters. What's your mother's name?"

That brought me up short. "Nadia," I whispered. Lily didn't seem to notice any change in me.

"And your dad?"

I cleared my throat and tried to conjure up the necessary memories. "I don't know my dad's name. Pavati's father was a musician. His name was Deepak something. Maris's and Tallulah's father was John Bishop. He was a biologist."

Her eyebrows pulled up in the middle. "Bishop sounds kind of ordinary for a . . . a . . . merman."

"No, not a merman. Mermen aren't allowed to be fathers."

"Not allowed?"

"It's not like there are a lot merfolk in the lake. It would get pretty incestuous, don't you think? My sisters' fathers were human. That's how we diversify the gene pool. Mermaids mate with human men, and that's how you make new merpeople. Well, at least, that's *one* way to do it."

"Did your sisters know their dads?"

"Not really. Newborns live with their human fathers for the first year of life, or I should say until they can walk. They have to learn that little skill on land and while they're still young. I mean, can you imagine an adult tottering around? Then, after

200

that first year, they're brought back to their mothers. So I guess my sisters knew their fathers at one point, but they don't remember them now."

This was going on long enough. I should simply pull Lily out of the kayak and stop her heart. Why was I prolonging this? It was agony. Her face, so trusting, made me hate myself more than usual. But I wanted her to keep talking. I wanted her to know me. I wanted *someone* to know me. Even if I had to kill that someone as soon as I laid it all out there.

"So, you said that was one way to make a mermaid. What's the other?" She was still talking, and I smiled at the forced casualness of her voice.

"The other way is lot more dangerous . . . and a lot less fun."

She blushed. "Which is . . ."

"A person would have to die. Their heart would have to stop. Then a mermaid would have to be there to reinvigorate."

"Reinvigorate?" She leaned forward on the seat of the kayak, her hands between her knees.

"That's what we call it when we bring someone back to life. That's the kind of merman I am. The reinvigorated type."

"You died?"

"I was three. I don't remember much. I was with my parents on our sailboat. My birth mom gave me a box of raisins. It's weird. I have a much clearer picture of that little red box than her face. I can just see her hands giving me a snack. The next thing I remember, there was a scream, and I was falling overboard. I don't even know who was screaming. . . . And then my new mother was there.

"I remember watching the shadow of my parents' boat.

And then the Coast Guard came, but by that time we were swimming away."

I glanced up at her and wondered at the shiny wetness of her eyes.

"Did they look for you?" Lily asked.

Shrugging, I said, "S'pose. For a while."

"Did *you* look for *them*?"

"Once I was reinvigorated, I didn't give them much thought."

"I don't understand that," she said, her eyes full of concern.

"Once someone is reinvigorated, they're connected to the family that changed them; it's more than just taking on a new name. There's a mental thread."

I pointed at her wrist. "It's like the charms on that bracelet of yours. They can slide away from each other, but they're still linked by the chain." I slid one of the charms to the opposite end. "During the winter I can get away from my sisters. They choose to stick together, but I opt for a reprieve. Once spring comes, though . . ." I slid the charm back to join the others. "We have to migrate back to this lake. This is where we reconvene.

"That's why we can hear each other. We're tied together as a family. Like a school of fish. There are a few merpeople in Lake Michigan. If one of them came here, I wouldn't be able to hear their thoughts. Different family. See?"

"So you're saying if you could break the bracelet, your mind would be your own."

"Exactly."

Lily nodded slightly. "And is that possible?

I lifted my arms over my head and dropped under the

water, clearing my thoughts. This conversation was going in a dangerous direction. When I came up, Lily's forehead was furrowed in thought.

"You said it was dangerous," she said. "Reinvigorating."

"Miss two heartbeats and it's too late. And we do it by shocking the heart. Sometimes there's too much electricity. Usually that part doesn't work out so well."

"Have you ever done it?" Her voice was sharp now, but I couldn't place the emotion.

"Never. Reinvigorating is a girl thing. The whole life-giving miracle and all." I chuckled. "I've never heard of a merman doing it. Not once in all the stories."

"You saved me that day I fell off the rock. I could be a mermaid right now. I just never tested things out."

I shook my head. "First, you weren't dead. Second, I didn't shock your heart."

Blood pooled in her cheeks. I could feel the energy radiating off her. I could see its color, a pink glow with a yellow rim. It was a happy, intoxicating excitement. I diverted my eyes. *Keep talking,* I told myself. *Don't look.* "Third, what I did was nothing more than basic CPR. Anyone could have done it."

"Maybe. But anyone didn't. You did."

The warmth of her voice flooded my heart and flipped it over. Maybe it was selfishness that turned the tide for me. My eyes focused on her neck. I wanted to run my fingers down its length, down her collarbone, over her shoulders. I wanted to raise the hair on her arms. I couldn't kill Lily. I would just have to make this work without killing her. I could hide her away and leave Jason Hancock to my sisters.

"So, do mermaids sit around waiting for someone to fall out of a boat and drown?"

I puzzled at her question.

"Y'know . . . to make more mermaids? Are they waiting for someone's heart to stop so they can be there to catch that window of opportunity?"

She seriously did not get this at all. She obviously had some Disney version of mermaids in her head. I wondered how she'd respond when I told her the truth. That we were murderers, monsters, fiends. That I'd lured her out here to kill her. That I was doing everything within my power to fight against nature. I tried to come up with the words to answer.

"No. We aren't that patient. And underneath, we're essentially predatory."

Her eyes widened. Her fear tempered the previously pink and yellow aura, and I was able to look at her more directly.

"My story is the exception to the rule. It was pure chance that a mermaid was there when I fell into the water. Generally speaking, when a mermaid is there to reinvigorate, it's not luck. They're there because *they're* the ones doing the killing. Mermaids kill just so they can reinvigorate. Sometimes they kill just to kill. It's like a crocodile, waiting in the shallows." I remembered the first night I saw her on the dock. "The zebra comes down for a drink and *snap!* The crocodile pulls it in, rolls it around and around, and then after a few moments, it's over."

"If they're not going to reinvigorate someone, why would they kill them?" She swallowed hard. "Do mermaids *eat* humans?"

"Don't be ridiculous."

"So why kill just to kill? That's so . . . so . . . wasteful."

"Envy. As a group, we're pretty jealous."

"Of what?"

"Happiness, usually. Love. Joy. Any positive emotion. It radiates off people. We can see it, feel it, taste it. . . ."

"What do I look like?"

I smiled, remembering our day on Madeline Island. "It changes, of course, depending on your mood. Today you look like melting orange sherbet. Delicious." A bitterness crossed my face, and I watched Lily's eyes tighten. "It's that positive emotion we crave. We don't have our own and we want it, need it really, to survive. So we take it."

She looked at me with confusion. I searched the ceiling of the cave for an explanation she could understand. "It's like any cold-blooded animal. Picture the lizard. He can't regulate his own body temperature. He would die if he couldn't find the necessary heat source, so he seeks it out, and then climbs up on a sun-baked rock and absorbs it until he's warm. Same thing with me. With my sisters. With all of our kind. We're attracted to the positive emotion. We seek it out and when we find it . . . we absorb it from its source."

"And by 'absorb,' you mean . . ."

"You know what I mean."

That was what had drawn Pavati to the old man the other day, and all three of my sisters to the college kids. That was what had drawn my mother to Lily's own grandfather. I almost wanted to tell her the story. How he'd been so happy he was a magnet to her. How she capsized his boat and brought him down, but he fought back. How he regained the surface and pleaded with her. How she offered him the life of a merman, but he rejected her, so she demanded an exchange, another life for his. How he offered his son—only one year old at the time. How she swam him back to shore and waited by the dock.

How a second later the family was running for the car and racing out of town. How she followed the road along the shore. And then finally how she was strangled in a fisherman's net.

What would Lily have thought if I'd laid it all out there like that? Would she have run away screaming, knowing that we were here to collect on that promise?

Lily wasn't so obtuse that she couldn't see something was bothering me. She leaned out of the kayak and draped her arm around my shoulder, laying her cheek against mine, comforting me without really knowing how wrong this was. I jerked away, not realizing I'd come close enough for her to touch me. A spark jumped through the air between her arm and my back.

I could choose not to kill Lily Hancock. That choice was still mine to make. I could protect her from my sisters. But there was one thing beyond my control. In the end, I would still deceive her. Jason Hancock was still marked for death.

27

BREATHING LESSONS

I was so caught up in my own selfish misery I didn't notice Lily untying her kayak and paddling it closer to me. It wasn't until its nose bumped against the rock that I looked up.

"You can't find happiness outside yourself, Calder."

I shook my head. "You sound like a fortune cookie."

"It's still true. Everyone's always trying to do it, y'know. They try to get with the right people, hook up with the right guy, join the right club—without ever asking what 'right' is."

"And this is somehow supposed to apply to me? I'm not

some identity-confused sophomore, Lily. If you haven't been listening, I turn into a thieving, murdering fish."

She smirked. "But you're not a murderer. At least . . . you don't want to be. I'm just saying, you wouldn't be jealous of happiness if you had some for yourself. If you had your own, you wouldn't want to rob others of theirs."

"You make that sound simple. Don't you think in centuries of merpeople that someone might have figured that out?"

"I'm thinking maybe no one's tried. Or cared."

I couldn't answer that. I was too distracted to reason it out, anyway. She was so close now.

"And I'd like you to try," she said. "That is, if you think I could make you happy."

A pink light shimmered around Lily's edges, that fuzzy-sweater look that was all her own. "Come on," I said, impulsively pulling the kayak into the dark arch of the sea cave. I lifted her out of the boat and set her on top of a sandstone shelf. "'She has a lovely face,'" I recited. "'God in his mercy lend her grace.'" I bowed my head and touched my hand to my heart. "'The Lady of Shalott.'"

"Am I that obvious?" She laughed, and my body naturally warmed. I soaked up the heat and marveled at how I was able to do it while she still sat, safe and dry, on her throne.

"So if I'm the Lady, then you're Lancelot."

"No, I'm better. I'm here to do your bidding. That's more than Lancelot ever did for the Lady."

"Very true. Then your first duty is to take me swimming with you."

So much for warmth. My body ran as cold as the lake. "Get a grip, Lily. I don't think that's a good idea."

"Why?"

"I've never done it before." The water agitated around me, and the cave amplified the sound of the water lapping against the rock.

"You've been in the water with me before."

"That was different."

"How?" She leaned forward, her hands on her knees.

"I don't know. It was quick. I didn't have time to think about you being with me. I don't want to hurt you."

She reached forward for me. "You won't hurt me."

"How do you know?"

"Because you're not like your sisters, Calder."

"I'm exactly like them."

"You've got to stop thinking that you're, like, some kind of monster."

"That's great coming from someone who hasn't once looked below the water. Not once since you got to the cave. Don't think I haven't noticed."

Lily pursed her lips and purposefully looked beneath the surface. Despite the shadows, bits of sun cut through the green veil at the mouth of the cave. The silver scales on my tail sent shards of light through the water as my tailfin stirred the sand below me. I watched as her shoulders relaxed and she looked back to my face with a triumphant smile. I shook my head and looked up at the cave ceiling.

"Fine. Let's say I don't hurt you. You'll be too cold. You couldn't survive more than a few minutes out there."

"Keep me warm, then." She slipped off her throne into the

water, so silently I wondered if *she* was now stalking *me*. Her thin white dress floated up around her waist as she propelled herself closer. The sleeves clung to her arms and shoulders.

I stiff-armed her. "Okay, that's good. You're close enough."

"What? Am I too happy?" Her eyes were teasing, and the pink glow billowed out toward me like a parachute. I couldn't understand her. Did she want to die?

"Can you see it, Calder? Because you're right. I am happy. But you don't have to steal that from me. I can give it to you." Her face brightened. "I have enough to share. Right now there's no happier person on earth."

She reached out and put her hand on my shoulder. My tail undulated gently below me, keeping us both afloat. She was so close now her chest was pressed against mine. Her fingers traced the silver ring around my throat and trailed the muscles in my shoulder and arm, which were tense and starting to burn. She closed her eyes. A crystalline drop of water clung to her eyelashes.

"Calder, do you like me?"

And then I laughed, breaking the spell.

Her eyes flashed open and blood flooded her cheeks. She pushed off, but I reached out and pulled her toward me again. That one second of physical separation was too painful a void.

"Sometimes you ask the stupidest questions, Lily."

Relief passed across her eyes.

"Do you see anyone else out here? Do you think I routinely reveal myself like this to people? Do you think you would have lasted this long in the water with me if I didn't . . .

like you?" I didn't need to tell her the rest—that I was obsessing about her, that I was risking my own sanity (maybe my own neck, if Maris found out about this), that my stomach was thinking about joining the circus and starting its own extreme acrobatic show. That, just as Pavati predicted, I might even *love* her.

"I still didn't hear you say it." She combed her fingers through my hair, and I closed my eyes, letting her drive me crazy.

"Yes, Lily Hancock, I like you."

"So you will take me swimming."

"Come on. It's too cold."

"If you haven't noticed, the cold doesn't bother me. You must be doing something to keep me warm."

I didn't know anything about that. If I was, it was unintentional. "Well then, forget the cold. You can't hold your breath that long."

"Then breathe for me."

A fluttery feeling ran through my heart before beating a path to my gut. I grabbed her before I could think about the danger. I wanted to take her. I wanted to show her things. It was that desire to show her my world that made me move too fast. I dove before she'd had time to fill her lungs, and the shock of it made her gasp. She convulsed, and I shot her toward the surface. She came up coughing.

"Sorry," she said. "I . . . didn't do that very well."

"No, that was all on me. I'll go slower."

She inhaled and exhaled two times before filling her lungs with air. We sank down into the water, face to face. I smiled at her puffed-out cheeks and squinty eyes. I put my palms out like I would with Tallulah and laced my fingers through hers. I controlled both our bodies as we hovered in the depths of the lake, almost like being in outer space, while constellations of bubbles rose from her nose to the surface. She pointed up. She needed air.

I pulled her closer, and she struggled against me in panic. It pained me that she would think I would hurt her now. I smiled, though I doubted she noticed, and tipped my head to the side. My mouth covered hers, and her lips parted. I sealed my lips tightly to hers and blew, filling her lungs. Her eyes popped open in surprise. I had no idea how long that breath would last. I hoped not long. I wanted another excuse to tie myself to her.

I watched her face. Her eyes were barely slits, but I looked for the smallest sign of panic. I glanced at my watch, counting the seconds. Twenty-eight, twenty-nine, thirty . . . *Oh, man, how long could this girl go?* Then her fingers dug into my biceps, and I brought her to the surface.

My mind raced forward, wondering what to show her first. I couldn't give her the whole *National Geographic* tour. The great lake was ten thousand years old, and there were more than thirty thousand square miles of ancient artifacts, shipwrecks, and geological wonders.

But then the Pettits' Sun Sport passed by. I pulled Lily back into the ivy, and we watched Jack troll the shoreline, binoculars held to his eyes.

"He's looking for his mermaid," she whispered.

I didn't acknowledge her assumption. Instead, I took her to the bottom. The water was only eight feet deep, and Jack's boat caused the fingerlike grasses to pulse gently around us, caressing our bodies like a thousand peacock plumes. I repeated the line she'd written for me: "'Where I'll find myself entangled in a merman's silken hair.'" She couldn't understand me, or hear me. Not really. But she pulled me closer, and I pressed my lips to hers again.

28

SWIMMING LESSONS

Lily should have been freezing. I couldn't understand what was keeping her warm. She said it was from being close to me, but being cold-blooded I wasn't in any position to warm her. I wondered if breathing for her stemmed the cold, but these thoughts were only in the background. The rest of my brain was preoccupied with the thrill of swimming with Lily, my arm wrapped around her soft waist, keeping her face even with mine for easy breathing.

I took her over the 1881 wreck of the fire-ravaged *Ottawa* and then swam her north to Stockton Island. The century-old remains of *Noquebay* lay just ten feet below the surface. We swam along the donkey boiler and rudder. Lily trailed her hand around the gears lying on the ruined deck. Bits of vegetation floated down around her like confetti. I marveled at her beauty. It rivaled any of my sisters', including Pavati's. With the exception of Lily's pale lower limbs, she looked every bit the mermaid.

Eventually I brought her to Manitou Island. As the water grew more shallow, she let go of me and stood up to walk to shore. She turned back with a questioning glance. I hovered in deeper waters, watching, wishing.

"Are you going to get out of the water, Calder?"

"Probably not."

"Why?"

"I don't have any clothes stashed on this island."

Her eyebrows shot up toward her hairline. "Oh, I hadn't thought about that. I could stay out on the water with you."

"No, that's okay. Go collect some kindling and then sit on that driftwood log. I'll just go over there a ways. Then—if you don't mind—I'll come from behind you and sit on the other side of that bush. We can talk then. I promise."

Lily walked up the beach, looking over her shoulder at me again, probably afraid I was going to swim off and leave her there. For a second I considered it. It wasn't a terrible idea. She'd be out of the way. Maris wouldn't be looking for her here. In a couple months, there'd be plenty of wild blackberries to eat. . . . That was about when the idea fizzled.

I swam up the shore, and when I was sure she could no longer see me, I floated into the shallows, willing myself to change. I took a deep breath of air and tensed my muscles, gritting my teeth as the tightening started. A spasm rippled through me, and then the ripping started. I doubled over and wrapped my arms around my middle. I strangled the yell in my throat and sat gasping in the shallows as my tail gave way to two legs still in the throes of the seizure. The agitated water around me slowly calmed as I stood up, letting the water run off my body. Then I staggered into the brambles, kicking up sand.

When I came up behind her, Lily was sitting on the log as I'd instructed, staring out across the lake, with a small pile of sticks in front of her. The wake of a passing Boston Whaler pushed waves up on the shore with a gentle pulsing. Her body shook uncontrollably as the wind sucked the water off her skin.

I was quiet. I walked slowly. I knew Lily would jump whether I made a loud noise or not. Her posture was rigid. She probably thought she was dreaming. Another hallucination— and here she was, sitting on an uninhabited island, wondering how in the hell she got here.

"Lily," I said quietly.

Her arms were wrapped around her knees, and her shoulders flinched infinitesimally at the sound of her name. Her pink skin showed through the wet linen.

"I thought maybe you lied to me, that you left," she said.

"No. I wouldn't leave you." The words—now out there, hovering in the air between us—were more true than I realized. "Besides, I promised you I'd be back. Merpeople may be great liars, but we can't break our promises."

She winced and whispered, "Where are you?"

"Right behind you." I rubbed my hands together to build

216

up friction, then ignited a small piece of driftwood with a spark from my palm. I handed it to her over her shoulder, and she lit the campfire. "Is it okay if we talk like this? Just keep your eyes straight ahead."

"It's okay." The pink glow from her body was fading into lavender. I recognized the sign: the excitement of adventure. The same color as my kayaker, the same color sailors put off before smashing their ships on the rocks. Purple Prows, the ancients called them.

Her hair was now pulled up in a ponytail, and it curled as a single unit into a spiral. The back of her neck was nearly translucent. I reached out and ran my finger along the bumps of her vertebrae. She shivered and turned her head.

"Eyes straight ahead, please." I secretly enjoyed doing this to her. Wasn't it what she had been doing to me for the last week? Unconsciously, maybe, but I still owed her.

I wrapped her ponytail around my hand and then released it, letting it snake around my palm.

"You're teasing me," she said. Goose bumps rose on her arms.

"Maybe."

"That's mean," she said, sighing.

"I'm a monster, remember?" I let my fingers trail down her arms, making the situation worse, no doubt, and enjoying every second of it.

"Calder, how come nobody knows who you are?"

"Who says nobody knows me?"

"The Pettits had never heard of you, and they've lived here all their lives."

I rubbed my palms up and down her arms, warming her

up as best I could. "First of all, I'm only here during the summer. Second, until I met you, I didn't have much reason to be on land."

"Are you and your sisters in Maine the rest of the year?"

I shook my head even though she couldn't see me. "I know you're really caught up in that whole Passamaquoddy legend thing Jack told you about, but that's not me. That was a long, long time ago. Maybe some ancestral connection, but that's it."

"You mean you're not immortal?"

"No," I said laughing. "Why would you think that?"

"You're mythical."

"I'm not mythical. I'm sitting right behind you. And other than the fact I turn into an enormous fish, there's not that much special about me."

"I don't think that's true."

"My body is just as fragile as yours. I bleed. And I will die. Maybe not as quickly as a human. I age more . . . slowly, about one year to every three human ones."

"How old are you?"

"Eighteen."

"I mean, when were you born?"

I closed my eyes so I didn't have to face her question. "I know where you're going with this, Lily. But my birth year is just a date on the calendar. Think of it like dog years, but in reverse. When it comes to aging, I'm eighteen. How many times I've seen the ball drop in Times Square . . . that's inconsequential. I'll get old—just like you—"

"Not just like me."

"Well, yeah, but we all get old and die. Eventually."

"Your mother died, didn't she? That's why I haven't met her."

My throat constricted. "Yes, my mother died."

"Was she as beautiful as your sisters?"

"Exceptionally beautiful. She looked most like Tallulah, maybe even a little like you."

"She was *Ariel.*"

"No. She wasn't. She was a *real* mermaid. Underneath."

"Right," Lily said, and I could tell she was smiling. "Monster. So if you're not the ones from the legend, where did your family come from?"

"They were born here, which is why the family comes back every spring. I'm tethered to them through our mother. I have to come back whether I want to or not. I bet if someone tied me to a chair and locked me in a room on the South Pole, I'd still manage to get back here." I remembered my last day in the Bahamas, Maris's annoying phone calls. If I'd known Lily was at the end of that path, I would have been back even sooner.

"I go to the Caribbean during the winter. There's a beach in the Abacos I like to hang around."

"Lots of girls there, I bet."

I paused. She was facing away from me, so I couldn't read her expression. There was something in her tone, however, that had my attention. It was sharp. Bitter. Mermaid jealousy I knew; I was weaned on it. If that was the emotion I was hearing in her voice, the human version was different. I could taste it on the air, like wine turned to vinegar. As I took the time to experience it, I failed to notice her anxiety growing.

"How *many* girls?" She started to turn around and I pushed her back.

"What?"

"Did you ever kiss any of them?"

I didn't know what to say. My mouth hung open like an idiot's.

"Because I've noticed that you've never kissed me," she said.

"What are you talking about? What have we been doing for the last hour?"

"Not the same thing. That was for survival."

My heart rate quickened as I realized what she was after. I could already see the excitement on her skin. I knew from experience what a kiss would do. The emotion would rise, then spill over the edges, light flooding over us like a tide pool. I'd never been able to resist that before, but I'd come this far; it was worth the risk.

Turning backward, I pulled up alongside her until my right shoulder aligned with her right, and we faced in opposite directions. I leaned in and pressed my lips to her collarbone and let my mouth slide down her shoulder. She lifted my chin with her finger and kissed me back, her lips warm and soft and absolutely bitable. I kept my eyes closed, tasting her excitement on my tongue but resisting the urge to take more than she offered.

She pulled away, touching my mouth with her finger. "Your lips are glowing."

"That's you. Your emotion left behind."

"And Jack was right. You do smell like incense," she murmured. "Patchouli, I think."

I chuckled softly. "We're supposed to be able to entrance our prey once we're close enough. I don't think smelling like a fish would help. Like I said, evolution has been good to us."

"Is that what you did to me? Entranced me?" She drew her finger across my lips one more time.

I laughed again, this time louder. "Believe me, I tried hypnosis on you. Truly gave it my best effort. You were amazingly resistant."

"No," she said. "That was acting."

"Survival of the fittest," I murmured.

She leaned against my shoulder and recited more Tennyson:

"I would be a mermaid fair;
I would sing to myself the whole of the day;
With a comb of pearl I would comb my hair . . ."

I shook my head. She was picking out the parts she liked. "Listen to what I've been telling you, Lily. It's not all pretty like that. You forget this part: 'Till that great sea-snake under the sea / From his coiled sleeps in the central deeps / Would slowly trail himself sevenfold / Round the hall where I sate.' Don't ever forget that part. It's the only part that's true. Slithering stalkers. That's what we are."

Lily humphed and wrapped her arms around herself. The wind had evaporated the last of the water off her skin, and she shivered.

The small fire was doing little to warm her, so I resumed my original spot and rubbed her back, trying to create some heat. Besides, I couldn't face her, knowing what I had to do next. No matter how much I cared about her, I was still tied to old family loyalties. No matter how much Lily told me I wasn't a murderer, I knew it was true in only a limited sense. I would never hurt her, but Maris would collect on the debt. I couldn't explain that to Lily. I couldn't even try. I was shackled to my sisters and my part in their plan—no matter how much it sickened me. Lily lay back against me, and the feel of her breathing filled me to the point of overflowing.

"Remember what you asked me before about my human family? Whether I ever thought about them?"

She nodded.

"What I should have said is that I didn't think about them, the actual people. They were strangers almost immediately after I changed. But I did miss the *idea* of them. After Mother died anyway. The idea of a normal family. Yeah, I missed that part. I still miss that."

Then I closed my eyes and said what I was compelled to say. "Your dad invited me and my parents over for dinner sometime." Each word was barbed, tearing my throat and tongue.

"Mmm-hmm. That would be fun." She reached up and behind her, cupping the back of my neck in her hand.

"Of course, you know I don't have any parents who would actually come."

"That's fine, too." She leaned heavily against me. I wondered if she was falling asleep.

"So should I come over again?"

"Sophie would like that."

I smiled despite myself. "And you would like that?"

"I would like that."

I could feel the stinging welling up behind my eyes as I led her down this path. In my head I could rationalize everything. I could be happy. I could even love her. But that didn't mean I wouldn't kill her father. And what would that do to her? I pushed the thought away. I could not fail in this. Satisfying Maris's condition, securing her revenge on Jason Hancock, was my only sure means of freedom. I could not give up on the dream, no matter what the cost.

"So, what do you think?" I asked.

"I'll tell them I've invited you for tomorrow night."

I nodded and then froze. Something else had my attention. They were only small dots on the horizon, invisible to the human eye. Maybe someone would think they were loons, or the tips of sunken timbers, but there were three of them, and I knew.

"Stay here!"

I got up, dropped two fistfuls of sand onto the tiny campfire, and ran into the brush, following my path back to the lake, fifty yards up the shoreline from where Lily sat. Sharp sticks and thorny plants cut my ankles and stabbed at the soles of my bare feet. I splashed into the water, running, my knees high, before diving in. It was my fastest transformation to date. When I came up again, directly in front of Lily, I was in full panic mode and bristling with electricity.

She was pacing in the shallows. "Calder, what's wrong? Are you okay?"

I took a deep breath and subdued the electric charge as much as I could before beckoning her to me. "Get in. Come out to me."

"What's wrong?"

"They're looking for me, and they can't find you with me. Not like this, anyway. They wouldn't want you to know, and it won't be good if they find out."

"Why? I wouldn't hurt them."

"For the love of God, Lily. I'm not talking about *you* hurting *them*. Would you please get it into your head that this is not a movie? Forget everything you think you know about merpeople. Forget that freaking Ariel; think *Silence of the Lambs,* think *Friday the Thirteenth.* Haven't you heard anything I said to you today? They. Will. Kill. You." The irony wasn't lost on me that I'd considered killing her myself just a few hours earlier.

Lily's face paled. "How do they know where you are? I thought you said you had to be in the water for them to hear you."

"They *don't* know. They're only looking. But it won't take them long. Please hurry."

She ran into the water and dove. She took three strokes, and I was there, slinging her onto my back like a duffel bag.

"I'll have to keep my head above water as much as I can." My voice came out high and thin. By the way her fingers tightened on my shoulders, she was finally understanding me. "That way they won't hear me and you can breathe. I won't be able to go as fast as before, but it's the only way." She ducked her head into my neck, and we were gone.

I plowed toward Bayfield, slogging across the rough chop, my shoulders pushing through the water as if it were mud. I didn't look behind me to see if they were following. Knowing couldn't make me go faster. I was halfway back when I saw a way out of this mess. Not that it was an attractive option, just the lesser of two evils. Jack Pettit's boat was crossing our path.

"Lily, it's Jack."

"Dive! You can't let him see you."

"I can get you onto his boat."

"No!"

Calculating our two paths and the point of intersection, I crushed the waves with newfound strength and stole up alongside the boat, smacking the port side with my tail. Jack jerked around from the wheel and killed the engine.

"What the—"

"Take her," I said.

Lily whimpered, "No," and tightened her grip on my neck.

"You," Jack said, pulling Lily from my back and dragging her up over the swim deck. "I knew it."

"Just get her home safe."

"Jack, please don't tell," begged Lily.

"*Ugh*. As if telling people's ever got me anywhere." Then his face twisted into a pained look. "Listen. I'll keep your secret, just tell Pavati I've been looking for her. Tell her I need to see her."

"I promise, but I really don't think it's in your best interest."

"All I need is your promise, and you can keep your opinions to yourself; by the looks of it, you've got a double standard on that point anyway."

Lily reached for me, not wanting to say goodbye, keeping her wide eyes on mine.

"You'll be okay?" she asked. She was always worried about the wrong thing.

"Go home. Don't worry about me."

"You're still coming over tomorrow?"

"Just go."

Jack turned the key, and the propeller churned the water mere inches from my tail. I recoiled and glared at the unlikely rescuer. Jack gunned the engine and bent the boat into a sharp turn, exposing its hull, spraying a rooster tail of water in his wake.

All I could do was wonder if Jack was as good for his promises as I was.

29

FACING MUSIC

Basswood Island was quiet. Nothing disturbed the water; nothing rustled in the thick understory; no squirrels bickered in the tree branches. I waited alone for a long time. The lights from the Hancock house shone across the lake and, as the sun set and the sky darkened, went out one by one. Lily's bedroom light went out last. She flipped it off-on-off-on-off before leaving the whole house in darkness. I took that as her "good night, good luck" wish to me. What else could it be?

The day's clouds dissipated and the stars came out. I

lay on my back and traced Orion in the sky. The Hunter. That was what we were, but somehow the nobility of Orion had escaped our lot. I worried that my sisters were hunting. They weren't anywhere near the Hancock place. I knew that much. But I couldn't find them in the water. A few times I waded in, submerging myself so I could listen for their voices. But it was quiet. They must have gone a long way.

It was midnight before three dark spots grew into long, thin figures emerging from the lake. None of them greeted me. Pavati and Tallulah walked past me in search of firewood. Maris scooped up her dress, which lay on the edge of the beach, and pulled it over her head, letting it fall over her angular body. She came to stand directly in front of me. She didn't sit, so I had to look up at her.

"There's a new smell on the water, Calder."

"Oh yeah? What's that?"

"Don't be cute."

"She was boating."

Maris cursed my name. "Were you in the water with her again?"

"No, of course not."

Maris's arms flew up in exasperation. The wind agitated the lake into rough chops behind her. "Calder, you are ruining everything. What makes you think she won't warn her father? If he's on alert, our whole plan is shot. I never should have trusted you with something so important. You've never grown up. You're for crap with responsibility. Do you have any idea how long I've been working toward this? Are you even on board?"

"Of course I am. The Hancock girl has no idea what we are. You're overreacting."

"Don't tell me I'm overreacting. I raised you. Do you think that was easy? Do you think I *needed* another sibling to look after?" She was screeching now. "We could have just left you. Mother didn't have to save you. But she did. So how do you think it feels to have you betray us now?"

"I haven't—"

Pavati and Tallulah returned with armloads of driftwood, which they dumped into a pile with a clatter. Maris and I both looked over at them. Tallulah wouldn't meet my eyes.

"Anyone hungry?" asked Pavati.

"What is your problem, Maris?" I fumed. "I thought that's what you wanted. For me to get close to her. Isn't that what you said?"

"Yes, but just how close are you getting?"

"Your smell is mixed with hers, Cal," Tallulah said. Her voice was small and unfamiliar. "It's all over Manitou Island."

"She took a boat over." I was making this up as I went. I prayed they didn't consider the unlikelihood of a human taking anything as rickety as the Hancocks' boat across open water. "I ran into her on the beach. I told her I'd done the same thing."

"Don't you think that was a little hard to believe, seeing as you didn't have a boat? And what about clothes?"

"I had clothes. I told her my boat was down the beach, pulled up into the bushes. She didn't ask many questions. She was glad to see me. That's a good thing, right?"

Maris's eyes narrowed. I looked over at Tallulah, but she still wouldn't look at me.

Pavati smirked and built the kindling into a teepee over a pile of dry leaves. She rubbed her hands together until sparks flew out of her palms and caught the leaves on fire.

"I'm invited over for dinner tomorrow." I was glad I had that bit to offer. I hoped that would improve their moods. I didn't want this to turn into a fight. *A fight?* The idea surprised me. Was that what it was going to come down to? Was I going to have to fight my sisters over the granddaughter of Tom Hancock? I could feel Maris's frenzy, electric on the air. She was like a piranha with blood in the water.

And how would I do in a fight against them? One-on-one I'd fare well. But three-on-one I didn't stand a chance. We were all fast, all skilled killers by nature. Or nurture? I'd never met another mermaid who lived any differently, but Lily's words haunted me. Was I the way I was because of Maris? Had she taught me to be this way? Was it possible to find my own happiness?

If there was a fight, I wondered whom Tallulah would side with. I couldn't imagine her letting Maris destroy me. Still . . .

"Dinner," Maris said. "I guess I'm glad to hear that much."

My resolve strengthened. With or without Tallulah, I would fight for Lily. She was good. And she was innocent. And she had no part in the sins of her grandfather. But I couldn't trust Maris not to take matters into her own hands. I would have to stay close to Lily to make sure she was safe. I couldn't leave her unprotected when it was all my fault that she was in danger.

That meant no longer sleeping on Basswood with my sisters. I'd tell them I needed to be alone to think—to keep my mind sharp on the plan. Because despite my feelings for Lily, despite my need to protect her, I needed the plan to continue for my own selfish desires. It was no longer about revenge. I needed Maris to be successful because only then would I be free to leave my sisters, without any obligation to do their bidding. That was our deal. I would be free. I could see if it was possible to be happy, as Lily had promised. And I could take Lily with me, and we could live like normal people. Or maybe . . . I stopped myself before my fantasies took over.

I knew I could never chance a reinvigoration with her. The likelihood of it working was next to nothing. Maybe I could practice on someone else first, just to see . . . but I had to stop that idea, too. While it might have made sense to me not so long ago, Lily had changed my way of thinking. How could I play Russian roulette with someone else's Lily?

I couldn't shake the fantasy completely. The idea of the two of us living together naturally, without any pretext, was tantalizing. I would have to push it far away before it could become too firmly rooted in my brain. Recklessness wouldn't do anyone any good. I was already walking a tightrope, balancing precariously between meeting Lily's needs and satisfying my sisters'.

I must have glazed over as these thoughts were tripping through my mind. Pavati was snapping her fingers in front of my eyes.

"Hey, Calder," Maris said. "Earth to asshole. How are you going to work out the fishing trip with Hancock?" Maris was bent over at the waist, yelling down into my face.

"Hancock is going to teach some kind of nature course at

the college," I said. "I'll ask him to take me out on the lake. He doesn't fish, but it could just be a boat ride. A little nature lesson or something."

The girls now sat in satisfied silence. Pavati elbowed me and said, "So, what are you going to wear to dinner?"

30

SHOPPING SPREE

Pavati parked our car at the far end of the JCPenney parking lot. Tallulah and I got out of the backseat, and Pavati tossed the keys over the roof of the car to me. I snagged them out of the air and pocketed them in my cargo shorts, which—now that I looked at them—had seen better days. The tip of one of the keys hung through a hole in the pocket.

"I think you're right about the clothes, Pav. It might be time to burn these."

She rounded the car and mock-appraised my T-shirt-and-shorts look as if she hadn't given it much thought before.

"Don't worry. When we're through with you, you'll look like a proper boyfriend."

Tallulah winced. "Come on. Let's get this over with. There's too many people here. It gives me the creeps."

I knew what she meant. The emotional tenor of each person blended with the next. Bring on a crowd, and there was a cacophony of sentiments and passions that created a constant buzzing and distortion of muddled colors. We'd all have decent headaches if we stayed more than fifteen minutes.

Pavati entered the store ahead of me and Lu, and I dropped my Ray-Bans over my eyes to fend off the glare. A group of shaggy-haired white boys in baggy pants and NBA jerseys backed up to give us a wide berth.

"Maybe you should ask them who their stylist is," Pavati whispered.

"Ugh," Tallulah said, slinging a bag over her shoulder. "Could you please stop kidding around? Where's the men's department?"

"There," Pavati said, pointing to the back of the store. "I'm thinking something classic. Maybe a simple oxford shirt, definitely new khakis. Your old ones smell like kelp, and the cuffs are all worn."

"Aw, Pavati, I had no idea you were paying attention."

We navigated between carousels crowded with children's rompers, junior fashions, then ladies' dresses. We passed a shoe display, and I grabbed a box of Sperry Top-Siders as Pavati pulled me toward the back. *Shoes,* I thought. I hadn't given any thought to new shoes. It didn't look like the girls had, either. I was glad I spotted them. Proper boyfriends probably didn't show up at the door barefoot.

Tallulah walked over to a display of shirts, all folded and pinned into tightly bound packages arranged by size and color. She didn't waste any time being particular. She yanked a medium in green off the shelf and slapped the package against my chest. "Here. That'll go with your eyes."

I grabbed the shirt before she let go. "Something bothering you, Lu?"

Her mouth twisted up to one side. She was just about to say something when a store clerk approached us.

"Can I help you find something?" the woman asked. She was wearing a name badge that declared her name was Jo-Ellen. She fingered nervously at her frosted hair as Pavati took a menacing step toward her.

"Actually, you can, Jo-Ellen. I was hoping to find a new dress for a cocktail party I'm attending next weekend. Something in pink, perhaps?"

Pavati held her gaze as the woman flushed and said, "Certainly, certainly. This way." Pavati wiggled her eyebrows at us before she followed Jo-Ellen.

Tallulah slipped my new shirt into her bag with the agility of a sleight-of-hand magician, then she pulled at my elbow. "Pants are over here."

I grabbed Tallulah by the shoulder and whipped her around. Her normally placid expression faltered, and the fluorescent lights reflected off her wet eyes. "What's wrong?" I demanded.

"Nothing's wrong." She faked a smile. "I'm getting a headache. That's all. Let's hurry this up, okay?"

I released my grip and watched her walk away. She stopped beside a carousel of men's dress pants and flipped through them all, making a scraping sound with the swipe of each hanger on the metal rod. "Too dark, too pleated, too old man–ish . . ." I had my back turned to her selection process, keeping watch. I didn't really have an eye for fashion. I was better suited as a lookout.

She pushed me into a dressing room with a pair of black pants. A few seconds later I tossed my shorts and the shoe box over the door at her. When I came out of the dressing room, she'd already stashed my discards somewhere for some unsuspecting clerk to find.

I held my arms out and waited for her opinion. She swirled her finger in a circle, and I turned around to model the pants.

"Nice legs," she said, ripping off the tags.

"Shut up, Lulah." I finished my last rotation and caught a glimpse of her dragging the back of her hand across the corner of her eye.

Pavati came up fast. "Ready?"

"Ready."

Jo-Ellen was trailing far behind. "I'm so sorry we have no Versace, Ms. Vanderbilt."

"Vanderbilt?" I asked.

Pavati winked, and we walked quickly toward the front of the store. The girls rubbed their hands together in a circular motion as we closed in on the doors. I snagged a pair of shorts off the rack and threw them in Tallulah's bag.

Several curious salesclerks watched us coming, but as we walked through the security gate, the girls pressed their electrified palms to the sensors, scrambling the system. No one stopped us.

31

DINNER

When I knocked on the Hancocks' door at six o'clock, Lily answered, her smile nearly reaching her ears. She'd pulled her hair back into a loose knot and covered her body in a high-necked lace blouse and a long black corduroy skirt. I missed all the skin and her pink glow from the day before. Tonight she was nervous.

Behind her, the house shone with wax and polish. A lightly stained pine plank floor replaced the old carpet and linoleum. Mrs. Hancock's paintings hung on the walls. The windows reflected the light from a dozen candles.

Lily noticed my new appearance, and her eyebrows rose in amusement.

"Shut up," I whispered. "It's called dinner with the parents."

"No. You look good. Very . . . normal."

"Perfect." I winked and folded my hand around hers. "That's exactly the look I was going for."

She pulled her hand out, and this time I was the one to be surprised.

"Don't overwhelm them," she said. "I've never brought a boy home for dinner before."

"It's not my first time here."

"This is different. They don't need to freak out prematurely."

"Got it." I yanked her close to me and kissed her quickly. "No freaking them out."

She laughed and led me into the living room. Hancock, Mrs. Hancock, and Sophie were standing in the room, as if they were posed and placed on marks.

"Good evening, Calder," Mrs. Hancock said. "Nice of you to join us for dinner. Sorry your folks couldn't make it."

"They said to pass on their regrets." I locked my teeth together and forced a smile.

"I hope you like chicken."

"Chicken," I repeated. I'd never tried it before. "Sounds great."

"Can we get you something to drink?" Hancock asked.

"Coke?"

"Coming right up. Sophie?"

"Got it, Dad."

We went farther into the room and took our seats on two small sofas. I couldn't relax. My muscles constricted, and I sat ramrod straight and still, ready to bolt. Lily kept an anxious watch on my face. Sophie returned and set the Coke down on a cocktail napkin on the coffee table. The glass was sweating in the humidity. I wiped my index finger around its edge, calming myself with the moisture.

"Do you golf, Calder?" Hancock reached forward and scooped a handful of peanuts out of a bowl. He tossed them into his mouth one at a time.

"No, sir."

"Play some football in high school?"

"Not really."

"That's too bad. You know what you're made of after playing some football. I was a running back in my day. Number sixteen."

"Calder was on the swim team, Dad," Lily said, putting a coaster under my glass.

"Uh-huh. Going to give that Michael Phelps a run for his money?"

I smiled, imagining the matchup. "Oh, I think I could hold my own."

"That's right. It's all in the attitude."

Lily sat next to her dad and pecked his cheek. I flinched and looked away. Sophie sat in a chair across from me. I hadn't been paying attention to her, but she was watching me intently. I smiled and raised my eyebrows at her. Her expression didn't change.

Hancock reached forward for another handful of peanuts.

Lily fiddled with a loose thread on her cuff.

The only sound was the crunching of peanuts. I shook the ice in my glass.

Lily looked at me and crossed her eyes with a comic expression. Salvation came when Mrs. Hancock called us all for dinner. "Here we go," Hancock announced, slapping his hands down on his knees to propel himself off the couch. "'Bout time."

Lily gave him a swat as he passed in front of her.

I sat where Hancock indicated, and Lily sat between me and her father.

"That's my chair," Sophie said as she shot dagger eyes at Lily. Mrs. Hancock redirected Sophie to the other side of the table while she wheeled her chair into her own spot.

Lily served.

The plate in front of me was covered with something I'd never seen. The large white piece of flesh, I presumed, was chicken. But it was covered in a gelatinous soup concoction that spilled over the edges and pooled on the plate. I smiled weakly across the table at Mrs. Hancock and tried to be inconspicuous as I scraped the sauce off the meat. I took a bite. The chicken was warm and chewy. I choked it down and drained my water glass.

Lily scooped some spinach salad onto my plate and passed me the salt shaker. I looked at her gratefully and shook it liberally over everything. The rest of the food was in constant motion, being passed from father to mother to child and back again. Hancock poured Sophie a glass of milk and handed it down to her. Mrs. Hancock ladled a yellow noodle dish onto Sophie's plate. It was all so . . . *normal,* exactly the way I imagined a real family to be. All that was missing was a dog lying under the table.

For a moment, I believed I could be part of this. I was born to this kind of life: the parents, the home, the meal. Maybe my human parents ate chicken, too. They were out there somewhere. They might have even loved me. Did they search for me still, all these years later? I couldn't imagine it.

Hancock asked, "You enjoy being up here for the summer, Calder?"

I passed the bread basket to Lily. "Very much so."

"My whole life," he said, "as long as I can remember, I've wanted to be here. It just kept gnawing at me. I've been to Erie, Michigan, Huron, Ontario." He ticked off the names of the Great Lakes while waving his fork in the air. "But up until this spring, I'd never been to Lake Superior. Hard to believe, isn't it?"

"Very. But Lily told me about that, sir. About your promise to your dad."

Hancock chewed, then swallowed. He leaned onto the table toward me. "One thing I've always stood for: When you make a promise, Calder, you keep it. No matter how bad it hurts."

"I couldn't agree more," I said. Best get this over with. "Get out on the lake much, Mr. Hancock?"

He looked at me, startled; then he lowered his lids to study me anew. "We have a couple kayaks. And there's a small fishing boat. But I never learned to swim, and I'm not a boater." He paused. "You seem shocked."

"Oh, no, sir, it's just that—"

"The Great Lakes can be dangerous—fascinating, too—but dangerous, particularly when you don't know what you're doing. I suppose you heard about those three college kids whose boat was found without them?" He shook his head and scraped his fork on the china plate. "I'll be surprised if they ever turn up." Then he pointed his fork at Lily and stabbed at the air with each word: "Lake Superior does not give up its dead."

Hancock grimaced and cleared his throat. "Anyway, I'd rather study the history of the lake than float on it all day. Did you know they discovered an underwater roadway? I've seen pictures. It looks like a paved Roman road. Now, *that's* a fascinating discovery. A real Atlantis of sorts."

I was aware of it. I didn't know any humans had found it. "A man-made road? Underwater? I'd like to see that."

Hancock nodded, chewing. "The theory is that it's part of an ancient copper mine."

"There are a lot of mysteries about the lake," I said. Lily squeezed my knee under the table.

"There's hundreds of sunken ships, too," Mrs. Hancock added.

I nodded. "Total ship graveyard. I've seen a couple of those. Some are in shallow enough water you can see them from your boat. Maybe I could show you sometime, Mr. Hancock."

"I'd like—" Sophie started, but Mrs. Hancock interrupted her.

"Oh, you'd like that, wouldn't you, Jason? Get out there for once." She reached over and touched Hancock's forearm.

Sophie pushed her chair back quickly and stood up to clear her plate.

Mrs. Hancock looked up at her younger daughter. "You all done, hon?"

"I'm not hungry." There was a strange expression on

Sophie's face. It reminded me of Pavati when she wasn't getting her way. Sophie sulked into the kitchen, and Mrs. Hancock picked up the conversation.

"Lily was telling me your family stays on your sailboat during the summer?"

"That's right. We keep things simple. It's sort of like an extended camping trip." I chewed a second bite of chicken slowly. The more I chewed, the bigger it seemed to get. Forks and knives scraped across plates while I reveled in the civility of the meal. Silverware, real cloth napkins . . . no sand in my food. I could get used to this.

"Sophie?" Mrs. Hancock called into the kitchen. "Are you going to rejoin us?" Then she turned back to me. "Six of you on one boat. I can't imagine living like that for much longer than a weekend. But I understand why your mother does it. It's hard to be separated from your family for even a short period. I don't know what we'd do if we weren't together."

"Not that you have to worry about that with a house *this* small," said Lily.

"You know what I mean," Mrs. Hancock said. "Calder, I'm sure you can understand. Your family must be close if you're able to live in such tight quarters. Take away one member . . . I just can't imagine the toll that would take on a family."

I dropped my fork, and it clattered onto my plate. I gripped the edge of the table. Mrs. Hancock's gentle voice, the memory of my mother, the way Lily looked at her father, "the toll that would take on a family," Pavati's warning . . . Pavati was right even before there was anything to be *right* about. I couldn't love Lily and kill Hancock, because I couldn't kill Hancock without destroying Lily.

I had to get out of here. I had to get out fast. My world was tumbling like pebbles over a dam.

"Excuse me," I said. Heat rushed into my face, and I bolted for the door.

32

CONFESSIONS

"Calder, are you okay?" Lily asked, following me away from the table.

"I'm sorry. I'm not feeling well."

Mrs. Hancock said, "Oh dear, I hope it's not the chicken."

Lily's bare feet followed closely behind me on the pine plank floor. "What's wrong?" she asked as the screen door slammed behind her. I was already over the porch steps and halfway to the car. Lily grabbed my shoulder as she caught up, and I could feel the electricity spinning out of me and into her palm. It must have been painful, but she didn't let go.

"I've got to get out of here," I said.

"What?"

"My sisters, Lily. I can't be here. I can't do this. This is so completely messed up."

"What are you talking about? What do your sisters have to do with anything?" She slapped her hand across her mouth. "They know? They know *I* know?"

"No, no. That's not it."

"Then what?"

"If that were all it was, I'd take you and we'd run. We'd go to the Abacos. We'd get a little beach house on one of the cays. You could write poetry . . . I could protect you."

"Would that make everything better? If it would, we should go."

"No! You don't understand. Even if I took you away, it wouldn't change anything. They'll still kill him."

"Kill him? Who's 'him'?"

I was pacing, my fingers clenched in my hair, pulling at the roots. My teeth ground together as I wrestled with the dueling loyalties. "Do you think any of this is an accident?" I asked. "A family of merpeople shows up on the doorstep of a family who's heard of a monster in the lake. More than heard of, tangled with."

"There are no monsters in the lake." Her voice was flat.

"I appreciate the vote of confidence, but you are seriously misguided."

"Calder, it's not your fault what happened to my grandfather."

"Of course it's not. Don't you see? My only regret in regard to your *grandfather*"—the last word spit from between my teeth—"is that he died before we had the chance to kill him ourselves."

Lily's brow furrowed. "What are you saying?"

I recounted the whole story, ending with my mother's last strangled breath; with each word, the blood drained from Lily's face.

"He promised to sacrifice your father."

"But Dad was a baby!"

"Age is irrelevant. And to a mermaid, a promise is a sacred thing."

"You were going to kill a baby?"

"Technically, my mother was, but that's beside the point. He promised his son in exchange for his life. It was a promise. They had a *contract*. Merpeople never break their promises. We expect the same in return. And your grandfather's broken promise killed my mother."

"He didn't know that."

"He caused that."

"So now what? What can I do to save my dad?"

"You? Nothing. I want you as far away from this situation as possible." I tried to wrap my arms around her, but she slapped at me and stepped back.

"And what exactly is *this situation*?" Her eyes practically glowed with fury.

"Lily, my sisters want to kill your father. They asked me to get close to you so I could get close to him. They want me to get him out on the lake so they can claim what is rightfully theirs."

"You got close to me on your sisters' *orders*?"

"What? Yes. At first. You're focusing on all the wrong things."

Lily's chin trembled. Her bottom lids filled with tears.

"But it's not like that now." I put my hands on her

247

shoulders and she threw them off. The air snapped between us.

"You were in there talking about a boat trip with my dad."

"I know, I know. But I can't do it. Don't you see?"

"Get out of here, Calder. Stay away from me, stay away from my family. And keep your sisters far away, too." She turned to run back to the house, but I spun her around and shook her by the shoulders.

"It's not that simple, Lily. They *will* get to him. Now that they've found him, they will trail him *forever*."

"I can protect him." She ripped my hands off her. "Get out of here. And don't come back."

Before I could open my mouth to protest, a child's scream reverberated off the lake and ricocheted through the trees.

33

COLLISION

The screen door flew open and Hancock was on the porch, his face expressing more panic than his words ever could. "Lily, is Sophie with you?"

"No."

"Help! Daddy!"

We all turned toward the lake and tried to locate the sound. Mrs. Hancock appeared behind her husband, her face ashen, helpless in the confines of her chair. Rather than run for the lake, Hancock stood motionless, his knees locked and his hands trembling.

"Jason," Mrs. Hancock cried, pushing him from behind. "This is not the time for your irrational phobias!"

With trepidation, Hancock staggered for the shore and pushed the aluminum fishing boat onto the water.

"Oh, God, no," Lily said under her breath. Her eyes locked on mine, her expression fierce. "Stay out of the water. Stay away from him."

Hancock pulled the cord on the outboard motor several times before he was able to get it to start; then he was flying out onto the lake.

I raced down the driveway, cutting into the woods, tearing my new clothes off as I ran. Tree branches slapped against my face and chest and thighs, cutting me, smearing me with pine sap. When I hit the edge of the land, I pushed off without stopping to visualize. I transformed midair. Far faster than Pavati ever had.

Perhaps it was because Pavati was in my thoughts, but as I hit the water, I could hear her voice. Pavati was trilling with excitement. She was at least a mile away, and Maris and Tallulah were farther still, but they were closing quickly and listening intently to Pavati's report.

The little girl had come outside, Pavati said. She was pouting because no one had been paying attention to her. She'd wanted to sit by me at dinner. Pavati had been watching from the channel. She called to her, asked her to come out on the lake. I could see it all through Pavati's mind's eye: Sophie pulling a kayak off the grass. Pavati promising her some fun.

Then I heard the echo of Pavati's memory as the kayak capsized. Sophie was clinging to the overturned craft and now—*finally!*—Jason Hancock was in the water. His boat was slow. The neglected motor sputtered as it ran out of gas.

He picked up the oars and started rowing. *"Hurry!"* cried Pavati. *"This is our moment."*

From under the water, I could hear Sophie's screams as she clung to the kayak.

Maris ripped through the water, Tallulah a silver streak behind her.

My mind tried to calculate the distance and their rate of speed, but there was something about having Hancock so close, and on the water, that pulled at my heart, too.

I shook my head to clear the ingrained urge for justice. I had greater desires. I had to stop my sisters.

Adrenaline pushed me faster than normal. But Maris was fast, too. And then there was something else. A new smell on the water. Lily in a second kayak. My heart leapt as Lily's face flashed in my thoughts.

"No!" screamed Tallulah. She twitched her tail and changed course.

"Why?" I called out to her. *"Tallulah, leave Lily alone."*

Hancock reached Sophie within seconds—just fifty yards from shore. He pulled her into his boat and tied the kayak to the defective motor. Maris was closing in, but I beat her to Hancock. I put one hand on the back of his boat and shoved it with more strength than I expected. The unexpected momentum threw Hancock and Sophie onto the floor of the boat.

A few seconds later their boat scraped across the sand as it hit the shore. Maris's curses and Pavati's fury muffled the sound.

Tallulah was quiet. I panicked when I realized I couldn't sense where she was.

I was forced to surface, not even caring who was watching.

I didn't need to look to know that Hancock was still near. The sun hadn't set, and if he wanted to know about the monster in the lake, he was getting a better show than we could have ever rehearsed.

Lily was twenty yards to my south. She'd stopped paddling when she realized her dad and sister were safe. Now she looked disoriented, like she was finding herself somewhere she'd never planned to be. She turned her head, searching for someone or something. I might have felt better if she didn't know what she was looking for. I imagined her searching for ripples, backs arching, and tails splashing against the water.

"You told her!" Tallulah was screaming at me. *"She knows. I can tell."*

"Leave her alone, Tallulah. She's mine."

"We've lost the element of surprise, Calder. You've ruined everything. And now you, you . . ."—her voice broke on a sob—"love her. How could you do this to me?"

"You? What do you have to do with this? Back off, Lu. Now!"

"No. I can't let you."

We collided just ten feet from Lily's kayak. The force of the impact sent us both sailing out of the water, entwined like a wild vine, before crashing back down. The water churned and the kayak rocked violently. My arm wrapped around Tallulah's neck, and I dragged her down to the bottom. My hand covered her mouth, and she sank her teeth into my fingers. I didn't stand a chance once Maris got there. Even Pavati would be impossible to fight off.

I dragged Tallulah across the rocks on the lake bottom, scraping her soft belly until there was blood in the water. She bit down hard on my arm. I put my tail against her back and heaved. The force did two things: it sent her deeper into the lake, and it propelled me closer to Lily.

When I surfaced, Lily screamed and scooped ineffectively at the water with her hands. I deserved her terror. I could only imagine what she expected me to do.

"Lily, it's me."

She still batted at the water.

"You're fine. Your family's fine. I'm not going to hurt you." I pushed her kayak into the weeds until the bow dug into the sand and my tail scraped along the rocks. "Please get inside, Lily. They won't touch you. Not tonight."

"Or Dad?" she panted. Her face was as pale as the moon.

"Or your dad. I won't let them."

"What about you?" she asked.

I looked nervously out on the now-stilled water. "Lily. If you don't see me first thing in the morning, you need to get your family out of here."

34

SHUNNED

As much as I wanted to, I couldn't stay out on the lake all night. I would have to go back to Basswood and face my sisters. It was almost an exercise in redundancy. I'd played the whole confrontation out in my head several times before I ever reached the island. It wasn't like I didn't know what they were going to say. There'd be no reasoning with them. I'd barely been able to reason it out for myself. I would be lucky to get through it without being maimed. Tallulah presented the only wild card in any of this.

Under any other circumstances, I could count on her

defending me. But I didn't understand her reaction to Lily. Sure, we never intended to make our true selves known to her, but for all Tallulah knew, the mission was all but accomplished. Why she'd pulled away from the pursuit of Jason Hancock and gone after Lily . . . I just didn't understand. Was it possible she was no longer interested in revenge? If that was the case, she would defend my decision.

I came at the island from a different angle. I could see their campfire burning, and someone was throwing stones out into the lake. My survival depended on a showing of contrition. A straight-on approach wouldn't signal an apology. I reached the island's northern point and followed the shoreline south, stopping one hundred feet north of where they sat. I stood up with my arms stretched out to them, palms up. I didn't say anything, but waited for them to notice me.

Tallulah turned first, and I could see she'd been crying. She nudged Maris. Maris and Pavati turned and looked at me. No one said anything. I couldn't tell if they were still deliberating or if they'd already reached a verdict.

Maris put her arm around Tallulah, and Tallulah laid her head on Maris's shoulder. They all turned back to the fire. There was no expression to read on their faces. The silence was worse than I'd anticipated.

I swam closer, my arms still laid out across the surface of the water. Maris hissed at me, spitting vitriol. I stopped.

"Maris," I said. "Let me explain."

"You've done enough tonight. We have nothing more to say to you."

I stuttered, realizing what she meant. "Y-you're shunning me? That's what it's come to? You won't even hear me out?"

"I can't imagine what you could possibly have to say, Calder. You have no idea how disappointed I am, how disappointed we all are. It's one thing to leave us for so long each year, to be so direct in telling us how little you care for us. It's quite another to betray us, to betray our mother. Do you think I enjoy being such a harpy? Do you think I come by this naturally? My only hope is that the end of Hancock will be my salvation from this hell. But you have chosen him over me. And you have chosen his daughter over your own sister."

I was about to ask what she meant when Tallulah looked up at me with wide, watery eyes, heartbreak etched across her face. I knew the look. A twisted horror snaked through me. Tallulah's aversion to Lily, her sudden and unprovoked attack . . .

"You're my sister," I said, still disbelieving. "It's vile!"

Pavati smirked and stoked the fire, shooting a sideways glance at Tallulah.

Another sob caught in Tallulah's throat, and Maris was on her feet. The closer she came to the water, the quicker I backed up. She stopped just as the edge of the water crossed her toes. "Stay out of our way, Calder." She bared her teeth and snarled. "Don't think I won't kill you if it comes to that."

I dove backward, arching my back, disappearing into the dark water.

An hour later I was still swimming. If I'd paid attention to the rocks, the sand, the sunken timbers, I would have known I was five miles north of Cornucopia. I could navigate this lake without ever looking for above-water landmarks. But the truth was, I didn't care where I was.

A school of coho salmon chased alewives around the underwater rock where I sat. I buried my face in my hands and dove to a depth they wouldn't go. But the silence at ten fathoms had its own snares; I was left with my own thoughts.

My stomach twisted unbearably with the knowledge of Tallulah's feelings for me. Not that it was *real* love. The closest approximation to love for a mermaid was obsession. If I was being honest, I'd always known Tallulah felt more for me than she should have. But Tallulah's affection was the only gentleness I'd known since my mother's death. What was I supposed to do with this information now? There was no way I would sleep tonight. I needed someone to talk to. Someone with good advice . . .

I followed the Madeline Island shoreline south and picked up the high-pitched vibration of the Ashland paper factory. Its tenor told me when it was time to cut through the pass between Long Island and Chequamegon Point. I bore southeast to Little Girl's Point, then north into the lake, along the Wisconsin-Michigan line, for the wreck of the *J.P. Brodie*.

The last time I'd come to this site, Reagan had been president, but not much had changed. I tasted the old oak on the water and circled the broken mast down to the hull. It was just as I remembered. Hand over hand, I trailed the starboard side to the third porthole window. I had to smile just a little to see Joe's gaunt face bobbing on the other side of the filmy glass.

It probably wasn't his real name, but I'd called him that as a kid. He looked as good as the first day we met, back in '74. Joe and his crew had already been dead ninety years by then, but the cold water preserved them. Bacteria couldn't grow at these temperatures, so the bodies didn't rot or bloat. The sleeve of Joe's peacoat was caught on something, which kept his face forever bouncing against the glass.

It was good to see him again. He'd always been a willing

ear, and he'd heard plenty from me over the years. After Mother died, I visited him often and pretended he was giving me fatherly advice. It helped sometimes when I was at my lowest.

"Hey, Joe," I said, leaning my shoulder against the exterior of the ship. *"Looking good, man."* Out of politeness, I waited for him to respond, then imagined the rest.

"Where y'been, kid?" he'd ask.

"Here, there."

"Staying out of trouble, I hope. I don't want to get any bad reports."

"Hmm," I said, smiling at his joke.

"What's bothering you?"

I ran my fingers through my hair. *"That obvious?"*

"Those sisters giving you trouble again?"

I nodded and pressed my hands to the portal glass.

"That bad?"

"That bad."

"Let me guess, you didn't let Tallulah beat you in a race? Put sneezewort in Pavati's hair again?"

"No."

"Snakeroot?"

"I'm not a kid anymore, Joe."

"Right. Right. Listen, you and your sisters will always butt heads. I suppose that's only natural." I didn't say anything, so Joe finally asked straight out, *"What did you do this time?"*

"I got between them and Jason Hancock."

Joe laughed a big, hearty laugh. *"Wow, kid. I didn't realize Maris had found him. You got a death wish or something?"*

"Something like that."

A long, morbid silence stretched out between us as he waited for me to elaborate and I waited for his sage advice. Joe spoke first.

"Well, I'm sure you had your reasons."

I rolled over my shoulder so my back was flat against the hull. *"Mm-hmm."*

"And this reason . . . she must have been very pretty."

"Very."

"Good conversationalist?"

I smiled and nodded.

"Then what the hell are you talking to me for, son?"

I turned back to face him and slapped my hand on the side of the hull as if to say, "Thanks, Dad." My place was with Lily. I'd promised her safety. I would keep that promise— whether she wanted me to or not.

My body whipped itself toward the surface, a wake of white bubbles trailing behind me. I cut straight west and looped the big island to my now familiar willow tree. From there I would watch and wait.

35

HAMMOCK

When I got to the Hancocks' dock, I hovered just outside the floodlights. The front door opened, letting a slice of light cut across the front yard. I held my breath. It was Lily. Of course it was Lily. She must have been watching for me. She was wearing a thin cotton nightgown. The light from the house shone through the fabric, revealing the curve of her legs.

She walked on tiptoe in bare feet across the porch and down the repaired steps, carrying a flashlight in one hand and pressing something else against her chest. The flashlight battery was weak, and the beam barely reached five feet ahead of her.

I started toward the dock. Slowly. I took hope in her coming to the water, but I still wasn't sure what she'd want to say. Regardless of what reparation I'd made for my sins in saving Hancock, I was sure she'd have more fury to dole out.

"Calder," she whispered, her voice carrying over the surface of the water.

"I'm here," I whispered back, bracing myself for what was coming.

She sighed and lay down on the dock, reaching out in the water for me. I swam in, tentatively, and she took my hands. She pulled me closer. As my chest came up against the edge of the dock, I saw what she'd been carrying. My new clothes were neatly folded beside her. How long had it taken her to find them in the dark?

"Are you hurt?"

"No," I said. "Not yet, anyway."

"I was so afraid they'd hurt you. How much trouble are you in?"

"Trouble doesn't begin to cover it."

She kissed me, and her fingers laced through my hair. "I'm sorry. I should have never doubted you."

An apology. It hurt more than her forgiveness, which I didn't deserve, either. What did she have to be sorry for? It was more punishing than her anger. I shook my head and pushed myself away. "I told you I planned to kill your father, Lily. You reacted exactly the way you should have."

She grabbed my wrist and pulled me back to her, wrapping her arms around my neck. "I'm still sorry."

"Please don't say that."

She kissed me, cupping my cheek in her hand, brushing her thumb across my bottom lip. "What will happen to you now?"

"I don't know." I could picture Maris plotting against me, pacing on the beach. "They've shunned me."

"You say that like it's a bad thing," she whispered, her eyes on my lips. "I thought you wanted to be free of them."

I almost laughed. "I'm hardly free. I may be shunned, but I'm still mentally tied to them, and Maris will never give me my freedom now. Worse, being shunned from the island, I won't have the benefit of knowing what their next move will be. If they attack again, I won't be able to hold them off."

Lily shook her head. "You're strong."

"So are they. And there are three of them."

"Not even Tallulah will side with you?"

Tallulah's name on Lily's lips was like a curse from an angel. I made a disgusted sound that she didn't understand. I had no intention of explaining that development. "We've got to keep your dad off the water, Lily."

"He never goes out on the lake. Well . . . except for tonight. But I don't think we have to worry. He's on the computer right now, posting a classified ad. 'Boat for Sale.'"

I dunked below the water and came up again. "Don't underestimate my sisters, Lil. Nobody ever plans to go to them, and yet so many do."

"You don't think they'd come to the house, do you?"

"That's one thing you don't have to worry about. A kill is only honorable on the water."

"Honorable?"

I gave a short laugh. "Yeah, that used to make sense to

me. I don't suppose you want to tell your dad the whole truth?"

"And let him know Grandpa planned to sacrifice him? No thanks."

"I thought so. So this is what I want you to do. I'm going to pull your boats out and sink them. That will be the easiest way to keep your dad off the water. But you need to convince him that being so close to the lake, almost losing Sophie, is too stressful for your mom. That it's bad for her health. You must convince him. You have to leave, Lily."

She looked panicked. "But what if he agrees?" she said, gripping my hands tighter.

"I'll be close behind."

She paused, considering my demands, then stood up. "Get out. Get dressed. Meet me in the hammock. It's freezing out here." She ran back toward the house, her hair streaming behind her.

A few minutes later Lily crawled into the hammock beside me and pulled a wool blanket over us. The hammock swayed, and we floated under the trees. I stared up at the blackened sky. She drew small concentric circles on my chest with her finger.

"Why did you do it, Calder? Why did you save him?"

"What else could I do?" My voice was low.

"You'd planned to kill him before."

"I did."

She stopped drawing circles and laid her palm flat against my chest. A patch of five-fingered heat soaked into my skin.

"I realized killing him would kill you. And *that* would kill me."

"Figuratively speaking," she said.

"I'm not so sure about that."

"So that's it?" she asked.

I didn't answer right away, trying to understand what she was really asking. "What more should there be?"

She had no response for me.

"Now *you* tell *me* something," I said, lifting her chin with my finger.

"What do you want to know?"

"How is it that you can be here with me? Regardless of what I did last night, how can you forgive me?"

"I like to think of it the other way around."

I waited for her to explain.

"What would happen if I didn't forgive you?" she asked.

"Hopefully, your family would take off and hide. I'd do my damnedest to sabotage my sisters' attempts to find you again."

"You'd go away?"

"Yes, of course." I answered easily, not thinking of the logistics, and twisted a lock of her hair around my finger.

"That's impossible to think about, but that's not really where I was going with this."

"I'm listening."

"Look at your sisters, Calder. They're bitter, miserable creatures who've now turned on you. They've spent half a century obsessed with nothing but murder. Do I want to sentence myself to that kind of prison?"

I understood. Hadn't I always felt shackled to them? "But how do you *do* it, Lily? What are the mechanics?"

"Forgiveness? I don't have a choice. Or at least, no other good choices."

"I'm not sure I can forgive them for what they tried to do last night—to your father, to Sophie, but most of all to you."

"Forgiveness isn't just for *them*, Calder. It's for you. For-giveness is freedom. It's something you do for yourself—to keep who you are intact. Now that I think about it, in some ways, it's kind of a selfish act."

I tightened my grip around her shoulders and pulled the blanket up under her chin. There must not have been any clouds because the stars burned unusually bright. I imagined, from their vantage point in the sky, they could see the ap-proaching sunrise. It made me wonder. Was it better to see the source of one's demise approaching or to be surprised?

"Look at the stars, Lily."

"I'd rather look at you," she whispered back.

"You can do that later."

She raised her head an inch, and her eyes burned into mine. Her hair fell in soft loops across my shoulder. "Can I, Calder? I thought you were trying to get rid of me."

My eyebrows pulled together as I frowned at her. "Why would you say that?"

"*Leave, Lily.*" She imitated my voice from back by the dock.

My face softened. "I also said I'd be close behind."

"Words," she groused, and she laid her head back down on my shoulder.

I reached over with my right hand and gently turned her chin so she'd look up at the sky. "See the stars, Lily?"

She sighed, surrendering. "Of course."

"Do you think they can see the sun coming?"

"I don't know. Probably?"

"Do you think they're scared?"

"They're burning balls of gas, Calder."

"Oh, c'mon. Where's the poet in you?"

She exhaled, and I sensed her smile. "I see. Well, in that case, yes. They've finally come home. They are triumphant in their midnight kingdom. But the enemy approaches. They have the numbers on their side, but the enemy is bigger, stronger, with a history of winning that goes back to the dawn of time. They're definitely terrified."

I nodded. She understood my analogy.

"But they don't run, Calder."

Air caught in my throat.

"I'd rather lie in a hammock with you—with nothing but happiness surrounding us—and be ambushed than run away."

I shook my head. "If I stay on the lake, I'd be like the stars watching for the sun. I could hear them, I could warn you, and you could get away." What I didn't say was that if I had never put on my human vestiges, I would not be here with her. And I didn't want to be anywhere else ever again. Lily lay on her side, her left arm draped sleepily across my chest, her left knee pulled up over me, as if she were the one protecting me from what lay ahead. My arm was her pillow, and she pressed her nose into the side of my neck.

"How are you feeling, Calder?"

"Happy."

She exhaled softly against my neck and her breath warmed my skin. "Me too. You do know what that means, don't you?"

Yes. I knew what it meant. I'd known it for some time. Ever since I saw the college kids dead on the beach and felt no urge to search for my own prey.

"You're not like them anymore."

"But I'm not like you, either," I said.

She gripped me tighter. "You're right. You're better."

I rolled my eyes. "I'm a prize, all right. I wonder what your dad would think about you snuggled up to a sea monster." I marveled at how I could think of—even mention—Jason Hancock with no thoughts of malice.

"Which reminds me," she said. "I read something else that might interest you."

"Not another poem."

"Not exactly. It's from the Bible."

I turned to face her now. "Now I'm interested. I had no idea you were religious."

"Oh, you've just begun to scratch the surface with me." She cleared her throat. "I memorized it. Are you ready?"

"I'm ready," I said. "Knock my socks off."

" 'Then God said, "Let the water teem with an abundance of living creatures." And so it happened. God created the great sea monsters and all kinds of swimming creatures with which the water teems. And God saw that it was good.' "

I pulled her on top of me. "Well, who am I to argue with God?"

"Exactly." Her mouth found mine. Her lips were warm and soft. She tipped up her chin, and my mouth slid down her throat to her collarbone and then her shoulder. Her natural scent mixed with the smell of herbal shampoo and freshly cleaned laundry. Nothing had ever been more right.

For the first time in weeks, I was warm. Very warm. The water couldn't touch that. No one could change that. Or, perhaps, one person could. If Lily took my advice and left, the cold would rush in like water into a sinking ship. I might not have been happy with my life before, but at least

I had accepted it for what it was. Now I could never go back.

I lingered on the details of the night, longing to reverse time and do it all over again, or speed up time to the next opportunity to be with her. Lily nestled against my chest. Her head sank heavier on my shoulder. Her eyes closed.

"I love you," I whispered, kissing her forehead. She didn't respond. "Lily?"

She slept more peacefully than anyone I'd ever seen—a stark contrast to my sisters' restless slumber. I wondered if this was the peace that forgiveness bought.

Behind us, the Hancock house stood silent and invisible against the black trees. Below us, the hammock was our cradle. The weight of Lily's arm around my chest reassured me. I was both exhausted and exhilarated. I would do anything to preserve this feeling, but I dared to close my eyes, and sleep overcame me.

36

PROMISES KEPT

I don't know how long I slept. Maybe an hour. Maybe only a minute. When I opened my eyes, it was still dark, but the birds had all gone quiet. A fish broke through the water with a small *pip*. Wind ruffled the trees. When something larger surfaced, just a hundred feet from shore, I was both surprised and disgusted that I had allowed myself to hope.

Someone raced toward shore with arms extended over the surface of the water, palms up, in a gesture of peace. At first I assumed Tallulah had come to explain herself, though I couldn't imagine what she'd have to say. But it was Pavati's wide, exotic eyes that burned through the darkness.

I gently extricated myself from the happy tangle of arms and legs that Lily and I had become. The hammock tilted as I rolled out, but I retucked the blanket around her before she had time to register my absence. She murmured softly as I walked toward the lake and listened for any sign of ambush.

"Pavati," I said, greeting her when she stopped fifteen feet out.

She said, "Peace, Calder," but there was a strange anxiety in her voice.

"Are you here on behalf of Maris or Tallulah?"

Pavati squirmed, and she spoke quickly. "It was Tallulah's confession to make. It wasn't my place to speak for her. Not then, not now."

I paused to consider Pavati's anxious face. "How am I supposed to look at Lulah ever again?"

"Listen," she said, looking quickly over her shoulder. "I'm not here to talk about her." Her tail lashed behind her.

"Say what you're here to say, then."

"Maris has taken the Hancock matter into her own hands."

Instinctively, I glanced behind me at the house.

"She's taken the little girl. She's accepting a daughter in the father's stead."

"You're a liar," I said, but despite my accusation, I couldn't help but listen for the sound of Sophie turning in her bed, a soft snuffle, a murmur. I heard nothing, but did that mean Pavati was telling the truth? The house was no quieter than before. Surely I hadn't allowed Maris to steal Sophie right under my nose. But was it possible? Oh, God . . . "Why would she do that?" I asked.

The sun broke the horizon behind Pavati, throwing her

face into shadow. "Please," she said. "Neither of us has time for explanations."

"I'm not stupid. This is just a trick so I'll leave Hancock unprotected. I suppose you wouldn't mind if I went inside to check on—"

"Look at me, Cal."

She pulled closer, and I could see her face again. My heart lurched with sympathy. For her. For myself. I couldn't tell. I couldn't even tell if the thought originated with me. My head felt light and detached. My legs swayed with indecision. Pavati stretched her arms toward me, and I could see only truth and panic in her eyes.

"She really took her?" I asked.

Pavati leaned north, begging me to follow.

"How do I know you won't attack Hancock?" I said.

"Maris and I got into a fight." She rose just enough so I could see the long red gouges across her neck and shoulders. "She knows I've had a soft spot for that little girl. This is Maris's way of punishing me for saying she was wrong to shun you. Please. I promise no one will touch the father," she said, her voice more even and calmer than it had been before. "Besides, I'm going with you. She's taken the child to Basswood, and it's too cold for her to be out there. For all I know, she's already dead."

A scream ripped across the water from my sisters' campsite to my ears. Pavati's eyes flashed, and the horror on her face was real. "Are we too late?" she asked.

I tore off my clothes and ran into the lake, leaving Lily alone in the hammock.

Once transformed, I searched Pavati's mind for some sign

of deceit. Though her thoughts were scattered and clipped, I could find no contradiction in them. My only choice was to cling to her unbreakable promise—*No one will touch the father*—and hope we weren't too late.

I shot through the water, whipping my tail until it all but blurred. Pavati followed, mere inches behind, her body bending and arching, plowing through the waves as Sophie's cries pierced the water.

My mind tried to tease out the possible terms of a truce, or even an exchange. What compromise could we reach? What did I have to offer her? How could I convince Maris to spare the child? It would go against her nature to release her claim on the Hancock family entirely. But hadn't I defied nature? Could that same peace be possible for them? And where was Tallulah in this? How could Maris possibly explain Tallulah to me?

As I approached the beach, I was thankful not to hear Maris's thoughts, which meant she was still on land. Presumably Sophie was with her. Alive. I turned to confer with Pavati, but she had surfaced. I followed her up, and my face hit the air just as she said, "Here he is, Maris. Give the child to me now."

From behind me, Maris said, "Gladly. She's more trouble than she's worth," and then, "Tallulah, you're up."

I turned just in time to see Maris raise a rock high above her head and bring it crashing down on my skull.

37

THE REPLAY

When I regained consciousness, I was trapped in a ghost net six feet underwater, my wrists bound, facedown in the sand. Pavati and Tallulah were gone, but I could sense Maris floating nearby, watching me. I turned my head as much as the ancient fishing net would allow.

"There, there," Maris said with mock concern. *"How's your head, little brother?"*

My eye throbbed and, as far as I could tell, my nose hadn't always bent to the right. I torqued my body to get a better look at her. *"What the hell is wrong with you, Maris? Where's Sophie?"*

She raised her eyebrows, surprised by my question. Her hair floated in a white halo around her head. *"Seriously? That's what you want to know? Pavati took her home. No harm done."*

I twisted and jerked, howling with unrestrained fury and searching for any breach in the net. *"Just like that?"* I asked through clenched teeth. And then I remembered Pavati hours earlier, promising me no one would touch Hancock, telling me Maris had agreed to take a daughter instead. The truth sank in, and I went still. No one *would* touch Jason Hancock, and Sophie was safe. But Maris *had* accepted a daughter as the father's substitute, and I'd been played for a fool.

Worse, I had no idea how long I'd been unconscious, and no idea whether I had any time left to undo my folly. I worked to rebuff Maris's telepathic replay of the time I'd lost. My efforts were in vain; she was too persistent. Maris burrowed her way into my brain like a parasitic worm until I could see Lily's face as clearly as if she stood in front of me. Now I would hear every devastating detail. This was Maris's intended punishment for me: to watch remotely and bear silent witness to Lily's destruction—and with Lily's, my own.

"See what you've missed," Maris said. *"Watch."*

With that word, Maris filled my head with everything I'd missed while I'd lain unconscious. She turned my mind into a movie screen, upon which she projected terrifying images and all-too-familiar voices I did not want to hear:

Tallulah swam back and forth along the shoreline. Distant thunder roused Lily from her sleep in the hammock. Sitting up, she looked around. Disoriented.

"Calder," Lily whispered. She rolled out of the hammock and tiptoed closer to the water.

From the confines of the net, I yelled, *"Stay back!"* But it was like yelling at a movie actor. The scene had already been filmed. How long ago I still didn't know. There was nothing I could do to change the past. Maris's mesmerizing projections continued, and I could not look away:

Lily didn't notice the pale, fervent face, the golden hair shadowed by the overhanging trees. She bit her lip and took a few cautious steps.

"Calder," she whispered again—more confused this time. "Calder, are you out there?"

Still no response. She wrapped the wool blanket tighter around her body. Her face contorted with worry as she stepped onto the dock. When she reached the end, she searched across the lake toward Basswood.

Maris inspected the ends of her hair, then looked up as I tried to yell my way out of the trappings. *"Fitting punishment, don't you think?"* she asked, her voice a syrupy sweetness. *"Who knew Tallulah could be so devious when scorned?"*

I refused to believe it, but I was convinced as Maris remembered Tallulah moving in on her prey.

Lily gasped. "Geez, Calder, you scared me."

"Not Calder. Tallulah."

Retreating, Lily tripped over the edge of the blanket.

Tallulah smiled and held out her arms. "I'm not here to hurt you."

"Another trick!" I cried out.

The eerie vibrations of Maris's laughter gouged deep tracks in the sand. *"Wait,"* she said, *"this is a good part."*

"What do you want?" Lily's voice came out cold and thin. *"Where is he?"*

"He left," Tallulah said, comparatively warm and velvety. "He was only using you. You must have seen that in his eyes. No? The flicker of deceit?"

Lily shook her head.

"Don't believe her!" I continued to yell. I hated that my agony was entertaining Maris, but I could not contain my pleas.

"Although I can see why he dragged things out," Tallulah said. "You are quite pretty. I hadn't really noticed before. Calder does like pretty things. For a while."

I watched, spellbound, as Lily readjusted the blanket, pulling it high and tight under her chin. The wind blew her hair in wild tendrils, making her look simultaneously romantic and tragic.

"Oh, that was a nice touch, don't you think?" Maris asked. "What she did there with the blanket. Did you see that?"

"But life isn't always pretty, now, is it?" Tallulah said. "We can't forget the past. It's not in our nature."

Lily took another step back, and hope rekindled in my shriveled heart.

"Stay," Tallulah said. Hypnotic. Lily stopped. Her shoulders twitched, as if she wanted to run but her feet were locked in place.

"I'm here to warn you," Tallulah went on, "but, as I said, I'm not here to hurt you."

"Warn me?"

"I'm sure Calder's told you we've been hunting your father. Do you really think after all this time, now that we have him in our sights, now that his scent is in our mouths, that we would just walk away? You look like a smart girl. A brave girl. How do you think this is going to end? Surely you can see it."

"Please," Lily said. "Please leave us alone."

Maris nudged me with her foot, and I rolled like a log onto my side. *"Hear how she begs there?"* She almost laughed. *"A family trait, I see."*

Lily clenched her teeth. *"Calder didn't lie to me. He told me everything."*

A clap of thunder nearly drowned out Tallulah's next words: *"Then you know what's been promised us."*

Lily's voice was little more than a whisper. *"My mom is sick. We need my dad. It's not his fault."*

Maris and Tallulah answered her in unison. Maris's *"No"* was angry, but Tallulah said *"No"* as if she was considering Lily's argument.

"You're right. It's not his fault. Calder said something about that once—that your father wasn't the debtor, merely the collateral. But you see, in the end, it's a distinction without a difference. In the end, we must take him."

"Collateral?" Lily's eyes scanned the water as if the solution lay somewhere under the waves.

"Stop looking for him," Tallulah said, her velvety voice giving way to hatred.

"What about me?" Lily asked.

"What about you?" Tallulah's lips twitched.

Maris chuckled, then muttered to herself while fear wormed its way into my stomach, twisting and curling.

"Would you take me?" Lily asked. *"In my dad's place."*

A slow smile spread across Tallulah's face. *"You're a smart girl. Just come to the end of the dock, and I promise you, we will release our claim on your father. Calder must have told you we cannot break a promise. You can trust me on that."*

"Not here. Not where my parents might see."

Tallulah's face turned stony, and the water roiled as her tail thrashed behind her.

"There's a rock just a little farther north," Lily said. "It juts into the lake about ten feet above the surface."

"I know it."

"I'll be there."

"I won't wait long, Lily Hancock."

"I won't be long."

"We'll see about that," Tallulah said, sounding bored now. "In my experience, Hancocks aren't known for keeping their promises."

"This time it's different," said Lily. A forked line of lightning split the sky like a broken dish.

"No!" I cried as Lily's promise echoed in Maris's memory. But I knew my plea would go unanswered, and nausea rippled through my belly.

38

SACRIFICE

Less than an hour after I found myself trapped in the net, the first raindrops pelted the surface. Maris's replay was over. While she and I waited for the story to continue in real time, across the cold channel, Tallulah waited for Lily to come to the cliff. Even from this distance, I could sense Tallulah's patience waning.

Maris swam closer to me. She circled the net twice and coiled her body close to mine, twirling one finger in my hair. I had long since given up trying to free my hands and had switched to using my teeth on the mesh of knotted ropes.

"Be patient," Maris said, sounding maternal and soothing. *"No need to expend so much energy. This will all be over soon."* She rested her hand on one of the stakes that held the net firmly to the sand.

For a second I thought she meant to free me, and my body slumped with exhaustion. *"Why, Maris? Just tell me why."*

"Two birds," she said, circling me again until we were face to face. *"One stone. I need to end the Hancock chapter in my life, and Tallulah—for some unknown reason—wants you in hers. We take out the girl, both missions are accomplished. Now, I'm sorry to leave you like this."* She clicked her tongue with pity. *"I can see you must be very uncomfortable. But I'm afraid I must go. On the off chance the girl is good for her promise, she will be arriving soon. Tallulah will need to surface, and I want to make sure you don't miss any details. Stay tuned, little brother. It's sure to be a cliff-hanger."* She laughed at her own sick joke and slipped away like the snake she was.

If I had ever hoped to convince Maris to let me go, that hope, along with the hope of saving Lily, had vanished. Straining against the bindings, I dislodged one of the stakes, but several more kept me anchored to the sand. There was no time. Maris was nearing the cliff, and through her mind's eye I could see Lily emerge from the pine trees. Maris's hatred distorted Lily's face, making her almost unrecognizable, but I knew it was her because she had changed into her Lady of Shalott dress. The poetic irony was too much for me to bear.

"Lily, no!" I cried as Maris panned the scene from prey to predator. Tallulah's eyes burned with fervor, the object of her desire so close now.

To my revulsion, Maris yelled, *"Action!"*

Hesitating just a second beside a paper birch, Lily draped her hand gently around its trunk and negotiated her first steps down the eroding embankment to the rock. She seemed to know Tallulah was there, but she didn't look for her. Instead, her eyes scanned the great expanse of water between herself and Basswood. My pain worsened when I realized she was searching for me. If she thought I was going to rescue her, I would betray those hopes. Even if I could get free, I had to assume Maris would attack.

Lily pinched her lips together and looked up at the sky. The rain came down harder, soaking through her dress and plastering her hair to her face. There were no sailboats on the lake. She knew no one would see her go in. Still, she walked with controlled, steady steps across the rock. Only once did her bare feet turn on the uneven surface. Within seconds she reached the end and curled her toes around the edge of the cliff. Tallulah nodded approvingly and swam closer.

"Very dramatic," Tallulah said. "It's fitting. I thought you might simply wade in."

"I thought of that," Lily said, still staring over Tallulah's head. "I thought about wading out like the Passamaquoddy Indian girls. But . . ."

I finished her thought. Leaping from the rock appealed to her poetic side. And something more: she hoped I'd know where to look for her.

"Calder won't save you," Tallulah said.

"Won't or can't?"

"I don't see the difference."

For the first time, Lily looked down and glared at Tallulah.

I had never seen such ferocity in Lily's eyes, and for a moment I wondered if Tallulah had met her match. But then Lily's equilibrium faltered, and she swayed. She caught herself from falling and stiffened her legs against any doubt she might have about jumping. A second later, I could see her mind go blank. She was no longer thinking of jumping off the cliff, or of anything she was leaving behind. The muscles in her jaw flexed.

"Time's up, Calder," Maris said from where she watched, her voice a combination of incredulity and mirth.

I strained against the mesh and did not shrink from the knots that tore my flesh. Thrashing and contorting, I wrestled with the net, which jerked upward and sliced my skin, scattering scales into the water like a shower of silver coins.

"Don't do this!" I raged.

"I don't have a choice," Lily replied, although it must have been in response to her own thoughts.

"No, you don't," Tallulah said. "Not really."

"You do," I whispered. *"You always have a choice."*

"Come to me," Tallulah said, her voice a seduction.

"If I do, that will save my dad?" Lily asked.

"I promise," said Tallulah.

"And Calder will be free?"

"If he still wishes."

With a gasp, Lily stepped off the edge—as easily as stepping through a doorway. Her hair streamed skyward as her body plunged. Her arms drew up alongside her ears, her toes pointed. She hit the water like an arrow, and the black water consumed her.

Tallulah dove, and now I watched Lily from my two

sisters' perspectives. Feathery particles floated like an underwater solar system as Maris lurked in the weeds and Tallulah counted out the seconds for Lily to run out of air. The bleakness of Tallulah's mind shrouded my heart. Like never before, I felt how low she'd fallen—how far my rejection had depleted her emotional tank. Tallulah was on empty, and Lily promised to fill her beyond measure.

None of us had ever witnessed a martyr's death before. Lily projected colors I'd never seen. Mesmerizing. Glorious. Unearthly. They intoxicated me, enraptured Tallulah, and lured Maris out of her hiding place. Tallulah sensed Maris encroaching on her prey, and she unleashed a feral snarl. *"Stay away!"* she screamed. *"The girl is mine to finish."*

A hissing sound rattled through Maris's chest. Tallulah bared her teeth and lunged for Lily, sleek and quick like the oily snakes of legend. Together, they rocketed to the surface, and Lily gasped for air before Tallulah flipped and dragged her down again into a death spiral.

"Are you watching, Calder?" Maris seethed as she slunk back into the weeds, her mind writhing with jealousy as Tallulah clutched the glowing Lily to her chest. *"This is what happens when you betray your family."*

Another second passed, and Lily was as good as dead. Maris's imagination flashed ahead to what she assumed would be my and Tallulah's affectionate reunion. Maris had no intention of sticking around to witness *that.* With Lily's sacrifice complete, there was no reason for her to stay. Besides, watching Tallulah had triggered her appetite. Maris took off in search of Pavati.

The vibrations of Maris's retreat found me where I lay

imprisoned, but I couldn't be bothered with her final thoughts. My mind was focused on Tallulah and the precious life between her hands. Heat flooded my body as Tallulah's mind whirled into a crazed obsession, overflowing with the thrill of the kill. She tightened her grip on Lily's chest as she prepared to absorb that vibrant rainbow of martyrdom.

"You are nothing," Tallulah said, though Lily could not hear her thoughts. *"Meaningless. Unworthy."*

Hatred boiled black and molten in my heart. I chewed the ropes, getting a mouthful of sand. I ground the grains between my teeth, creating white-hot sparks that snapped on my tongue.

"You were never his," Tallulah said. *"Never. But now you are MINE."*

With that last word, my mind exploded with fury. A blue flash of electricity shot from my eyes and my heart. The sheer energy of my revolt raced down my arms to my fingertips, slashing through the ropes that bound my wrists, and shredding the net into a thousand pieces that shot, blazing, across the sky.

I didn't know whether I was swimming or flying. Water trilled like piano keys as it streamed past my ears. The smoldering tatters of my prison fell back to earth. Fish scattered.

And then there was blood.

Far in the distance, Maris's laughter faded to an eerie thin note. Tallulah shut her eyes. And Lily was no more.

39

SILVER RING

I'd never known Tallulah to break the skin, but this was not
the Tallulah I knew. The image of Lily's broken body fueled
my rage and pushed me faster. I would kill my sister. Tallulah
would know my pain. I bent my body toward the surface,
the metallic scent of blood flooding my senses, and prepared
myself for what I would see. But I had made all the wrong
assumptions.

High atop the cliff, Jack Pettit stood at the rocky edge,
the scope of a hunting rifle pressed to his eye. He pointed the
barrel at Tallulah, whose lifeless arms floated an inch below

the surface. Her silver tail hung low while a dark red line spiraled out of her body, then dissipated in the churning water. Tallulah's blood filtered through the water, across my lips, coppery on my tongue: her macabre parting kiss.

My shoulders tensed and my muscles hummed with adrenaline. I suddenly couldn't remember if Tallulah was to be hated or mourned. Despite everything, I felt only pity and wondered if Maris had encouraged Lulah's misguided affections for me, *used them,* like any other tool in her box of manipulations. I could not abandon my sister's body to the carrion birds. Or worse, to Jack Pettit. Most importantly, I could not allow Tallulah's body to be discovered.

Jack lowered the rifle, and his eyes locked on mine. "All mermaids ever do is hurt people," he shouted. "Not anymore." Then he raised the rifle again, centering me in his scope.

Before he pulled the trigger, another voice yelled, *"Stop!"* and Jason Hancock collided with Jack's shoulder. There was a grunt and a clatter as the rifle slipped from Jack's fingers, hit the rock, and fell into the lake. Jack ran away before the splash.

Hancock and I spotted Lily at the same time. Waves had pushed her against the face of the cliff—arms splayed wide, palms pressed back against the precipice. Her heart slogged out a lazy rhythm I could feel in the water. Her pale face tipped back against the onslaught of waves, like a battered water lily. "D-don't," she said.

Hancock swayed, and his legs trembled. He bent his knees in preparation for a jump his mind could not force his body to make.

"Jason!" I called up to him. "I've got her."

Why I said it, I will never know. If I thought my words would be reassuring, I was wrong. I'd forgotten how different I was—that I was not human, that my presence would not provide him comfort.

When Hancock saw my tail twitching and slapping at the waves, he yelled, "Stay away from my daughter!" and searched reflexively for the spot where the gun had gone in.

I held up my hands, palms out. "I won't hurt her. I would never hurt her."

"She's gone!" he cried. "Oh, Christ, she's gone!"

I dove.

And I dove.

Down.

Deep.

Lily hung in suspended animation, her arms extended softly in front of her. The last blip of air—a thin line of bubbles—trailed from her nose to the surface. The lake was as silent as a grave.

Fifty feet separated us. It would take mere seconds to reach her. My fingers tingled with a new flow of electricity as I prepared to reach out and reinvigorate her, not really knowing if it would work. Another part of me wondered if it was better to let her die. Was a martyr's death really so much worse than the life of a mermaid? Was it selfish of me to save her? Could I condemn her to the life I hated, and could she still love me once the damage was done?

All these questions melded together until they were a jumbled patchwork of hopes and fears. I reached for her, closing the last few feet. My fingertips charged with a brilliant blue light.

There was a splash from above: Jason Hancock, submerged for the first time in his life, swimming with powerful, purposeful strokes to save his dying daughter. The man had no tail, but it was only a matter of time. I'd witnessed thousands of transformations, and I knew the signs. A silver ring already shimmered around Hancock's throat, and his eyes glowed with an unnatural fire. He showed no awareness of his impending change. Only I bore witness.

My confusion caught me up short, if only for a second. Just enough time for a stone to skip across the surface. Really no time at all. But in my hesitation, two arms wrapped around Lily's chest and pulled her to safety.

And they weren't mine.

40

NIGHTMARES

Lily's lips parted silently, and her head dropped backward over someone's arm. With the jerk of her head, I woke from the dream, gasping beneath a canopy of trees, calling "Lily!" I tried to pretend it was only a dream, but I'd never felt such an all-consuming rage. I'd been shunned, set up, betrayed, and now left alone to die, brokenhearted. I begged anyone, anything who would listen, to rewind time, to put things back the way they were before. I'd do anything.

But who was I kidding? There was no response, and I sank deeper.

It had been twelve hours since Hancock pulled Lily from the water. Twelve hours since I'd witnessed his glowing eyes and the silver ring around his throat. Eleven hours since I'd reasoned out the truth. Tom Hancock hadn't promised to sacrifice his son in exchange for his own life. He'd promised to return Mother's son—*their* son—to her at the end of his first year.

Jason Hancock was my brother. It explained his yearning to return to the lake all these years. It explained his inability to break his promise to his father. It answered everything except why Mother had allowed us to grow up with a lie. What did she think we would do? She couldn't have wanted us to kill her son. But Maris . . . Maris should have known the truth. These questions would have to wait for later. My mind was too tired, my heart too sick to think it through.

I was now lying in the thickest part of the forest, covered in a blanket of wet and decomposing leaves, preserving myself from the heat of the sun. I breathed in the smell of last year's rot and let the little gray beetles climb over my body.

This was my penance for being such a worthless hero. There was no point to any of it. Why couldn't Tallulah have just talked to me? Told me how she felt? I could have made her see reason. It didn't have to end this way.

Each time I closed my eyes, the dreams returned: Hancock plunging into the water. Hancock pulling Lily from my fingertips. Hancock pumping her chest and blowing saving air into her lungs.

I heard myself pleading from the water, *"Please, Lily, Please."* I measured each heavy second, counted along with Hancock as he pushed blood around her body, exhaled with him as he blew oxygen into her wasted lungs.

The sound of Lily coughing and sputtering against her father's knee was the only reprieve from this nightmare, but it plunged me into the next:

Me, dragging Tallulah into the depths of the lake, searching for a place to hide her body, digging a hole under a sunken pallet. Me, wedging her into the chasm and repositioning the pallet over her, closing my eyes to the shameful burial. Me, tucking in her arm, which—even in death—reached for me. Me, squeezing her hand before letting her fingers slip away.

Then Lily's head jerked back, and I was awake again, gasping—*Lily!* This continued for three days. Hour sixty-one. A new record.

From the cool shadows of the forest, I watched her bedroom window. There was no movement. No flip of the lights. No brushing against the curtains. I wanted to go to town to see if there was any talk. I doubted Hancock would have told anyone the truth, but even a lie would be worth knowing.

But I couldn't have made it to town even if I'd tried. My body grew weaker with each minute of my self-imposed exile from the water. My skin pulled tight across my cheeks. My tendons thinned and turned brittle. My muscles cramped and sent stabbing pain from my thighs to my toes.

Defeated, all I could do was watch from the trees. I whispered Tennyson through cracked lips. When my skin split in long, thin lines across my cheeks and shoulder blades, I wondered how long it would take to completely mummify, and as my body dried, my mind slipped into hallucinations.

At first I thought the trees were watching me—or at least, one thin, pale birch, which leaned forward with the breeze as if getting ready to speak, or wanting to speak but wondering if it should. A glimmer of reason reminded me that birch trees didn't talk—even in my nightmares. I pushed myself to allow my mind to clear and my eyes to focus, but in retrospect, I should have left my hallucination alone. It didn't take long to realize it wasn't a talking tree. The thin, pale figure was Maris. And she was coming closer.

"Stay away from me," I croaked through my cracking larynx.

"Don't be such a baby," Maris said. "Obviously Tallulah wasn't going to keep you in the net forever. Where is she?" She scanned the woods. "Why are you out here?"

I narrowed my eyes. She didn't know? Of course she didn't. Tallulah hadn't seen the danger at the top of the cliff. She hadn't seen Jack Pettit pull the trigger. Tallulah hadn't had time to alert Maris or even project her own fear or pain. The secret was mine to bear alone. For better or worse.

"You need serious help, Maris." My voice was like chalk.

She picked at the bark on a tree, and the corners of her mouth twitched into a sad kind of acknowledgment. "I assumed you and Lulah would be riding off into the sunset by now," she said.

"I won't be riding off into any sunsets with Tallulah. Or anyone else, for that matter."

She rolled her lips inward and nodded knowingly. "I guess that's why I'm here. Isn't there something you want to ask me?"

"Me?" I coughed.

"Yes, you. We struck a bargain. The deal is complete. I assume you want to collect on my promise."

I didn't know what to say. "Our bargain . . . ?"

"Okay. I get it if you want me to say this out loud. Will that make up for the lump on your head?" She almost sounded sorry. "We asked you to seduce the girl. I admit you accomplished the seduction, *although*"—she nudged my shoulder with her foot and appraised me—"you're not much to look at now. But I digress. We asked you to get Hancock out on the water so we could take him down."

I opened my mouth to say something, although I wasn't sure what.

She leaned one hand against a tree. "Yes, yes, I know, it ended up being a different Hancock, but it's not your fault Tallulah changed my mind. As I think Pavati told you, one dead Hancock satisfies the debt as well as any."

I stared at her, afraid to blink. It was too good to be true. Was Maris really unaware Lily had been rescued? Had my own thoughts been so addled she hadn't seen any of it? Or—I dared not think it—did she know something I didn't? Had Lily not survived after all? Surreptitiously I glanced at the dark house, the darker window.

Maris didn't notice. "Damn it, Calder. You know I don't have any choice in this. A promise is a promise." She sighed. "Although I don't see what good your independence will do you. I've never known a loner who survived for long, and if you keep up this landlocked melodrama, you won't have much time left. Still, it's not my place to judge."

She shredded a sheet of birch bark in her fingers, then dropped it like confetti onto the ground. "You made good on your end. I'll make good on mine. From this point on, you get your wish." She locked her eyes on mine and said, "We are no longer family."

With her words, I felt the click in my mind—as easy as flipping a switch—the breaking of the cord that bound me to the family White. I wondered how she did it. There was barely a flinch of her shoulders. But she wasn't ready to leave me yet.

"She was just a girl, Calder." Maris looked down at me with a combination of irritation, pity, and incomprehension.

"The truth," I said.

She chewed on the insides of her mouth and debated her words. "What do you want me to tell you?"

"About me. Hancock. The whole story. I want to know the truth before I die." I did my best to glare at her, though my eyes creaked in their sockets.

She crouched beside me, her skin still glistening with water droplets. She snaked a wet fingertip down my arm, leaving a trail of temporary relief.

"Why the lies, Maris?"

"Hancock confessed?"

"You could say that."

"Tom Hancock promised to give the baby back to Mother as soon as he was walking. He broke that promise."

"How is that Jason Hancock's fault?"

"He grew up, didn't he?" she snapped, her eyes flashing. "Years passed, Calder. Decades. He could have come home at any time. He had to feel the pull. He had to know where he belonged."

"He did."

Maris looked smug. "Of course he did. You have no idea what it was like to watch Mother die. Slowly. Slipping away from us every day. I was twelve. Pavati, Tallulah, you— you were all too young to understand. I shouldered this. Me. On my own."

"Mother died in the nets," I reminded her. "I saw it."

"She died of a broken heart. It was no accident."

"But I saw."

"You saw the memory I planted there for you, Calder. For all of you. She hoped, by making you, she could replace the son she lost."

"She was wrong," I said, barely a whisper. Every inadequacy I'd ever felt multiplied in that second. I hadn't saved Lily. I hadn't saved Tallulah. I hadn't been enough to save my mother. I stared up at the night sky, flat and matte without any stars. "But why kill Jason Hancock?" I asked. "He was your brother. Even more than me."

Maris chuckled.

I used every bit of strength I had to roll over and look at her more closely. "What was my part in this, Maris?"

She drew her fingernail across the palm of my hand, slicing it like a scalpel. The brittle skin split neatly in a hairline of red that thickened and filled every crevice. "Neither the truth nor the lie really matters," she said. "Brother or not, Hancock is the reason Mother is dead. He needed to pay. I wanted you to feel useful. I hoped helping us execute his murder would draw you closer to us.

"Then, when we discovered you'd fallen for the girl, Tallulah suggested it was a family debt and any member could pay it. The girl's suicide would torture Hancock more than his own murder ever could. Let him feel the loss of a child—just like Mother did. And it had the bonus of getting the girl out of the way so you and Tallulah could . . ."

Maris turned and looked at the lake in confusion. The night breeze dried the ends of her hair. When she looked back at me, she clicked her tongue as the blood from my hand seeped into the wet leaves and stained the tips of her toes. "Pavati was harder for Tallulah to convince than I was. . . . I don't understand. Where is she? We can't hear Tallulah anywhere. What did you say to her?"

I closed my eyes. Despite the deceit and treachery, the loss of Tallulah still gnawed at my heart. Until recently, she had been my closest confidante, my dearest friend. The memory of her lifeless body was too raw for me to lie to Maris with any confidence. But I need not have worried. When I opened my eyes again, Maris was gone. No goodbye. No love lost there.

41

THE MERMAN

I would kiss them often under the sea,
And kiss them again till they kiss'd me
Laughingly, laughingly;
And then we would wander away, away
To the pale-green sea-groves straight and high,
Chasing each other merrily.
                    —Alfred, Lord Tennyson

I crept out of the woods. Not because I was suddenly brave, but because I could be a self-pitying idiot for only so long without disgusting myself. And Lily deserved better.

The motion detectors on the floodlights were disabled; the lights were left on permanently now, illuminating the water. I crept down to the Hancock dock, dragging myself when I couldn't stand, and lay prone at the end. Raking my fingers through the ripples, I yanked them back before the temptation grew impossible to resist. I wasn't ready yet.

I didn't doubt that my thoughts were safely my own. I didn't doubt that I could hide Tallulah's fate from Maris and Pavati. The radio frequencies of our minds were no longer the same. I could feel it, even on land. There was no one in my head but me.

But I couldn't leave without knowing what had become of Lily. The house behind me was just as dark, just as quiet as before. My mind reached back to my last night in the hammock, Lily tracing my chest with a light touch, her calling my name.

"Calder," she whispered.

I smiled to myself. My body might be withering, but my imagination was as sharp as ever. Her voice was as clear as if she were right behind me.

"Calder, are you out there?"

I jerked around. There was a light in Lily's room and her familiar shape leaned through the open window.

"Lily." I staggered to my feet and limped up the dock to the house, my legs stiff, not responding as they should. "I'm here."

Exhaling, I released the tension caused by our separation, not really feeling its intensity until I began to let it go, bit by bit. "Are you okay?" I asked the question, dreading the answer.

"Better. Were you worried? You look worried."

I searched her face for some sign of trauma. She was ghostly pale and for a moment I wondered if I was seeing her apparition.

"Calder, did you see?" She gestured at her neck. "My dad. Did you see?"

"Yes, but I'm surprised *you* did. What does he know? He had you out of the water so fast he never finished the transformation."

"He knows my grandpa wasn't crazy after all."

"But he doesn't know what he is? That's good. There's no reason for him to find out. What happened—it should give him even more reason to stay on dry land."

"No," she said. "He has no idea. He thinks some freakish adrenaline rush kicked in and allowed him to swim, but, Calder, he knows what *you* are. He's forbidden me to see you ever again. He's sending me back to Minneapolis tomorrow."

Good, good. I couldn't risk Maris's discovering that Lily lived. "Your dad thinks I'll hurt you."

"No. Yes. But . . . what I really want to know is . . . what I need to know is, if my dad is like you, then what am I?"

I shook my head to assuage her fears. "You're not a mermaid, Lily. I think maybe you've inherited something—some trait that makes you comfortable in the lake. I always knew it wasn't normal."

"Are we related?"

My eyes closed. "Not at all. If anything, you're related to my sisters." I laughed one hard laugh. "I'm sincerely sorry about that." She didn't smile at my attempt to joke. "How is Sophie?" I asked.

"Fine. Why?"

Ah. So Pavati had shown some mercy. She might have

allowed Maris to use the little girl as a pawn, but she had not allowed Sophie to remember. "Nothing. Forget it. Now please, Lily, come out to me. I can't stand it anymore."

Lily looked over her shoulder, then disappeared for a second. Returning to the window, she flung one leg over the sill. I watched nervously as she climbed out onto the porch roof, crouched low, and inched herself to the edge. She jumped, landing softly on the balls of her feet.

She grabbed my hand and dragged me, stumbling, across the yard to the edge of the woods, then down toward the shore by my willow branch. I groaned as the waves lapped at my ankles. She reached down and cupped the water, rubbing it gently into my bare arms and chest, as if afraid I would fall apart at her touch.

After splashing my legs and shoulders, she filled her hands and let me drink. It helped, but it was only a superficial relief.

"Why did you do it, Lily?" I asked, my voice dry and rough.

She stopped splashing and her face flushed.

"How could you do that to yourself? To me?"

"It was the only way to end it," she whispered. "It worked, didn't it? They promised if I gave myself to them . . ."

I took her into my arms and rested my chin on the top of her head. "You did fine. You fulfilled the promise. They heard that much in Tallulah's mind. The rest . . ." I struggled to finish the sentence but couldn't.

"I should have never left that goodbye note for Mom and Dad," she said. "It was so stupid, but I wanted them to know what happened to me. I didn't know Jack was working at the house. He saw it first. Poor Jack. Will they go after *him* now?"

300

"It happened too fast for Tallulah to project any kind of fear in her thoughts. Maris and Pavati don't know."

Lily looked up at me, her eyes glossy. "Have I made everything worse?"

I pulled her closer. "What did I ever do to deserve you, Lily? You are the hero. You saved us. Your dad . . . me . . . You freed us both."

"Not Tallulah," she whispered.

"No. Not her." My voice caught in my throat.

"I'm so sorry."

I pulled back to get a better look at her. She was the most unbelievable girl. "They tricked me, Lily. If I'd known what they were planning, I would have never left you. I almost got back in time. Your heart stopped beating." I felt her tense under my hands. "I was there. I was right there. For a moment, I considered . . ."

She nodded.

"But I was too afraid to try. And even if it worked, I couldn't bear the thought of ripping you from your family." I dropped my chin to my chest. The water pulsed against my ankles. My whole body vibrated with the urge to dive, and I swayed dangerously. I was at my limit.

"You're leaving," she said. It wasn't a question.

"But I'll be back."

"At the migration?"

I looked up at her quickly. "Actually, I was referring to you. I don't think I have much choice in this anymore. I'll be back for you. Wherever you are."

"Is that one of those merman promises?"

"No other kind."

"Well, if that's true"—she closed her eyes and pressed her forehead to mine—"we better get you out of here before you turn to dust." She looked back at the house. "And before my dad wakes up. He's had enough revelations for a while." She laughed despite the tears welling in her eyes. Then she said, "Wait here."

I watched as she ran back to the house, then focused my attention on my feet in the water, the ripples rolling away from my ankles as I twisted my toes in the sand, a lump rising in my throat. She came back with a small drawstring bag.

"I don't suppose you'll be able to ditch your clothes in the car anymore," she said.

I held her close and drank in the scent of oranges and pine. A rose-colored light spread from her arms and soaked into my shoulders, my chest, my legs. . . . It warmed me to a point where I almost forgot my own name. Then her lips met mine.

Too soon she broke away, turning her back on me. I stripped down, shoving my clothes into the bag, and slung the straps across my chest.

"Go," she said, still facing the house.

And I dove.

Instantly there was a burst of light and heat that surely lit up the night sky. Every cell in my body broke open, crying with relief, welcoming the water that flooded through me. I seemed to expand—in fact, I was sure I did—like a wasted sponge submerged. Burning with pent-up energy, my legs knitted and fused, exploding into the silver tail that bent the water and propelled me like a bullet from the shore.

I arched and turned, breaking the watery plane, the midnight air on my face. Lily watched from the dock, her hand raised. The memory of her kiss was still fresh on my lips, and I knew that with Lily, I was both free and imprisoned for all eternity.

ACKNOWLEDGMENTS

This is the scary part where I get to thank all those people who helped me bring Calder and Lily to the world (and pray I haven't left anyone out). In chronological order of events (because I'm a linear thinker) they are:

Everyone who introduced me to Lake Superior when I could barely walk—and who rescued me when I tumbled in;

My sister, Elizabeth, who told me to get off my butt and write something, for cripe's sake;

My first three novels, which taught me what works and what doesn't;

My parents, Steve and Deede Smith, who read the first draft of the first chapter of what would someday be *Lies Beneath* and told me to keep going;

The talented writers of the Minneapolis Writers Workshop, who caught my every misstep as I read Calder's story aloud;

My beta readers and all-around cheerleaders, including Stephanie Landsem, Laura Sobiech, Beth Djalali, Weronika Janczuk, Therese Walsh, Elissa Hoole, the Apocalypsies, and my critique partner, Nina Badzin, who said, "I think this is the one!";

Ian Baker, for forgetting his book at home and loving *For Weasel* (which won't make much sense to anyone but him, but I am sincerely indebted, kid);

My enthusiatic agents, Jacqueline Flynn, Jenny Meyer, and Rich Green; and

Françoise Bui, for her keen insight and finely tuned

questions, as well as all the good folks at Delacorte Press and Random House Children's Books.

Big hugs to my three beautifully weird kids, Samantha, Matthew, and Sophie, whose joy and creativity brighten my world. Let this be a lesson to you. Never give up on your dreams.

And finally, thanks to my husband, Greg: at the end of the day, it's always you.

AVAILABLE NOW!

The story of Calder and Lily continues in
Deep Betrayal—and this time around,
it's Lily's turn to narrate.

ANNE GREENWOOD BROWN

*Deep
Betrayal*

the sequel to *Lies Beneath*

DELACORTE PRESS